I0760992

JAIME CASTLE

CJ VALIN

HARRIER

THE TRENCH

aethonbooks.com

Aethon Books
www.aethonbooks.com

Print and eBook formatting, and cover design by Steve Beaulieu.

Published by Aethon Books LLC.

ALSO IN SERIES

NOTE: RAPTORS and HARRIER stand alone with no need to read the other for enjoyment.

Raptors

Sidekick

Superteam

Scions

Baron Steele

Mega-Mech Apocalypse

Harrier

Justice

The Trench

Invasion

For Valerie Beaulieu. It's been a tough few years, but you'll always be a superhero in my mind.

—JC

To my mom, who started supporting me before I was born and hasn't stopped a single day since.

—CJ

PROLOGUE

ERIC

Truth time.

There was an era when the name Battlegear meant something—granted, primarily due to headlines about me getting thwarted at every angle. But occasionally, "Supervillain robs First Union National. Gets away with $1.2m" or something similar hit the web. I've clicked every one of them. Some even gave me the dignity of using my moniker. Felt good to get a little credit now and again.

But all those years as a so-called supervillain? I was miserable. I know, I know, it seems like it would be such a glamorous life, right? Money, fame, ladies... But it's not. The money was fine, but I couldn't spend it without first laundering it, and I'm terrible at laundering. No Marty Byrd in this human vessel, let me tell you.

But fame? No one even knew my real name. True, that's part of it—not giving away your identity—but I've always envied Eaglestar. Every person on Earth knows the name Jonathan Powers.

And ladies… I admit the money got me girls. But that always felt one step shy of prostitution. No one warmed my bed because of me.

Now comes the truth I mentioned. Supervillainy is mostly work: planning, heisting, getting the crap kicked out of me, and then replanning how to do it without that last bit. If I'm *really* being honest, the most fun part of the gig *was* getting the crap kicked out of me.

And that was usually by Eaglestar—who, of course, got all the praise. Being the most powerful person on the planet has its perks. That's not just something people say. He holds that title, hands down.

That's what I always wanted. Power. Okay, and money. Power and money. Sick combo if you ask me.

When I strapped on the suit and equipment and stepped onto the streets of New York, I knew the chances were high that my face would be meeting his fist in the near future. He could've killed me with a look. Literally. By shooting laser beams out of those glowing red eyes of his. But he didn't. Was it just because he's one of the "good guys"? I like to think it was more than that. In fact, one time, he basically told me as much. I remember it like it was yesterday—sort of.

The doorbell rang. I ignored it, figuring it was someone trying to help me find religion or a neighborhood girl selling cookies. Even the prospect of Thin Mints couldn't sway me into opening the door.

Ding-dong, several more times in a row, followed by a pounding fist.

"Eric! I know you're in there!"

Crap. It was Jocelyn. We'd only gone on a few dates, but I liked her. Of course, my line of work requires a certain level of discretion. She was supposed to be at work. Why was she here?

I took a deep breath as I rushed to open the door. "Look, Jocelyn, I—"

Smack! Before I could finish, she gave me an open-handed slap across the face. I shook my head to try to clear it. Tears streaked Jocelyn's hazelnut skin, but she seemed more angry than anything else. "I received a rather cryptic message from Eaglestar."

"Eaglestar?" I asked, my stomach sinking.

"Yeah, imagine my surprise when it was about *you*!"

"Me?"

"Mmmmhmmm. He said you were hiding something. It's true, isn't it?"

"I don't know wh—"

Jocelyn shoved past me into the house. "How could I have missed it? It was right there. Right in front of me."

Double crap. She knows. She's figured out my secret.

I rubbed my cheek—mostly for show—and went into the bathroom.

Jocelyn kept talking from the living room. "And to think, I was about to introduce you to—are you even listening to me?"

I grabbed my mask—a black cloth—from the towel rack. Like her or not, I'd have to make sure she kept her mouth shut. "Yes. I'm—"

"I knew it was too good to be true. Nobody with a body like yours is as smart as you are."

"Thanks? I really can't—"

"And don't even get me started on the outfits!"

I looked down at my leathers. "Well, yeah, but—"

"You're gay, aren't you?" she shouted. "Just tell me the truth. I'd rather know now than—"

"Wait—what?" I replied as I returned to the living room, hiding the mask behind my back. "You think I'm gay?"

"If that's who you are, that's who you are. But why me? Why toy with me like this?" She glared at me. "What the hell were you doing in there? What's behind your back?"

"Nothing," I said, slowly turning as she circled me, trying to see.

I'd had enough. My frustration finally boiled over into anger. "Yes! I'm gay! So why not just leave."

I wasn't, but it seemed the best story to tell to get her to leave and go far away, never to return.

She slapped me a few times, light little love taps. Then, she made a huge mistake. Reaching around, she pulled the mask from my hands.

“Give that back,” I told her, but it was too late. She’d used her lithe little legs to dart across the room before I could stop her.

“What is this?” she asked, holding the mask up to the window’s light. The look on her face told me she recognized it.

“Why do you have this? This is Battlege—”

The truth hit her like one of Eaglestar’s punches.

Oh, why did you have to do that?

Jocelyn was taken aback by the change in expression on my face. It was one part fury, one part pity. I started toward her, knowing what I had to do now.

“What the hell is wrong with you?” she demanded.

She was frozen in abject terror by the time I reached her and snatched my mask back. I slowly pulled it over my head.

“You have no idea,” I growled.

Jocelyn backed away, clearly thinking I’d lost my mind and she’d made a terrible mistake by confronting me. She came here thinking I was using her as a front to hide my sexual orientation, and now she realized it was far worse than she could’ve imagined.

Did she think I was going to kill her? Chop her up into little bits and feed her to my dog, Ace?

She stammered for a response. “I’m… just gonna go.”

I gave her my best supervillain laugh as she tried to retreat for the door. I wasn’t going to hurt her, but my cover was blown. I had to make damn sure she didn’t tell everyone who I was.

"Oh, I don't think so." I reached into the front closet and pulled out a gun I'd designed to resemble a *Star Trek* phaser.

"You don't have to do this," Jocelyn said. "I'm sorry. I really am."

I shook my head and raised the weapon. It wouldn't kill her. I had it set to stun. She was mid-plea when I zapped her with a blue pulse. Gentleman that I was, I caught her as she fell unconscious. Then I proceeded to carry my—now ex?—girlfriend over to my couch to lay her down. What a pity. I liked this girl.

"There, there," I said in a soothing tone. "We can get through this."

That was when I heard a sonic boom powerful enough to rattle the walls. "No, no, no, no. Not yet." I grabbed my goggles off the coffee table and fitted them over my eyes.

What followed was a whistling sound like when Wile E. Coyote plummets off a cliff as the result of a misguided attempt to make the Road Runner his dinner. I lifted my entire sofa—Jocelyn and all—and tossed it aside with only the slightest effort. Then, from a hidden hatch in the floor beneath it, I pulled out a big-ass weapon.

Just in time.

There was a tremendous crash as something burst through the ceiling of my single-story home with the force of a demolition ball. Once the debris and dust began to clear, I could see the silhouette of a man.

But not just any man.

Ripped muscles, red-white-and-blue spandex, and an iron

jaw framing an impossibly handsome face. And a cape. A cape that somehow billowed behind him despite the absence of any breeze.

Eaglestar.

"Surrender, Battlegear." He always spoke like he was doing a voiceover for an action movie. Or maybe a truck commercial.

"You'll pay for this," I snarled back at him. I always loved this part. The witty banter. He was never this way with anyone else, as far as I know, which made it even better.

"You can't defeat me."

"No, I mean you'll *literally* pay for all this damage. There's no way my insurance is going to cover it. How did you find me?"

"It was all too simple. I had my suspicions. Gave her a little intel. Then, I heard her voice. Heard her mutter your filthy name," he said. "That's all it took for me to discover the truth of who you are and where you live. Don't you feel small? Where is she? Where's the woman?"

He stepped toward me but stopped when I trained the giant weapon on his chest. Then Eaglestar noticed Jocelyn on the couch and turned a furious glare toward me.

I was defiant. "That's on you. This was between *us*."

Eaglestar frowned. "She had a right to know the truth of who you really are. *What* you really are."

"No. No way." I flipped a switch on the weapon, and a slight hum indicated it was powering up. "*Plus*, it's against the Code. She could tell the world."

Eaglestar ignored the remark and pointed at the weapon. “That thing again? Last time, I barely felt it.”

“I’ve made some improvements,” I said, pulling the trigger. The weapon jolted and kicked back against my shoulder as a lightning blast erupted, slamming Eaglestar through the exterior wall. I approached the hole in the side of my house and peered through. Outside was a burnt, fallen tree and another smoking chasm looking into my neighbor’s garage. I could only hope *they* had insurance.

With a proud smile, I slung the weapon over my back and returned to Jocelyn. I prepared to put her over my shoulder when I heard a crackle behind me.

Turning, I saw Eaglestar standing there, seemingly untouched except for the front of his costume being burnt away. Which only made him look more impressive with his giant pectorals and washboard abs—Wait. *Am* I gay?

His eyes—the source of the crackling—shone red as steam poured off his body like a steak hot on the grill.

“Nobody… messes with… the costume…”

Even though I wore my goggles and knew to close my eyes, I still saw the bright flash of Eaglestar’s laser vision as I felt the searing heat and pummeling force of the blast.

The next thing I knew, I was being slapped again. I woke to a stinging face and something warm against my back. My eyes opened to Jocelyn standing before me, tears streaming, arms crossed. We were in my basement. I tugged on the chains, which were firmly secured to the furnace.

Behind Jocelyn stood Eaglestar, who wore a smug look of satisfaction.

"I think I need to go to the hosp—"

"You don't deserve anything except to rot in jail, you sonovabitch," she said. "How could you not tell me?"

I tried to focus. "I can expl—"

Smack! Another slap from Jocelyn. "No. I am never speaking to you again after this. I gave you the best six-and-a-half days of my life, and this is how you repay me? Zapping me with some kind of... of... whatever the hell that was?"

"Well, I—"

Smack! "Shut up!"

While I'm super-strong and tough as a woman giving birth, I'm not invulnerable like Eaglestar. That means I can still feel everything. "Can you maybe stop doing that?"

"No. I will not stop." She punctuated each word with another slap.

Finally, but not with any sort of haste, Eaglestar interrupted. "Miss, I'm going to have to take him in now."

Jocelyn turned to him. "Fine. I'm done. Go ahead. Make him pay."

Eaglestar tossed me over his shoulder effortlessly and spoke to me under his breath. "I would *not* want to be you right now."

As Eaglestar flew up, we burst through the ceiling—which was actually the floor of my house—I could hear Jocelyn calling after me. "And you can forget dinner at my parents' on Sunday!"

Neither she nor Eaglestar realized that the stun I gave her was slowly erasing her short-term memory. She wouldn't remember confronting me or being zapped when she woke up the following day. Besides, I'd never told her my real last name anyway. I'd move... again... and it would all be over.

Another sad attempt at a relationship down the drain.

Police officers cheered as Eaglestar entered the station dragging me behind him. But unlike most law enforcement, Detective Fernanda was not a fan of Eaglestar. She tried to turn to avoid him as we approached, but he plopped me down right in front of her desk anyway.

"Good afternoon, Detective. I want to make a citizen's arrest," he said.

Fernanda tried to hide her annoyance. "That's... great. Why don't you take him right down the hall to booking and—"

Eaglestar simply smiled and shook his head. For someone with super-senses, Eaglestar is often oblivious to the obvious.

She sighed and clicked around on her computer. "Okay, then. Name?"

Eaglestar answered for me. "Battlegear."

Fernanda struggled to maintain her composure. Her

mouth moved silently, counting to three before continuing. "I was hoping for his *real* name."

"Sorry, I can't do that. It's against the Code."

I looked up. "Oh, sure. *Now* he follows the Code."

Eaglestar turned to me. "You didn't deserve her. She's strictly hero material."

Fernanda ignored the banter and addressed me directly. "Oh, good. You're lucid. Wanna tell me your name?"

"No, ma'am," I said. "And you won't find anything if you run my prints or picture, either."

"Why's that?" the detective asked, placing both palms on her desk.

Eaglestar interrupted yet again. "He's a whiz with technology."

Fernanda stared daggers at both of us.

"Look, you're wasting your time anyway," I said. "Ask him what you're supposed to charge me with. Go ahead. Do it."

Fernanda gave Eaglestar a questioning look.

The smug bastard smiled heroically. "Attempted world domination."

Fernanda looked back at me, and I was now sporting a knowing grin. She returned to Eaglestar. "First of all, there's no such crime as 'world domination,' never mind '*attempted* world domination.'" Eaglestar looked incredulous as she went on. "And second, if there *were* such a thing, it would be *way* out of my jurisdiction. Or any jurisdiction I even know of."

"But he told me his entire plan in a detailed monologue...."

I leaned toward the hero. "You never read me my Miranda rights. Besides, you broke into my house and took me away without a warrant."

Fernanda tried to correct me. "He's not an officer of the law."

"Sorry, but you're wrong there. The president deputized him as a federal agent last month."

Eaglestar pulled a badge from *somewhere* and proudly flashed it around the room. Several of the other officers started to clap.

"Everyone shut up!" Fernanda shouted. "Just shut the hell up!" She stood and pulled Eaglestar aside. He dropped me, and I landed hard on the laminate floor. That dumb smile never left his face.

She tried to speak quietly enough that I couldn't hear, but my mask had built-in sound amplification around the ears. "Listen. The way things are looking right now, we're gonna be lucky if he doesn't sue the hell out of the city and have you charged with breaking and entering *and* assault and battery."

"But what about all his illegal weaponry?" Eaglestar asked, smile fading. "He has all sorts of gizmos and gadgets. And would you look at my costume? Do you have any idea how expensive this material is? It's imported from Italy."

Fernanda looked me up and down. "But he doesn't have any—"

Eaglestar darted back to me in the blink of an eye and

grabbed my forearm, yanking me to my feet in the process. He pointed to a metallic wristband covered in buttons and touch-screens. "Does this look like an Apple Watch to you?"

"Can you get it off of him?"

I started to panic. "No-no-no-no-no—it's not a weapon!"

Fernanda nodded to Eaglestar, and he gave the wristband a sharp pull. I tried in futile desperation to keep it on. "Please don't. Don't take it off. *Please*."

Eaglestar pulled it free and handed it to the detective.

"What is it?" she asked, turning it back and forth.

I slumped over, totally defeated, already starting to shimmer and fade. "It's a device that jams locator and transporter tech—"

Fernanda and Eaglestar looked at each other as they faded out of my sight.

My next vision was the inside of an airlock, with windows showing a field of stars outside and a beautiful view of Earth, miles and miles below. "—nology."

I turned to see several menacing figures in colorful costumes beyond a transparent plasti-steel door. We were in a super-futuristic space station control room of my own design, all chrome and black with flashing lights and holographic displays. This was my pride and joy—a real thing of beauty.

A moment later, Dr. Delay turned toward me. His face showed a mixture of horror and delight. Then, the horror disappeared, and only unparalleled elation remained.

"Uh… hey, Doc," I said.

Soon, half a dozen more of the world's worst villains

joined him. They stared at me, none offering a response except ear-to-ear grins.

"Look, I know you guys must be angry, but just… just keep your hands away from that button, okay?" I pointed to the giant red square that activated the airlock. "Okay?"

If they decided to push it, I'd be toast. Well, more like ice cubes, frozen in the vacuum of space after my head popped. Or is that just what they do in movies? Anyway, it wouldn't be pleasant, no matter the details.

Dr. Delay, a professor whose schtick was creating traps, watched as I screamed at the top of my lungs, but they couldn't hear me. I know they couldn't because I designed it that way.

I could hear *them*, however, with my mask.

"What's he saying?" Delay asked. It was then that it finally dawned on me that the symbol on his chest was supposed to be a stylized "don't walk" sign. Wow, is that stupid, especially for a guy with a Ph.D.

Music Master, who was fidgeting with the mess of bright red hair sticking out of the top of his orange and green mask, was the first to answer. "Don't know. Probably pleading for his life, if I had to guess."

Creeping Death, an arachnid-themed villain who'd gotten started during the Great Depression and was somehow still active, tried to talk but released a hacking cough first. His formerly-black costume was frayed and had turned a medium gray after being worn for so long. I knew how much the ancient criminal hated me since he had fought Eaglestar since

World War II but had lately been replaced by me as his arch-nemesis.

The old man finally took in a wheezing breath and spoke. "Could be entertaining."

Delay flipped the intercom switch, and my voice immediately burst forth from the speaker at full volume. "You're going to regret this! I guarantee it!"

The villains stood in silence for a moment, then all burst out laughing simultaneously. Repo Guy pulled his goggles over his curly hair and leaned toward the intercom. His costume was just mechanic's overalls covered in the patches of car companies, as if they sponsored him, which they didn't. At least, I hope they didn't.

"Bro, you're a walking cliché," he said, sounding like a dopehead. "You act like you're one up on us."

My eyes narrowed as I eyed Repo Guy. "What makes you think I'm not?"

Repo Guy looked flustered as he flipped the intercom switch off. "I *hate* that dude. He thinks he's better than us just because he's, like, smart and stuff. You know, I can build cool stuff, too. You dudes should see my—"

Delay cut him off. "We don't want to hear about your damn car again, Repo. *None* of us wants to hear another word about your freakin' car. *Ever.*"

Repo Guy crossed his arms in a huff while Delay flipped the switch again. "Surely you can't be serious, Battlegear."

Megadude, nearly twice as tall as Delay and built like a Mack truck, suddenly let his rage get the best of him. He looked like he was going to rip right out of his blue and white tank top and bicycle shorts. "You... are the one... who screwed it all up!"

Sinsation always has a way of calming Megadude down. She put her hand on his arm, and his breathing slowed. I'm not sure if it's one of her powers or if she's just so hot, no man could resist following her every command. It helps that her costume is practically non-existent, also. "Calm down, big boy. Don't want to crack the door."

Megadude turned away from the airlock and took deep breaths but continued shaking. Delay put his hand above the airlock's decompression button. "I think we're done here."

My demeanor changed immediately. "Wa-wa-wa-wa-wait. Please. Just listen to me for one minute."

Delay was about to press the button anyway when another member of the group spoke up. Med-Evil is the creepiest person I've ever seen—basically a zombie dressed in a warped version of an old-fashioned doctor's uniform. Y'know, like Dr. Frankenstein in the old movies. And his voice sounds like a goat choking on a tin can. "Let's hear him out."

Delay's finger hovered just centimeters above the button. "Hurry it up."

I tried to look as humbled as possible. "I know I've been a little... defensive. I get that way when I know I'm wrong. I apologize."

The others looked at each other and rolled their eyes.

"No, seriously, guys. You know how Virgos are."

This time they grudgingly nodded.

"It's true," Sinsation said. "I've dated Virgos."

"Right? Yeah. Well, I screwed up. I made a *huge* mistake. I realize that. But we've all been there, haven't we?"

Through the transparent door, the others looked a little embarrassed. Most of them wore sheepish expressions, and a couple looked away.

I cautiously continued. "I mean, Dr. Delay, you told Brave Badger your plans to carve your face into Mt. Rushmore while he was hanging over a shark tank. And we all know how that turned out, right?"

Delay lifted his left arm and looked at the hook that replaced the hand Badger shoved into the shark tank after he'd escaped. As much as he hated to admit it, I was onto something.

"And Music Master, how about the time you sent that video to all the networks explaining how you were the new Emperor of Mexico... just a tad too early?"

Music Master's face turned almost as red as his hair. I still remember seeing the video on the news of the massive Mexican anti-hero, La Cucaracha, chasing Music Master around and smashing his electric keyboard over his head several times.

"There was even that song," Repo Guy said, laughing.

Music Master turned to him and growled, "La Cucaracha was a lot tougher than I thought he'd be."

I pulled off my mask and revealed a furrowed brow and watery eyes in a last-ditch effort to survive. I'd never been so happy for those acting classes I took in college. "Was my blunder really that much worse than what the rest of you have done? I mean, we all grew up on comic books and Bond movies, right? How can we resist the monologue when we have them in our clutches?"

Repo Guy leaned in toward the intercom microphone again. "But it was Eaglestar, dude. *Eaglestar*."

"Can I help it if my arch-nemesis is a little more powerful than the rest? You're saying that's somehow *my* fault?"

Creeping Death glared at me. "I never screwed up this badly with Jonathan Powers."

"What about when we infiltrated the Guild and got caught because of your smell?" I asked.

Sinsation snickered.

The others seemed swayed by my arguments—all except Med-Evil, who shambled closer to the door and lifted a skeletal finger. "It was flawless. World domination was but hours away. I may be undead, but that doesn't mean I have forever. Decomposition isn't pretty, you know."

I know I wasn't the only one looking at him and thinking, *Oh, I know*.

"Hey, so we came up with a perfect plan once. Who's to say we can't do it again?" I said as I put my hands together in a prayer position. "What'aya say, guys? We can have our minions crunching the numbers within the hour."

Med-Evil reluctantly waved his hand in dismissal. "Fine! Let him—"

Beep, beep, beep. A warning light flashed along with the alarm as the space station computers went into overdrive.

Video screens sprang to life as the space station's cameras focused on the threat.

Delay hit a few controls and looked at the readings. "Incoming!"

Eaglestar bolted toward the station on the monitor behind them at incredible speed.

Megadude looked scared for someone so big and strong. "It's him!"

They all turned back to me, and I grimaced and sucked in air through my teeth. "Did I… forget to mention I also revealed the location of our super-cool new headquarters? My bad."

I saw Eaglestar approaching through the airlock windows and hoped the idiots could figure out how to fire all the powerful weapons I had installed and financed. If all those months working undercover in the tech department at that stupid bank had gone to waste, I was going to be pissed.

I tried to get their attention as they fumbled to the control room.

"Hey!" I shouted. But they were gone.

Since none of them seemed smart enough to think of letting me out so I could actually do something about the most powerful being on Earth coming to throttle their necks, I pulled the panel off the door controls. It only took about thirty seconds, but without a hand hovering over the button, it gave me enough time to work on the circuitry inside to get it unlocked.

A shudder rolled through the station. He was here.

The airlock whizzed open, and I rushed to the control room. But I was too late. A cacophony of screams, wrenching metal, and small explosions overwhelmed every sense I had. I pulled on my mask and went through the hatch.

By the time I entered, some of my fellow supervillains were already on the floor, while others fought in the corridor —presumably as they tried to make it to the escape pod.

I searched through the wreckage of our armory and found one of my giant weapons, a ray gun the size of a bazooka. I smiled and powered it on, but the hum quickly died, and the lights faded.

So did my smile. "C'mon... c'mon..."

I opened the weapon, pulled out a cartridge, and then tossed both aside. I tore off my mask again, then slumped to sit, back against the wall, amidst the debris. This was my lowest of low points.

I must admit, from here on out, my memories are fuzzy. You try almost losing everything you've worked for in a matter of seconds. But, I'll do my best to recount my conversation with Eaglestar.

"Battlegear."

I looked up, dread scrawled across my face. In the flickering light of the damaged space station, I saw Jonathan Powers approaching.

"Call me Eric. I'm done with all that stuff."

Eaglestar's expression changed from stoic to one of shocked disbelief. "You're not even going to take a shot at me?"

"I thought you had super-hearing. I said *I'm done.* My colleagues are out cold. Our station is toast. My plan is ruined. What else is left? You won."

I thought Eaglestar actually seemed a little worried. He looked around at the destroyed room. Then, in a move that surprised me more than anything I'd ever experienced, he sat next to me.

"You must have *something* else in the works," I think he said.

I picked up a broken piece of technology and turned it around in my hands. "Nah. We threw everything we had into this latest scheme."

"I can't believe that. You're a super-genius. Surely, you have more ideas."

Tears welled in my eyes as I tossed the gadget. "What's the point? You know? I mean, you mop the floor with us every time. You don't even need the help of those other heroes anymore."

"Yes, well... It *is* easier to fly solo. Some of those others have some serious issues."

I nodded at my fallen teammates. "Tell me about it."

He slapped his thigh and stood. "You can't give up."

"What?" I asked, looking up at him.

"What am I supposed to do then?" he said.

I was confused. "Wouldn't that make your life a lot easier?"

"Easier? Everyone needs a challenge," he said. "Even me."

I was hesitant to speak, but then I opened up. "You

know... you were the reason I got into this biz in the first place. I thought about being a hero, but it was like, 'Why be just another second-rater living in Eaglestar's shadow?' Seriously. I figured if I was a good enough villain, I could become your arch-nemesis, and our names would be linked forever."

Eaglestar seemed genuinely touched. "Wow. I'm honored."

"Really? You know, maybe I *could* come up with something new."

"See? That's the spirit." Then I think he said something like, "We're like yin and yang. You cannot leave me to fight guys like Creeping Death and Music Master all the time."

I smiled. "I *was* doodling some schematics last night for a device that would create tsunamis and wreak havoc all over the Pacific Rim."

"There you go. Just dump these has-beens and do it. They are not even in your league."

"For real?"

"They are just holding you back. Who came up with the plan to shrink the Eiffel Tower?"

I shrugged. "*Moi.*"

"And whose idea was it to turn me back into a baby last year?"

"Mine. But you still kicked all our asses."

Eaglestar chuckled. "How about that zero gravity emitter? That was something else. Took most of the Guild to keep things from flying off into space. That was truly inspired."

I raised my hand sheepishly. "Guilty."

I can't remember his actual words, but the gist of it was,

"See? You are the man," or, "You're awesome." Something like that. I'm paraphrasing, but he was really complimentary of me. That's what counts and what I recall best.

"You know what? You're right!" I pulled my mask back on. "Battlegear's back, baby!"

"Fantastic! What do you say we wrap this gig up?"

I was about to stand, but Eaglestar lifted me by the front of my costume and held me high as he pulled his fist back. "Now, you might want to close your eyes, buddy. This is going to hurt...."

Ah. Memories.

And now, just a short few years later and everything is different. Now we're on the same side. Yeah, right? I can hardly believe it myself. I'm one of the guys running the Counter-Vigilante Taskforce. The whole freaking thing. Like a boss, too. Things are a lot more fun. And a lot less painful. And you know what? I still get to fight superheroes most of the time. Only now, I'm on the side of the law, and they're the ones breaking it. What a world we live in.

Instead of giving powers to criminals to commit crimes, I now provide them to government agents to take down the guys I used to risk going to prison for fighting. Did I mention the money? Yeah, buddy. I've got myself a *huge* government contract. No plans, no heists, no waving weapons at innocent people and hoping no one smashes that little red button under the teller's desk. I'm making beaucoup bucks that I won't be imprisoned for keeping. It makes so much more sense. I'm having the time of my life.

The social aspect isn't so great, though. All my old friends were criminals. And none of the so-called "good guys" want to be friendly, that's for sure. Alex Garner has been a decent dude, though. Tolerates me, at least.

I've never been so great with others. Pretty sure I'm just too smart for them. Smarter than almost anyone else around. No cap. So I adapted by adopting a persona to accompany my buff physique and devil-may-care attitude. People don't like it when they think they're being talked down to. So I speak in a way that makes them think they're superior to me: like saying stupid stuff like "no cap."

The frat-boy schtick works. Now I get why blonde chicks act dumb. People feel bad for dumb people. It's innate in their DNA. *Aww, look at the little three-legged dog. I just want to take him home.*

Why? Why would anyone want a mutt that's more work than a regular four-legged dog?

I digress. The heart wants what the heart wants or whatever.

Anyway, Alex Garner. I'm trying to butter him up a bit, get him to give into the friendship, even though we used to be enemies. I think he has a difficult time dealing with that and moving on. Especially since I'm basically his boss, or his co-boss. I'm not really sure. Eaglestar wasn't very clear when he sent me to work with him, and I don't want to ask in case I'm wrong. I'm supposed to "handle him," whatever that means. Keep him in check, I guess.

Is it a bromance? No. Not yet, anyway. But I feel like I'm wearing him down.

And I was freaking paramount in helping him capture Black Harrier, the CVT's primary target. If that doesn't buy me an in with the dude, I don't know what will.

We'll see.

CHAPTER 1
SAWYER

Under the Sea.

When I was a kid, my mom used to sit me down in front of the "babysitter"—AKA, the TV—while she drank in the kitchen or entertained a "gentleman caller," as they used to say in ancient times. We couldn't afford cable or satellite, so she'd pop in one of the DVDs she'd found at Goodwill or garage sales. Never anything new.

Out of that limited selection, *The Little Mermaid* was my favorite, and when Sebastian the crab sang about living under the sea, I never failed to pop up to dance and sing. As a kid, all I wanted was to join him on the ocean floor and spend the rest of my life there. I was too young to understand that you can't even talk underwater, never mind sing. Also, spoiler alert: mermaids aren't real, and neither are talking crabs.

When I got older, those Disney movies turned into somewhat more adult content. Not like *that*, perv. I had one called *Wishmaster*, where an evil genie distorted every wish. Like, you want a million dollars? Sure, your rich grandma dies, and you get your inheritance. You want eternal beauty? *Bam*! You're a mannequin—that kind of thing.

Little did I know I'd one day have my own evil genie, and all my dreams would come true in some warped perversion of my childhood wish. I get to live on the ocean floor. And I can even sing if I want to.

I used to love the idea of the Trench. Locking up the worst of the worst—supervillains, scumbags, assassins, terrorists—and throwing away the key. They say the Trench is impossible to escape from, and I believe it. There are so many security measures taken, then backups of backups, it's almost ridiculous.

And even if someone miraculously managed to break from the prison itself, there's the ocean to deal with. When you're that deep, there's a lot more to it than just holding your breath and swimming to the surface. Which would be impossible anyway unless you're someone who doesn't breathe like a normal human. We're not talking about feet or meters here... the Trench is almost seven *miles* down from the surface of the ocean in the Mariana Trench. And that's among the least of the reasons why it's so secure. So for me to—

Maybe I better back up and remind you how I got here before I continue rambling...

Quick recap: Being a superhero became illegal. I did it anyway. Surprise!

I got busted and arrested by my former friend and partner,

Alex Garner, my evil genie—who now heads up the New York division of the Counter-Vigilante Taskforce. And then there was court.

My trial was pretty much an open-and-shut case. They had everything needed on me for a quick conviction. Even with the most expensive lawyers money could buy—and with my dad being Franklin Douglas III, I had those—my chances of staying out of prison were chiefly zero.

The only thing my attorneys were able to negotiate ahead of time was that my identity would be kept confidential in the interest of protecting my family and friends from any criminals and supervillains I'd fought and put away over the years. I guess it's better—and cheaper—than putting everyone into protective custody for the rest of their lives.

Keeping the true identities of former superheroes classified was already part of the deal the government had made with Eaglestar in exchange for him helping enforce the international ban on masked crimefighters and ensuring they don't rise again. But he seems to have less pull the longer this goes on, and my attorneys warned me that it wouldn't be a given.

The main question was whether someone like me would lose that privilege if we continued to break the law, especially once convicted.

Which... surprise again! I was.

In a rare act of non-egotism on Eaglestar's part, he insisted no one learn my real identity, which went far in helping me to get the deal. They even kept my face out of the press, which is extra important now with AIs everywhere utilizing facial recognition software.

And trust me, it's everywhere. AIs writing books, doing artwork, and voiceovers. Did you know James Earl Jones sold his voice to Disney to use forever as Darth Vader, even after he dies? Crazy world.

I even heard about this comedy club in Spain where cameras detect when a person laughs, and the club charges them a small fee. Not something I have to worry about though, since nothing I'm dealing with is very funny.

Now we're in the present, so let me start this thing out right...

Claustrophobia.

I never really had that problem before, but now it's getting to me. I'm stuck in a tiny cell with a thick transparent wall. The special submarine I've been stuffed into is small and cramped to begin with. I guess it's sort of like the one James Cameron took down to explore the wreck of the German battleship *Bismarck*, only slightly bigger.

Apparently, when you go far enough under the ocean, you can't just breathe normal air anymore—even inside. They have to start pumping in some other mixture of gases, or air bubbles blow up in your brain or something. I don't know the exact details, but I don't *want* to know them. It freaks me out too much to even think about. As far as I'm concerned, it's one of those "ignorance is bliss" types of things.

I've never minded small, enclosed places before. Maybe it's just because I had no reason to worry about them. But here, now, in a submarine made from some alloy most Americans don't know exists, I'm worrying... a lot. Imagine the tallest mountain, Everest. Now keep going. As I said, seven miles... Seven miles below sea level. That's how deep the Mariana Trench is. That's how high a commercial airplane flies—bonkers when you think about it. If something went wrong, even if you could get to the surface in time, it would cause a stroke because of depressurization or something.

Not even Sebastian would be singing down here.

In addition to the manacles on my hands and feet designed to inhibit superpowers I don't have and the small cell I'm confined to, there are also numerous guards armed with everything from heavy-duty firearms to lightning sticks to pepper spray. Depends on the situation and who they're trying to contain or put down, I suppose. They probably don't consider me much of a threat since, as I said, I don't have any powers. Not really, anyway. I doubt my memorizing and copying ability is anything they'd worry about.

One of the many ways the Guild of Masked Crimefighters used to monitor and regulate us was to give every hero and villain a "Power Rating." It went from zero to ten, with zero being a normal human and ten being, of course, Eaglestar. No surprise there, considering he was the one who came up with the system. Even the idea that someone could be more powerful than he was never even entered his mind. When I registered with the Guild, they tested my abilities and asked me a bunch of questions. And, when it was all said and done, I was given a Power Rating of one. I mean,

Cupid was a *two*, for crying out loud. I tried complaining to Frank about it, but he said I was lucky even to get a rating at all. He mentioned something about them considering a more accurate system that went from one to a hundred, in which case I'd probably still be around a one. So I never brought it up after that.

Wow, it's crazy to think about some of the stupid things I used to worry over. I'd give anything to go back to the days when my biggest apprehensions were my Power Rating and trying to get everyone to call me Red Raptor instead of Red Kite.

These guards have treated me with nothing but contempt since we left San Francisco. I guess none of them were ever fans of Black Harrier, or they decided after I broke the law, they weren't. I had a glimmer of hope that maybe as law enforcement themselves, they'd feel some small connection to me, pity even... but there's no sign of it anywhere.

We continue our plunge into the dark depths of the Pacific Ocean, diving farther and farther from the unmarked ship that carried us. With the claustrophobia I'm experiencing, the trip down feels much longer than it actually is. Dropping down thirty-five thousand feet under the ocean's surface takes a couple of hours, but it feels like a couple of days. I'm finding it hard to breathe and feeling a bit of panic settling in.

Soon, there's no light coming from the surface. The only illumination is the vehicle's front headlights and the occasional glow of one of those weird fish with the lamps on their heads. Other than that, it's just eerie, damning blackness. A gigantic eye appears as I stare through the porthole, sending me toppling backward off my cot.

I swear loud enough for one of the guards to show up. He also sees the whale as it swims by and looks curiously at the sub, probably deciding whether or not it's edible. Luckily, it decides not to make us into a snack and wanders off.

"Keep it down, criminal," he says, slamming his lightning stick on the bars. A few sparks pop.

There's that word again: criminal. My whole life devoted to stopping them, and now, I'm treated like one. I shake my head and sit, burying my head in my manacled hands.

As I ponder how I ended up here, I realize this might be the first time I've ever truly been alone in my life. As a kid, I always had Mom. Then, Frank showed up, and even before I knew he was my father, he'd always just... been there for me. I missed Amy, Mr. Chen, and everyone else. Hell, I'd probably even give Logan a big hug if I could.

Okay, fine, that's going too far. Really, it's his fault I'm in here in the first place.

But, yeah. I'm alone.

Other than the two sub-pilots and several guards, the only others onboard are the other prisoners also making the trip: the giant intelligent gorilla known as Royal Rampage and the no-holds-barred vigilante who calls himself Justice. Yeah, I know you're probably thinking, *That name can't possibly be something available for just anyone to use.* It's become like a running joke. He just doesn't care. That's kind of the whole point, that he does what he wants in the name of justice—or his idea of justice, anyway. If that means putting down criminals so they don't keep hurting people, then he doesn't hesitate. So you can see how he ended up on his way down here with me.

Also, if I'm not reading the signs completely wrong, he's probably my brother—well, half-brother—whom I'd never met until just before I got arrested. In the same way that I inherited my father's ability to mimic things I see, Justice also appears able to copy stuff from watching someone do it. And Frank and I are the only ones I know of with that particular gift. And he doesn't know anything about his father, which was the same situation I was in until a few years ago.

Do I tell him? Would that be a good thing or a bad thing? Especially considering he's gonna spend the rest of his life cut off from everyone on the surface. I just can't see any benefit to it yet. Even worse, what if I'm wrong?

"Almost there," I hear the guard say to one of his fellow torturers.

I stand and peer out the window again. If I smush my face just right and strain my neck to the point where any chiropractor would wince, I can barely see the Trench. Even at such a distance, with such low visibility, it's quite a sight, all things considered. If I weren't headed there for the rest of my life, I'd probably be excited to see it in person. Like everyone, I've seen pictures and even videos before, but they don't live up to the real thing. It sits on the deepest part of the ocean floor, lit by floodlights, as well as the light from the numerous windows and portholes. A massive, shining complex of sections and tubes, like a futuristic space station that fell into the Pacific and sank to the bottom.

"Home sweet home, Spandex," the guard says, returning to my cell.

He's a big guy but nothing like some of the punks I've taken down over the years. One-on-one, he'd be begging for mercy. But those days are over, I suppose.

"Hands against the wall," he orders.

"I'm handcuffed, and you have a weapon, yet you're still afraid I'm gonna pull something?"

"Shut it," he warns.

"No, really. Do you think I'm gonna try to make a break for it?"

He angrily pulls a ring of keys from his side and starts fumbling to find the right one. Guess he's upset. Imagine how I feel.

The door swings open, and I honestly consider dropping the dude. My hands and feet might be tied up, but I still have a little movement. More than I need. But that wouldn't be a great way to start my stay at the Trench. Instead, I play the role of good prisoner and let him manhandle me, tossing me against the wall as he reverses the orientation of my handcuffs.

Then, he ushers me out of my cell and down a long corridor toward the hatch. It's only a few minutes before I feel the rumble of the sub stop, and I know we're docked. The hatch opens, saltwater trickling down on me.

"Is it supposed to leak that way?" I glare at the ladder. "And I'm supposed to climb that without hands?"

"You're a superhero, ain'tcha?" Guard numero uno says. "Let's see you be super."

I wanna remind him that I was powerless *before* the cuffs took away powers, but instead, I shimmy up the ladder backward with more grace than he'd probably have, doing the right way. As I reach the top, I feel two sets of hands grab me, and I'm airborne.

"Don't try anything *smart*," a voice tells me.

"That's probably easier for you than me," I mumble.

"What was that?" guard number two demands, spinning me toward him.

"I wouldn't think of it," I say.

"Keep your comments to yourself. You're a maggot now."

About fifteen men in gray guard uniforms run past me as I'm escorted in. A few seconds later, I can hear strains behind me. Peering over my shoulder, I see all of them trying to lift a sedated Royal Rampage from the sub-hatch.

"You'll have plenty of time to meet the inmates," the guard says, giving me a shove.

We stop at two large metal doors. A red light above blinks, and a buzzer sounds. The doors whoosh open like a sci-fi set. Strangely, once we're inside, it looks like an ordinary prison. Gray walls and gray floors that match the guards' gray uniforms and gray guns, and… you get the point. Someone around here got ahold of some seriously boring interior design magazine.

Standard lighting along the ceiling and a few panels on the floor. All pretty mundane, except there are a lot of windows made out of what must be some *extraordinarily* thick transparent material. I'm not sure why because outside, you can only see a few feet until the prison lights don't extend any farther.

"Stupid monkey!" a guard yells as they enter behind us.

"Maybe we need to lead him in with a banana," another guard jokes. "Want a banana, Curious George?"

Rampage growls, but it's weak since he's still groggy.

"He's so stupid, we could probably just show him a picture of one on my phone, and he'd think it was real." They all laugh.

"Hey, you don't have to be jerks," I say. "He understands everything you're saying, you know."

"Shut up, fresh meat. Nobody asked for your opinion."

"I'm sure nobody asked your parents why first cousins were having a kid together, but that doesn't mean they shouldn't have," I say.

My detainer wrenches my arms hard and pushes me forward. "You're gonna learn some respect, kid."

"Wait, Ernie," the guard I'd insulted said. We turn around, and he's traipsing toward us, hand on his lightning stick. He gets in my face and says, "What the hell is that supposed to mean?"

"It means you're an inbred piece of sh—" Then I get my first lesson in how things work around here when the guard backhands me hard across the jaw.

The other guards laugh at their friend's embarrassment. Even Royal Rampage smiles sleepily.

I spit some blood from my mouth, then nod toward Rampage. "See? He gets it."

I guess Ernie's had enough too. He slams me in the solar plexus with the butt of his weapon and knocks the air from my lungs.

This gets Royal Rampage fully awake and aware. The giant gorilla makes a move like he's gonna attack, but I look him in the eye and shake my head, warning him off. As much as I'd love to take these guys down, I have to remind myself that they're the good guys—technically speaking, of course. Or, at least, they're on the right side of the law. From what I've seen so far, "good" may not be the best way to describe them. Either way, I don't need to make what's sure to be a miserable time in here even more miserable by getting into it with the guards right out of the gate.

I keep my mouth shut the rest of the way as I'm shuffled down the passageway. We stop at a booth protected by opaque plexiglass with a round speaker in the middle.

"Wait here. I won't warn you again," Ernie says.

"I know. Nothing smart."

"Well, you already did something dumb, didn't'cha?" He points to a camera mounted in the corner. Then to the guards standing a few feet away. "Smile."

I lean down to see if I can see anything through the small slot at the bottom of the booth's window.

"You all right, man?" a voice behind me asks.

I turn to see Justice, tattoos covering most of his body, red mohawk… Red hair. Oh, man. Of course he'd have red hair. Frank's never dated a woman *without* red hair.

"Yeah, I'm fine," I say.

"Hey, don't worry," he says. "I'm gonna have your back in here. I hope I can count on you to do the same."

I answer Justice with a simple nod since I don't know what else to say. The guy seemed like a total psycho before, but the more I learn about him, the more I realize he thought he was doing the right thing in some twisted way. Besides, I've been thinking about what I'm gonna do in here to protect myself. I feel like there aren't a whole lot of options.

"Step forward," a voice crackles through the speaker.

The intake process takes a while, but I don't know why I'm even worried about things like that anymore. It's not like I'm ever getting out of here. I have all the time in the world. They have me confirm my inmate number. It feels odd that they don't mention or ask me for my name, but that was the deal my lawyers got me, and they stick to it. Then they issue me my jumpsuit, which is what I'm gonna be wearing from now on. Guess that saves time picking out clothes in the mornings. Gotta look on the bright side of things, right?

After that, they take us to our cells. They're not much bigger than the ones in the sub we arrived in, which is disappointing. Plus, mine has a funny smell that I'm really not enjoying. I guess, eventually, I'll go nose-blind to it. I hope it doesn't take too long.

Each cell has a small bed attached to the wall with a thin

mattress and a pillow that's so flat, it looks like it's been the victim of a Zamboni attack. And the folded-up blanket they hand me is so thin, I could rip it like a tissue. There's also a small sink and a tiny metal toilet with no lid molded into the floor, which seems to contain salt water—sort of makes sense.

And then there's the tiny porthole that I suppose is meant to serve as a sad excuse for a window. Or maybe it's just a reminder of how hopeless it is here. If it's true what they say about people getting depressed when they don't get any sun, this place is the most depressing place on Earth.

From what I understand, they used to leave everyone in their cells most of the time, but the prisoners started to go stir-crazy, and there were complaints. Lawyers got involved, followed by humanitarian organizations. Eventually, the people who ran the prison were forced to give the prisoners a yard to exercise in, a library, and access to books and entertainment.

Other than that, the only thing in the cells is a writing desk attached to the wall. The stool to sit on is also connected to the floor, like the toilet. It looks like they don't want too many things that can be thrown or used as a weapon during a riot or whatever. I wonder how many riots they get in here? It seems most of these prisoners have nothing to lose, so I feel it's probably a lot.

Then again, I guess I don't have much to lose at this point, either. *Yay, me.*

CHAPTER 2
ALEX

Disaster.

That's where Frank's campaign for mayor is heading. Ever since I arrested Sawyer and sent the Resistors on the run, he's stopped his circuit and stayed holed up in his penthouse atop Douglas Tower. No rallies, no press conferences, nothing. He's also started drinking more than I've ever seen him drink.

Wait. That's not quite true. After Toby—his Red Kite sidekick between me and Sawyer—was killed by Chef Maléfique, he was pretty bad. But this is close.

Sawyer being sent to the Trench hit him hard. I know he feels responsible for it. Sawyer's life may not have been great before he became Frank's sidekick, but at least he wasn't rotting away in a prison at the bottom of the ocean. I can't prove it, but I'm sure Frank was helping Sawyer continue as Black Harrier despite the ban. Probably even encouraging it.

And then there's the spyware scandal that just hit the

news. At first, it seemed like something that might just blow over. People don't generally get all that upset anymore about companies mining data and finding out everything about us. Whether through social media, our shopping habits, or the searches we perform on the internet, someone out there knows it all. And even when someone gets pissed off about it, they tend to get over it fairly quickly. It's become one of the realities of living in the modern world. But there was something different about this. Douglas Industries was selling it to governments, including our own. They also sold info to some pretty evil regimes around the world in the name of law enforcement. With a lot of places around the world, that can be a very gray area.

When journalists started digging into it, they discovered people had been arrested, "disappeared," and even killed after being spied on with this software. Frank apparently wasn't behind it. Claims he didn't even know about it. But that's irrelevant. Even if it was Luis Chen—his right-hand man running the company—who was responsible, Frank still has two things working against him: First, he's both the face of the company and the name behind it. And second, he's running for mayor, which opens up a new level of scrutiny and theoretically forces him to take responsibility.

I'm standing in front of his penthouse door. Last time I was in the building, I arrested a kid named Javier. Something I still regret. Sawyer was the kid's only friend, and we forced Javier to turn on him. I can't even imagine what kind of mental torment the kid must be putting himself through now.

And Frank may blame himself for all this, but the onus falls directly upon my weary shoulders. I wanted to be a cop for so long, to do the right thing, but it seems like the longer I do what I always wanted to do, the more miserable I become.

In the old days, before Frank lived at the bottom of a bottle, he'd know I was here. He'd already be opening the door, having seen me on his security system. Today, I don't even know if he's conscious in there. He's become a shell of his former self. Less than a shell. More like a ghost. I hesitate to say he used to be a "great man" because I'm aware of so many of his flaws. But in many ways, he really was.

After a long, labored breath, I ring the doorbell. I'm not here to arrest or question anyone. Quite the opposite. I just want to clear the air. We may not be on the best of terms, especially after Sawyer's incarceration, but still, when I was a kid, Frank was like a father to me—sort of, anyway—and I don't like seeing him this way. I don't think I've felt this bad about anything since my parents were killed.

The door cracks open, and some woman I've never seen before pops out in a dress more revealing than most swimsuits. She looks just like the model on the cover of the latest *Sports Illustrated* swimsuit issue. Is that still a thing people pay attention to? I, uh, saw it on the rack next to the register at the bodega when I was getting a bag of Doritos. I'm really getting old, aren't I?

Oh, wait. I think it *is* her.

"Uh, hi there. I was looking for Frank?" I'm surprised I even got that sentence out; my mouth is so dry.

"He's here somewhere," she says, words slurred almost to the point of incoherence. "*Frank*! Some guy's here to see you."

"What guy?" Frank shouts back from another room. Though I can tell he's been pounding down whiskey as well, his voice is loud and clear.

"What guy?" she asks, turning back to me. I can tell she's having trouble even focusing. I hope alcohol is the only thing they're partaking of here.

I practically need to shout because of the loud music and the fact that everyone else seems to be shouting.

"Alex Garner. *Detective* Alex Garner."

"Al the gardener!" she yells toward the other room.

I begin to correct her, honestly doing my best not to laugh, but it doesn't matter. Frank comes stumbling in, his hair and clothes disheveled, looking confused.

"I don't have a gardener. I don't even have a gard—!" He looks over at me, and his eyes come into sharp focus. "Oh, it's you. What happened—we get a noise complaint? I told the band to turn it down from eleven."

Then, he does something so *uncharacteristically* Frank that all portends of humor washes from me like a deluge had hit me. He cracks up at his own joke. When he finally stops, he glares around at us, surprised no one else is laughing. With a dismissive sigh, he wrangles his arm around the swimsuit model. "You know—eleven. Like in that one movie...."

Blank stare. She doesn't get it. At all. Probably because she was raised on *Toy Story* films.

"Never mind. It's wasted on you. You're too young."

She shrugs.

"What's, uh… What's going on here, Frank?" I ask.

"Not that it's any of your business, but it's a party. We're celebrating."

"Celebrating what?" I ask, stunned. Not much to celebrate these days, if you ask me.

"It's Giselle's birthday," he says as he points to the model.

"Who's Giselle?" she asks, looking insulted.

"Who's Giselle," he repeats, snickering and doubling over. "This one—always trying to be funny."

"I'm Gigi."

Frank looks up, confused but still smiling. "Then where's Giselle?"

"I don't know who Giselle is." She shoves him away a bit.

"Then whose birthday is it?"

"Mine."

"But you just said you weren't Giselle!" God, that drunk laugh is awful. I thought Serious Frank was bad, but Drunk Frank is the worst. The absolute worst. I've only met the *real* Drunk Frank a few times—as opposed to the act he sometimes puts on for the paparazzi—but he's as obnoxious as all get out.

"Ahhh, I'm just kidding," Frank says. "I know your name. You know me. Funny Frank."

Funny Frank? Yeah, right.

After a slight hesitation, Gigi laughs along with Frank, giving him a playful slap.

When she's not looking, he gives me a *wow, that was close* look.

I finally have to put a stop to it. "Hold on. Gigi, can you please excuse us for a minute? I have to talk to Frank in private."

As she shrugs and leaves the room, Frank watches her go like he's a hormone-raging teenager. "I could swear her name was—"

"Frank, we have a problem. I need you to sober up and listen to me."

"Sober up?" he asks incredulously. "I'm fine." He takes a big gulp of whiskey from his tumbler. "What kind of problem?"

"Got a call from your campaign manager, Gina."

"Gina! That's what I was trying to think of. Maybe it's *her* birthday. I can't keep all these 'G' names straight anymore."

"And I'm sure it doesn't help that they're all attractive redheads, either."

"Are they? I hadn't noticed. Who the hell *is* Giselle, then?" Frank asks as if I would know.

"Frankie!" Another woman's voice comes from the other side of the penthouse—a very loud, very whiny voice.

A look of anger crosses his face. "Why's she calling me that? Nobody calls me that."

Understandably, he has a thing about being called by that name. His grandfather was "Franklin," and his dad, "Frankie Jr.," happened to run the majority of organized crime in this city. When Frank was a kid, they called him "Trey"—as in "the third"—but that's worse than Frankie to him. He does *not* like being reminded of whose son he is.

Frank is just Frank or Franklin. That's it.

I try to avoid what I know is coming next. "Listen, I have to—"

"*What*?" He shouts to the other room, all playfulness now replaced by annoyance bordering on rage.

"When are you coming back? We miss you," the woman says.

"I'll be back when I'm ready! Can't you see I'm busy talking to my old sidekick here?"

My heart skips a beat, and I can feel panic set in. I whisper-yell at him.

"Frank, what the hell are you doing? 'Sidekick'? Really?"

He waves it off. "They don't know what the hell I'm talking about, and they don't care. They're just here because I'm rich. It's not like they're suspicious that I'm Black Harrier or something."

"*Keep it down.* Dammit, Frank. That's one of the reasons I'm here. Your campaign manager said there are rumblings of *another* big story coming out about you, but you're ignoring her calls. She has no idea what the story could be because—I *hope*—she has no idea you were Black Harrier."

"So what? What does that have to do with you?"

"Chen's blowing her off, too, and she didn't know who else to contact," I say. "So she asked for my help. She had my card from when I came by during your campaign announcement dinner, and she knew we had known one another previously. So, knowing I'm a *cop*, she asked me to check on you and make sure everything's okay."

"Everything's fine, *Officer*," he insists. "Can't you see?" He spreads a hand out behind him. "What else could a man want?"

"Oh, I don't know, perhaps to be mayor of New York?"

He puts a hand on my shoulder, and I feel the full weight of it. "Alex, my campaign is done. Over with. *Kaput*."

I slap his arm away, causing him to lose his balance and nearly collide with me. Then, before I can stop myself, I growl, "This is about a lot more than your campaign, you selfish bastard."

He squints at me, trying to focus. "*What* did you just say to me?"

I grab him by the shirt, and he's so surprised that he almost spills his tumbler of Scotch. I'd smack him in the face to get him to snap out of it if I thought it'd help rather than have him try to deck me.

It takes everything to keep my voice low enough that the party girls don't hear.

"I *said* you're being selfish. We're talking about a lot more lives than yours being affected if this story turns out to be about you being Harrier. Think about Megan."

"Don't you say her name," Frank stammers. "Don't you say her damn name."

"Okay, what about *mine*? As well as Sawyer, the entire Guild, Chen, and everyone else who works for you."

Frank's expression is still one of anger, but I think I can see in his eyes that I'm finally getting through.

He drives his forearms upward into mine, breaking my hold on him. "Oh, that's rich, coming from you. Worried about Sawyer, huh? Now that you put him away and threw out the key?"

"Frank—"

"Don't *Frank* me, traitor. That boy looked up to you," he says. "You were like a brother to him."

I can't breathe. The words catch in my throat. I think I stutter out a few syllables, but that's all I can manage.

"What's wrong? Cat got your tongue, little birdie?"

I shake my head. "Look at you, Frank. Look at you."

"Look at *you*," he says, a typical drunken response.

I ignore him. "Running for mayor was a stupid idea, no matter what good you thought you might accomplish if you won. You're too rich and too public. You were already the target of paparazzi all these years, and you lucked out that nobody ever found out and exposed who you really were. But running for office took it to a whole new level of scrutiny."

"Too rich," Frank scoffs as he tries to smooth the wrinkles out of his shirt like it wasn't already a mess.

Silence lingers for longer than I'm comfortable with before he finally says, "Alex?"

"Yeah?"

He opens the door. "Get out."

"What?"

“You heard me. Get out of my house now, or I’ll have security throw you out.”

I shake my head. “Glad to see I was able to get through to you.”

He moves forward to force me out, but I don’t give him the satisfaction. The door is already slamming shut as I take the first step into the hall. Definitely not one of my most successful missions.

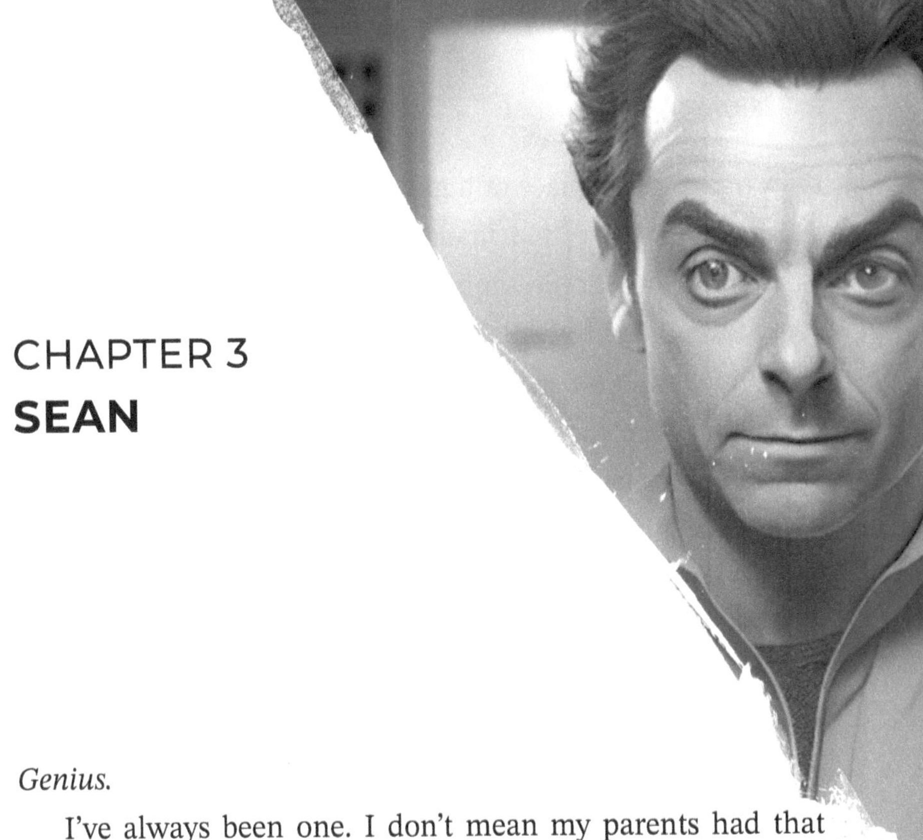

CHAPTER 3
SEAN

Genius.

I've always been one. I don't mean my parents had that bumper sticker: *my child is on the principal's honor roll* or similar. I mean a genuine *bona fide*, smarter-than-anyone-alive genius. I can see the look on your face right now. And you're not special; I've seen that face my whole life.

"True geniuses don't need to tell people they are geniuses," I've heard said. But in reality, stupid people need things explained to them. Most of the time, more than once.

I'm not explicitly saying *you're* stupid—although your synapses are not firing on the same level as mine. I obtained my first degree at nine years old from a little school called Yale University. While you were discovering boogers could be different colors, I was learning typology maths. Never heard of it? Hmm. As I was saying...

I was, without a doubt, the youngest student to which

they, or any other place of higher learning, had ever presented a degree. I'm sure that made them feel superior, as if they were somehow the pre-pubescent brainchild who'd mastered every form of study available.

Why Yale, you ask? Quite simple, really. Harvard and Princeton were too far a commute for my mother to drive. Sure, I could have driven; driving is little more than making basic calculations. But alas, being a child has its disadvantages. I couldn't see over the steering wheel. And there's that pesky little thing called "the law." Proof, in my mind, that the decision-makers haven't a clue what they are doing. Even at nine, I was more qualified to operate a vehicle than any man in a jumpsuit who turns left for a living.

My mother gave birth to me in Manchester, Connecticut. I was told it was a cold evening, but I looked it up, and it was average. She also said I was difficult, but at fourteen hours in labor, I was utterly average as well. But that was the last time 'average' would be used to describe anything about me.

When I came out, I hit the ground running. A typical newborn can barely focus on the dark shapes before its pitiful eyes. Everyone—the doctors, nurses, all of them—could tell I was fully aware of my surroundings when they put me into my mother's waiting arms.

Glory Meyers was the most extraordinary woman the world has ever known. Many kids believe that about their mothers, but she was a saint. I say "was" because she died, and her death made me who I am today. My dad died too, but it was my mother's death that destroyed me.

I know it's difficult to fathom, but I can still remember the first hours of my existence. I remember the smell of ammonia in the hospital halls, the white sterility of the walls with the gray chair rail, and those awful pink curtains. I recall my mother's nurse, Jenny. And most of all, I remember my father, absent on all accounts.

Before you get the wrong impression, this isn't one of those "Daddy didn't love me" stories, but the truth remains: Daddy didn't love me.

As a kid who has those early years of life committed to memory better than most, I can tell you he wasn't around much. The worst part, it wasn't due to him being some big-money CEO. He drove a milk truck.

He wasn't a drunk or an addict. He didn't beat me. He simply… didn't care. He'd come home after a long day slinging milk crates, remove his pants at the front door, and plop down on the stained recliner with the tan and blue fabric by the TV. He had the *worst* taste in television too. He would watch hours of *Gilligan's Island* repeats. How many times can you watch a bunch of imbeciles fail to succeed before winding up defeated and depressed yourself? At a mere four years old, I could have told you every way they could have left that island, and some of them were right beneath their noses the whole time.

Little did I know my future would look a lot like *Gilligan's Island.*

Ironically, here I am, stranded in the Trench, unable to escape for the past decade and a half. I've concocted plan after plan. The problem is all schemes require more than just myself. And so far, the pickings here at the bottom of the ocean have been slim.

Do you know how difficult it is to be the world's most intelligent person, imprisoned with a bunch of supervillains who can't spell villain? It's A before I, simpletons!

Yes, I know I'm considered a supervillain myself. But everyone is a hero in his own mind. And I *am* a hero. The greatest hero the world has ever known. It's just that everyone is too stupid to realize it yet.

Harrier? Just a has-been. Besides, as I understand it, he's coming to join me now.

As for Eaglestar, I don't pay attention. Eaglestar? A puppet. A government man through and through. He mostly fights relics from the past. Oh, and Battlegear. Let's not forget that cretin. He thinks he knows tech? That he's super-intelligent? Puh-lease. He's minor league compared to me. Single-A, even.

And most of those "heroes" have sidekicks! And men in chairs whispering in their ears, telling them where to go and what to do. Little boys and girls soaring around in bright colors, just begging to be cannon fodder. What do I have? *Robots!*

But more on that later...

Around two years of age, my mom started taking me on "special trips" to the doctor. In other words, I became something of a lab rat. At first, it was a lot of fun, like I was playing with costly toys meant for grownups. Really, it's the same story you'd hear from any super flying around these days. The thing that made my story unique—not special, just unique—was I was informed my mind was already as developed as a fifteen-year-old's. And not just any fifteen-year-old—a brilliant one.

Two years old. I even impress myself.

I skipped grade school entirely—never even stepped foot through the doors. My hands were never dipped into paint so my mother could hang my unimpressive handprint on the fridge. I never had to play with bins of beans or glue elbow macaroni to construction paper.

At three years young, I sat under the tutelage of some of the brightest minds in the world. All this and more at the expense of the United States Government. If only they knew, someday I would be the president of the world! President might not be the correct term... ruler? King? Lord? Lord. I like that—Lord of the World. I'll have to get cards printed. Sean Meyers, Lord of the World.

I was a good kid. I fell in with a good crowd in college. I was valedictorian of my graduating class. They had to stack ten phone books so that I could reach the microphone. Even then, I strained to see my comrades in the congregation. Nine years old, and I was told it was the most encouraging and well-spoken speech they'd heard in all their years. But I was humble—I still am... I know, I know, saying you're humble is the opposite of humility, but truth is important to me.

Without truth, what do we have?

"You are a work in progress," I said with the vocal cords of a boy barely out of diapers, "so don't expect perfection. Even as a graduate of one of the greatest schools in this fine country, you will not get everything perfect every time. You're not me, after all."

They laughed at that point, thinking I had made a joke.

"Extend grace to others," I went on, "but most importantly, to yourself." It was true then, and it is true today. "Nothing will be handed to you. You'll have to work hard for it all."

For years, I fought for the good guys. I didn't realize how even the phrase "good" was relative to the individual's thought process. You must remember, this was the early 2000s—years before every university in America elevated self-reflection higher than academics. I wasn't taught that truth was relative, and still I don't believe it is. Truth is absolute. But perspective determines what you *perceive* truth to be, and I believe perception creates one's reality.

When I became a "villain,"—A before I—I saw things from two opposite ends of the spectrum and quickly found the absolute truth. I had experienced both sides of the proverbial coin and realized that the best position a penny could be in was upright and spinning.

Imagine determining which company would produce the best product at any given moment and using history to prove its success? To play the stock market as if counting cards at a hole-in-the-wall riverboat casino?

I'd met a handful of masked villains over the years—even befriended a few. But they all held one thing in common: they were dirty, thieving, greedy monsters—even the nice ones. A few years after I graduated from Yale, I decided my gifts should be used for something *good.*

Then, it hit me.

It was my birthday. I figured I owed it to myself—like a rite of passage. I was becoming a man. But I still wasn't old enough for a driver's license. Riding my bicycle down a deserted road, which I often did while thinking to myself, I came across a scene that would forever change the trajectory of my life.

I love to paint word pictures, so imagine this: A man standing beside the road, screaming into the sky. At first, I assumed him a vagrant with some undiagnosed mental illness, but then I realized he was nicely dressed, standing beside what I presumed to be his car—a very elegant luxury sedan. It was dark, so I had to concentrate whilst following his gaze. Only then did I see what he was shouting at—lights in the sky—colorful lights rotating rapidly.

I quickly made calculations to deduce what it could be. Nothing known to me made sense. Hence the "unidentified" part of UFO. The general populace has a huge misconception about what that term means. "Unidentified Flying Object" does not automatically imply a space vehicle manned by alien lifeforms from another world. It simply means it's flying in the sky and is not immediately identifiable. Most of these "objects" are assuredly prototypes and test vehicles from the United States or a foreign government. However, I had never come across anything like this. That's not to say it couldn't have existed here on Earth, but my hacking skills were—even at the time—without par, and it's highly doubtful information about something such as this had slipped through my research.

Then the man spotted me.

"Do you see them?" he bellowed, clearly distressed. "You see them, too, right?"

I nodded, still unable to determine what I was witnessing. Furthermore, I couldn't rule out the possibility that the man *was* mentally unstable. If so, a bad reaction to the vision before us could've proven fatal to me.

He pointed upward. "They keep coming back for me. Ever since I was a kid. They're studying us. We can't let them succeed. They're going to—"

A bright, white beam burst from the nucleus of the spinning lights and vaporized the man mid-sentence.

To this day, I don't know if he was taken up or wholly destroyed. I suppose I'll never know. I would like to say that I stood my ground and tried to do something helpful, but that's not what happened. The truth is important. And the truth is, I ran. I threw my bike down and fled into the woods. In fact, I didn't stop running through the thick trees until my lungs burned and my legs gave out.

I was changed.

After that night, I wiped the stupid off my face and began preparing. It was like any other form of education. Study, memorize, apply. I researched UFO and alien sightings. Yes, there are certainly a lot of crackpots, liars, and drama-seekers out there. But a relatively large percentage of the stories check out under the sort of scrutiny only one such as I can provide.

My discovery: there is an invasion force preparing to visit Earth. They've come before and left behind artifacts. Even fought some of this world's most powerful beings. But those were just scouting missions. These aliens are sending their entire fleet to conquer us, and their arrival is imminent.

We are in danger, and no one is doing a damned thing about it. I tried to sound the alarm, attempted to warn the government, the Guild, the media. I was mocked, scorned, and marked as a crazy conspiracy theorist. Tin foil hats arrived in my mail from undisclosed senders for weeks on end.

No one cared. No one that matters, anyway.

It's up to me.

Between everything I've learned and the billions of dollars I've invested in equipment, I can promise that no force alive—including extraterrestrial—will defeat my army of robots and other machines currently hidden away around the globe, no matter how technologically advanced they may be. I've tested my mechanical creations against the most powerful beings on the planet, including Eaglestar. Their abilities have been strained against the military might of the wealthiest nations on Earth as well. And each time said tests conclude, I improve my robotic children.

If those trials and experiments caused the world to see me as a villain, then so be it, a villain I will be. They eventually got me into trouble, arrested, and thrown into the most challenging place on Earth from which to escape.

But I know the truth, and the truth has made me free. Free to do what's necessary. Free to stop worrying about laws, norms, and rules that do nothing to protect us from the most significant threat humanity has ever faced.

The time has come to escape from the Trench and make final preparations for the impending invasion. I am going to save this planet the way I know it needs to be saved, no matter how many lives I have to take to do it.

So how are my plans going thus far?

Perfectly.

If the Black Harrier thought he would come in here and suddenly be in charge, he was sadly mistaken.

As I stroll through the cafeteria to obtain my daily fill of the garbage they get away with feeding us in here, the other prisoners step aside. Some probably don't even know why they're getting out of my way. They just see the others doing it and assume there's a very good reason for it. But they're in the minority, mostly newly incarcerated individuals who haven't yet heard through the grapevine whom they should fear and respect. Most of them know better, which is why I can skip to the front of the line, and no one—not a single individual of any size, shape, or ferocity—says a single word to me about it. I even get extra helpings, which is something they never do for anyone.

It's good to be the one pulling the strings.

How, pray tell, did this situation come about? I'm so glad

you asked. In case it's escaped your limited attention, I adore talking about myself. The thing about possessing my intelligence is that I'm able to deduce things from myriad angles. I have not managed to become the most influential person in the Trench because of any *one* reason. Some follow because of simple subornation. Using the library computers, I can access their commissary accounts and keep them flush with whatever small luxuries they're able to purchase within these walls.

For others—primarily guards—I have ingress to their outside bank accounts, which I fill with just enough extra cash to keep them in my pocket without the IRS becoming suspicious. And I should know how much that is since I do most of their taxes. Then there are others about whom I have acquired pertinent information that keeps them doing my bidding. It would be a shame if security officer Ubong's indiscretions involving his commanding officer's wife were to somehow find its way onto social media or the national news.

The only thing I *can't* manage from here is escape. No matter how many carrots or sticks I may have with the guards, it would take far too much for any of them to liberate me. This is going to have to be a coordinated effort between the guards on my payroll, prisoners over whom I hold sway, and a certain bird-themed hero who recently took up residence here himself.

A number of individuals have already been lined up as part of my prison break. Bullshark, of course, will be the muscle if that part isn't already evident to you. This is a man who allowed himself to be experimented upon in harrowing ways to garner an advantage against the law. He's perfect for the task and as dedicated as they come. But he's not exactly the brightest bulb in the chandelier.

I also require the unhindered abilities of one of the few women incarcerated here: Sinsation. That's not a typo, by the way. It's a play on words. I suppose she thinks it's clever, but in my dealings with her, I've found she's anything but. She's also not quite "all there," if you get my meaning. In fact, she probably belongs in an asylum instead of here, but I doubt any hospital would be able to hold her for long, no matter how secure. However, I believe she will prove useful nonetheless.

Sinsation was a chemist working with pheromones for a perfume company when she discovered a formula allowing her to influence men almost to the point of control. After a bad breakup with her life partner, she went off the deep end and became a criminal, using her ability to take whatever she wanted. She has had more plastic surgeries than Michael Jackson and took to wearing a costume so revealing a Kardashian would balk. All this to further enhance the effects of the pheromones.

Using that to our advantage, however, will demand a bit of work on my behalf, reducing the effects of the power dampeners within the facility. It's something I've pondered long and hard throughout my incarceration. I already have several working theories on accomplishing the task, and I should find it quite simple.

Next, an expert marksman. Superhuman in that regard. This person will also have to be ruthless to a level even most criminals here would find appalling. I've treated with Deadeye on more than one occasion, but he has yet to swear his obeisance. I'm confident he'll come around, but apparently, he still performs the odd job for the government despite his criminal background, and he's concerned their partnership will be nullified should he find himself on the run.

If they've found no fault in their arrangement despite all he's done thus far, I fail to comprehend how absconding from the Trench would make a difference. However, he's still a bit hesitant.

Lastly, the key is going to be our newest guest. Why is Black Harrier so important to my plan? I wouldn't want to spoil it for you. You'll just have to find out along with everyone else.

Including him.

CHAPTER 4
SAWYER

Lunchtime.

After I settle in for a little while, the cell doors slide open, and we're told to file out into lines to head to the cafeteria. The dining facility is pretty much what you'd expect under the circumstances. The whole place looks like it's made of stainless steel, which I used to think looked old-fashioned when I was a kid, but now it's in, I guess. Now it looks pretty classy. In a kitchen, I mean. Not here, covering every single surface. Here, the monotone look just adds to the hopelessness of the situation, which is probably part of the design. Cold. Sterile. Lifeless.

I follow a line of prisoners to the food pick-up area, where we each grab a tray, paper napkin, and a plastic spork thing. I suppose they think that a spork is good because it'll do the job of scooping up food and still has the tiny prongs on the end, but it's not as dangerous as a fork or knife. You could still probably excavate someone's eyeball with it, though. Wow, that's dark. Where did that come from? Has prison already changed me after only a few hours?

They've got inmates serving inmates. Guess that saves on payroll. A man with eyes like a pug's and only a few wisps of hair plops some mystery food onto my tray, and I honestly don't even look at it. I'm too busy trying to figure out my strategy. In every movie or TV show I've seen about someone entering prison, they're advised to find the biggest, toughest guy there and kick his butt to show dominance—prove they shouldn't be messed with. The problem is this place is full of supervillains, and it's difficult to figure out who the biggest, toughest one is.

Also, once I do decide, there's a good chance they'll kill me before I can actually beat them up. I'm a good fighter but rely heavily on body armor and equipment. Wearing nothing but an orange jumpsuit doesn't exactly make me feel powerful.

My first thought is to go after Royal Rampage since he's an easy target. I doubt anyone in here looks more imposing than a giant gorilla. But there are a couple of problems with that. First, Rampage is actually a good guy. He did nothing wrong. He's down here for the same reason I am: continuing to fight criminals as a vigilante. Second, because he's new, he doesn't have a badass reputation for me to use in my favor. Sure, most people presumably know who he is and what he can do, but they also know he fought with the Guild. They might think it's a farce.

Plus, there's the fact that he would probably rip my arms off and leave me spurting on the floor until I died. So there's that.

That leaves me back at square one.

The place is sprawling with guards. However, most look busy enough to at least give me a good start. We were warned upon arrival that the Trench is equipped with power-dampening emitters in triple redundancy. The devices are securely placed within the metal walls. The chances of someone getting through that mystery material to find even one of them before security pounced are slim. For me, that's good news. It's possible the technology might have some effect on my ability to almost supernaturally recall anything I've seen or heard, and replicate the action—but what good would that do me here other than always knowing what was being served for lunch?

Anyone else would be at a disadvantage.

As I walk through the cafeteria, I spot a famous villain from the '80s named Ion. His ability was to build up kinetic energy in his fists that would release like an explosion upon impact. One punch would have the power to level a building. Unfortunately, he's barely bigger than me and probably pushing sixty.

In front of him, getting her tray is Maestra Mal. I hardly recognize her without her sexy teacher costume, but the beauty mark below her right eye is a dead giveaway. I honestly don't even know what her power is, but I'm not about to pick a fight with an unarmed woman.

After waiting in line between Doctor Defiant and some guy with his face tattooed to look like snake scales, I grab a carton of chocolate milk and move toward the tables. I can feel the eyes following me. They may not know my real name, but everyone here knows by now that I am—was—the Black Harrier. And a lot of them are here because of me, either when I actually *was* Black Harrier or when I was Frank's sidekick, Red Kite.

I pass a guy called Bullshark, who I helped put in here about five years ago when I was still Harrier's partner and was calling myself Red Raptor, even though I couldn't seem to get anyone else to do it. He was the bodyguard of a criminal scientist named Med-Evil, who worked on some really shady and extremely risky genetic research, trying to create super criminals for a price. Bullshark—whose real name is Jerry Zambezi—was willing to be a test subject in hopes of gaining superpowers for free. I'm reasonably sure this next part was inspired by Doctor Evo way back when in an event involving actual sea creatures growing legs and arms. Med-Evil somehow spliced his DNA with that of—you guessed it—a bull shark, which some consider the most dangerous shark on Earth. Even if they're not the most deadly, they're, without a doubt, nasty creatures you don't wanna mess with.

The results weren't pretty. As a human, the guy was already giant, but now he stands over seven feet tall, armed with razor-sharp teeth the size of steak knives. We got lucky when we took him down, partly because he isn't the brightest crayon in the box. I'm hoping I can do something similar in here and knock him down before he kills me. It's a risk, but I think he's the best option. He's big and dangerous enough to make a statement but dumb enough to fall for some tricks I have that could probably beat him.

I stop by his table, his all-black eyes staring holes into me. At least, I think they are since it's hard to tell without any irises or pupils.

My heart is pounding, ears ringing, palms sweating. But hopefully, none of that is showing.

Here we go.

"*What* did ya say to me?" I snap at him.

Bullshark goes from smiling—or at least baring his teeth—to looking around, confused.

"Ya talkin' to me?" His voice sounds like a dying boat engine.

"Yeah, I'm talking to you. I heard what you said." I'm starting to think the power-dampeners are harshing my vibe because, try as I might to put on my best Dwayne "The Rock" Johnson, this whole thing feels like a lame spaghetti western.

He looks confused. "I didn't say nothin' to ya."

"You sure about that?" I ask.

He turns to the guy next to him, an Asian ex-masked crimefighter known as Tokyo Drift—hey, he named himself that, not me!—and says, "What's wrong with this guy? I didn't say—"

Clang! I smash him in the face with my tray, and my lunch—something resembling chicken a la king on toast with mashed potatoes—drips down from his shark snout.

"Hey! What'd ya do that for?" he yells, rising to his impressive full height.

My response is to put everything I have into a full-force kick to the groin. I can only hope that the genetic re-sequencing didn't alter that part of his anatomy.

Uh oh. Judging by his lack of doubling over in agony, it may have. I didn't feel anything... uh, *squishy* when my foot connected, either. In fact, my toe is now hurting a lot. This is bad. This is very, very bad.

Bullshark's brain finally seems to catch up to the situation, and he sneers, his multiple sets of saliva-coated teeth on display. "You're a dead man, Tweety."

Everyone else backs off. Bullshark has a habit of literally biting people's heads off, and I'm sure nobody else wants to get in his way. He's strong—super strong, in fact—and it's not a superpower, which means those dampeners won't do squat to help me. The only thing I can count on is that he's not very fast, which is one of the reasons I chose him as my "victim."

His giant Schwarzenegger arms attempt to grab me. I leap onto the nearest table and do a handstand flip to the next one. Now that I have some breathing room, I can try to figure out how to get out of this fun predicament I just put myself in.

Thinking I'm safe with the long, heavy table between us is a mistake. He smashes it in half like it's Styrofoam and tosses the halves aside. Then the ground shakes beneath me as he stalks forward in a straight shot for yours truly.

I could keep leaping from table to table, but at this rate,

we'd run out of dancing room after a few minutes, and I still wouldn't know what to do next.

A group of inmates I recognize as Fate's Foursome decide they're gonna help Bullshark out, probably to get him on their side. Can't say I blame them, but that's not good for me. Luckily, none of them are great fighters without their powers. I grab the nearest one—Spinner, I think. I never bothered to learn. I wrench him in a headlock to choke him out while I elbow the second guy in the jaw, knee the third right across the bridge of his nose, then kick a fourth in the gut, putting him down, gasping. When Spinner—now unconscious—bangs his head on the edge of the table on his way to taking a nap on the dirty floor, the rest of them back off, not wanting to be next.

But it's not enough to scare Bullshark, who's still circling the waters. The prisoners caught in his path quickly part like the Red Sea as he moves through them, causing my time to come up with a solution to shrink down to nothing.

As soon as he's close enough to snag me, I leap back onto a table farther back, and this time, the criminals surrounding it scatter instead of trying to swarm me.

"Quit runnin'," Bullshark growls. He makes short work of another table, denting it to the floor with one swipe of his giant fist. I can't keep this up forever, and my number of options—and tables—is dwindling. I'm all the way back near the wall now, but I can't let him get anywhere near me, or I'm gonna end up like one of said tables, if not worse.

I remember a story I've heard more than once about

sharks. If you hit them on the snout, they shy away. I don't know if it's true, but it's all I've got to go on at this point. So, I make a move that both incorporates that fun fact and hopefully takes him by surprise. I head right *toward* him.

I launch myself up and do a flip, timing it so my feet come down right on his face. While airborne, I realize that I'm throwing myself into the mouth of the beast, but it's too late to change my mind. The good news is he doesn't bite me or grab me, probably because he wasn't prepared for such a dumb move. The bad news is he's so big and solid that his face is basically just a diving board for me to bounce off. No shying away whatsoever.

And, *wow*, does that toe hurt now.

Time to reassess the situation now that nothing I've tried has worked. If I met Bullshark on the streets of New York, what would I do? My mind automatically races through the list of equipment I usually possess, but then I again realize *I don't have any of it right now.*

To make matters worse, I've been assuming this was gonna stay a one-on-one fight, and that's not the way things work in here. While I'm standing on another table trying to figure out what to do, two other prisoners catch me off-guard when they grab onto my ankles and yank me down onto my back, knocking the wind out of me and causing my head to slam on the metal table. Several other prisoners join them and secure my arms and shoulders. All hope of kicking my way out evaporates.

I struggle against the ever-increasing mob of inmates, but

there are way too many of them. Bullshark takes his time now that I'm restrained, a frightening smile stretching across his gray, slippery face.

Da-dun, da-dun, da-dun, da-dun-da-dun-da-dun.

Two massive shark hands—yes, I know how dumb that sounds—dig into my shoulders with his vise-like grip, and his cavernous gaping maw opens. I squeeze my eyes shut and wonder how long those teeth will hurt before I lose consciousness and die. Or maybe I'll just go straight to the dying part.

"Stop!" a voice shouts.

I open one eye enough to see that Bullshark is no longer bearing down on my scalp. Turning my head, I see a tall, skinny guy with crazy, black Christopher Lloyd hair standing with his arms crossed, the center of everyone's attention. The place has become so quiet now that it's disconcerting.

Crosscircuit. Wow. I didn't know the guy was still alive.

He and I came to blows, along with virtually every other hero in America, back when I was like thirteen years old—well, technically, it was a long-distance battle since he was controlling robots from here in the Trench. An event that had come to be colloquially called Mega Mech-Apocalypse brought the world's greatest heroes together to stop this very man from destroying everyone with robots of all shapes and sizes. It was the first time since I'd started crimefighting where I wasn't sure if the good guys were gonna win.

For some reason, at Crosscircuit's command, Bullshark lets go of me and backs away, albeit reluctantly. So do the rest of the prisoners. Apparently, this guy has a lot of pull around here, which is surprising since he's definitely not the physical type.

Crosscircuit approaches me and looks into my eyes. "The Black Harrier, I presume?"

I nod. No sense trying to hide it since everyone in here already knows.

He smiles wide. "It's so nice to make your acquaintance. I thought you'd be... older."

"You're the so-called genius. I'm sure you can figure it out," I say.

His smile somehow turns even smugger, which I wouldn't have thought possible. "It truly isn't much of a mystery, though, is it? Either way, you're just the person I've been waiting for."

As he says this, I hear the guards coming through the cafeteria, shouting for everyone to stand down and shoving inmates out of their way as they go. A few give them lip, but for the most part, they're surprisingly compliant.

"Waiting for? Why?" I ask.

The guards grab Bullshark first, and he complies without a fight. They put oversized, high-tech cuffs on his tree-trunk wrists and take him away.

"Because I need your help," Crosscircuit says.

The guards make their way over to me. "On the floor, hands behind your head!" security guard Ernie yells.

The whole fight had only lasted seconds, though it felt like hours.

"Hold on," I tell him. I turn back to Crosscircuit. "Need my help with what?"

"On your knees!" Ernie yells again. "I knew you was gonna be trouble."

I still ignore him, eyes fixated on Crosscircuit.

"Why, escaping, of course," he whispers to me so the guards can't hear it.

Just then, Ernie strikes me at the base of my skull with his lightning stick, and the world goes black.

CHAPTER 5
ALEX

Done.

I'm so ready to be done with all of this. Frank's BS, the campaign, Battlegear, Eaglestar. All of it. Who knew the simplest time of my life would be when I used to dress up in a bird costume and run around punching people in the face?

Ah, the good old days.

After my stint as Red Kite at Frank's side, I'd decided to go out on my own in Boston. I was Redhawk. It was my city. Unless I'm missing cues, that was when all of this started—everything going on in my brain. It's when I took on the mantle of a real hero, not just a sidekick. It's when I started seeing how wrong it was to take the law into my own hands.

That said, I'm beginning to realize it's not exactly cut and dried. It's not black and white. There's room for gray. There has to be a happy medium between law enforcement and masked crimefighters. Greater regulations? Sure. But I'm not totally convinced outlawing them should be the official stance.

Perhaps Frank as mayor would have been a good thing. Maybe he had the solution. Having seen what he's been reduced to after so long serving the city, my gut is roiling. I've said it before; he was a great man. He truly cared about the people of New York. Now... I digress. I'm not sure how we recover from this, and I'm not convinced I'm the right man to develop a cure, either.

Leaving Douglas Tower, I get a call on my comm—Captain Fernanda. Oh, right, add her to the list of things I'm done with right now. Can I just ignore it? If I want to come up with a reason I don't answer. I weigh whether I'd rather deal with her unpleasantness now or even more unpleasantness later.

I let out a deep sigh—something I find myself doing more and more as I get older. Forget LOL. S.O.L. is my thing now. Sighing out loud.

What the hell? It's not like I'm scared of her or anything. I tap the answer option on my comm screen before it goes to voicemail. "Hello, Captain. And how are you this fine morning?"

Am I laying it on too thick?

"Laying it on a little thick, don't you think?" *Whoa, can she read my mind or what*? Now I *am* scared. "Were you planning on gracing us with your presence here at the station today?"

"Yeah, just following up on a case uptown." Well, it's *kind of* true.

"Oh, you have cases you're working on? Because from what I've seen, there hasn't been much action happening with your task force lately."

"More like I'm trying to wrap up some loose ends."

"Oh, now I get it," she says. "Let me guess: the Harrier case again?"

Dammit, why is she so good at this?

"Um... well..."

"Never mind. I don't care. I'm calling because I need you to do some PR during this downtime you've been lucky enough to have. According to the polls, the CVT is one of the most unpopular agencies in the whole country. I'm texting you a link. People miss their masked heroes, and they blame *you* for them being gone. You need to get those numbers up."

"How am I supposed to do that?" I ask.

"I don't know. And, again, I don't care. That's not my job. It's yours."

"Right. Well—" There's a beep.

My screen shows the call has ended.

"Well, have a nice day yourself, Captain," I mutter to myself. Another increasingly frequent occurrence for me as I get older. I really need to loosen up before I turn into a grumpy old guy. At least at the rate I'm going, I'll never have my own lawn to yell at kids to get off of.

I tap the link to the poll numbers she sent me. Ouch. Worse than I thought. But I don't have the slightest idea what to do about it. I don't remember public relations being in the job description when I took it.

I jaywalk across the avenue to my parked car, pulling my sport coat back to ensure my badge is clearly visible on my belt in case anyone gets it in their head to honk at me. It doesn't stop them. Of course it doesn't. Why would I be stupid enough to think anyone would respect a badge in this city?

Based on the poll numbers I just saw, if they knew I was CVT, they'd probably swerve to try to hit me.

Before I reach my car, I hear a woman's voice behind me —a strangely familiar one.

"Detective Garner?"

I turn around, and Summer Valentine, up-and-coming TV reporter, and Sawyer's former girlfriend, approaches me slowly. Although I've seen her on TV plenty and even in person, this is my first look up close, in the light of day, and undistracted by a million other things. People on TV shows and movies tend to be less attractive than expected in real life without all the makeup and lights or look even better than they appear on screen. Summer definitely falls into the latter category. Not that she's not utterly captivating on TV, but in real life, she's so lovely, I find myself almost speechless.

"Summer Valentine," she holds out her hand to shake. "We've met, but I wasn't sure if—"

I find myself stumbling over my words as I shake her hand. I'm even tempted to kiss it, old-school style, then realize how stupid that would be. "Yeah, I, uh, know. I've seen you on the… you know."

Smooth as gravel, Alex.

She pouts like I've done something wrong as she raises a perfectly shaped eyebrow at me. "I never got that interview you promised me after the chaos at the mayor's gala."

Oh, *right*... the mayor's gala. I'd been so focused on trying to corral the Resistors and bust Sawyer for being Harrier that I must admit, I hardly remember speaking with her, much less promising her anything. But now, standing enraptured before this angelic beauty, I can't believe that could be possible. How long have I been standing here silent like an idiot? Answer her, doofus...

"Oh, sorry about that. I guess the busyness of the night and things with Saw—" I clear my throat. "Things with the CVT, it just totally slipped my mind."

"I went to MoonMoney in the morning."

"I'm sorry."

"And all the messages I left you?"

She's got you there, lover boy. "Yeah, about that... Look, I promise I'm not trying to avoid you. It's just that—"

"I'm surprised to see you exiting Douglas Tower." Why do reporters love to interrupt people so much? I guess getting people to talk when they're off their guard and confused is easier. At least until they get so annoyed by it that they walk away.

"Right. Police business." I show her my badge on my hip as if she'd somehow forgotten.

"With Frank Douglas, perhaps?" she asks.

"Sorry, I can't talk about it. Ongoing case. You know how it is."

"Yes, I do." She puts her hand on my arm as I turn back to my car. "Well, how about it?"

"How about what?" I ask, skin going clammy.

"The interview. Are you available now?"

"Oh! Yeah, that," I say, feeling like a dumbstruck teenager. God, is this how Sawyer always feels? Garner, you're a former adult superhero-turned-cop. Get it together, tough guy.

I shift my brain into overdrive to think of a reason I can't oblige that won't sound like the lame, fabricated excuse it'll truly be. She's staring intently at me, affecting a look I've only seen in Anime. Man, those eyes sparkle. Despite my best efforts, I come up empty.

Fernanda's voice echoes in my brain. "You need to get those numbers up."

This is it. Summer is a big fan of the CVT. She can help paint us in a light the public will find appealing. The solution to my problem just fell into my lap.

"Uh, sure. How do we do this?" I ask.

A few minutes later, I find myself sitting in a small café in Greenwich Village, sipping an Arnold Palmer while waiting for the waiter to take our order. Summer sticks with plain water with lemon, which I never understood. I get that people have to drink enough water, and I certainly drink my share. But if you're in a restaurant, live a little, you know?

I keep trying to focus on the menu, but I find myself looking over the top at Summer as she peers down at her own. She glances up, tucking her hair behind her ear, and catches me staring. I quickly shift my eyes behind her, trying to play it off, but her smile tells me she doesn't buy it—but also doesn't mind.

She lowers her menu. "Any progress with the Resistors?"

"The Resistors?" I laugh a little and return my gaze to the lunch options. "They haven't shown their faces since Harrier and Justice were arrested."

"Does that mean they shouldn't have to pay for their crimes?" she asks.

"That's an interesting take on it, Ms. Valentine."

"Please, call me Summer." She takes a small sip of water, brushes her hair back again, and although I can't see below the table, by the way she shifts, I can tell she's crossing her knees.

Here we go…

"The whole point of the law is for them not to be out there committing acts of vigilantism," I respond. "And they're not. Why is it so important to you that they're punished for past transgressions if they seem to have learned their lesson?"

She doesn't provide an answer, but from her eyes and the way her jaw clenches, it's clear there's a long story behind her feelings on the matter. "Then what's next for the CVT?"

"We keep doing our jobs."

Uncrossing her legs, she leans forward. “But if there aren’t any vigilantes out there, what exactly *is* your job?”

Why is this going south? I place my menu down and cross my hands over it. Then, I remember hearing in body language training that people who lace their fingers during a conversation appear untrustworthy. So, instead, I place them both face down on the white tablecloth.

“I hardly think the lull in masked crimefighting is going to last forever.”

“But what if it does?” she asks. “What if everyone out there still willing to risk imprisonment has been arrested, and everyone else has finally decided it isn’t worth it?”

I hadn’t even considered that. It didn’t seem possible, but it *has* been a while since we’ve had to go after anyone. Maybe seeing the Black Harrier get nabbed did finally clue the rest of the community into how serious we are.

“That doesn’t seem very likely.” Even *I* don’t believe my own words.

“You’re probably right.” She smiles. “But even if someone who tries to take justice into their own hands *does* show up every once in a while, it hardly seems worth the enormous budget the city provides for your task force at taxpayer expense, does it?”

This line of questioning is making me uncomfortable, and if I’m not careful, she’ll notice.

“I’m not sure what you’re getting at,” I say. “Weren’t you the CVT’s biggest cheerleader not so long ago? And now you’re—what? Questioning our purpose?”

If our biggest supporters are turning against us now, no wonder our poll numbers are so low.

"I'm just doing my job, Detective Garner." Now her face is expressionless, making it impossible for me to get a read on her.

"Alex."

"Okay, I'm just doing my job, *Alex*. And I'm hoping you're going to do yours. The Resistors are still out there. Somewhere. And you're obviously not very busy."

I look around the quaint little café, wondering for a moment what I have in common with all of those eating around me. It's barely 10:30 in the morning—squarely between breakfast and lunch—when most people should be in their respective offices. It's then I realize her little jab worked.

"If you recall, I was leaving a very important visit pertaining to a case," I say, unsure if I was convincing her or myself. "As for the Resistors, I'm sure we'll get them eventually."

I take a long sip of my Arnold Palmer.

"Even your ex?"

I spit out the half-iced-tea-half-lemonade goodness like a comedian doing a bit on a late-night talk show.

"Would you like to hear today's specials?" a voice beside me says.

I hadn't even noticed the white-clad waiter approach. Hopefully, he hadn't heard any of our conversation. Though, I imagine servers don't care what most customers talk about.

Or maybe they do. I have no idea, considering this is the first "real" job I've ever had.

I calmly lift the napkin from its place folded on my lap and dab my lips. "Give us a minute, please," I tell him. Then, as he nods and leaves, I turn to Summer. "My... my what?"

"Oh, please. Once I discovered who Sawyer was, connecting all the dots wasn't complicated at all."

I clear my throat. Great. Probably another tell.

"I don't know what you're—"

"Frank Douglas was Black Harrier. You were Red Kite. Then Sawyer took over for you when you got older. I assume you were Redhawk after that. And that would make Osprey Amy Chen. Any of this ringing a bell?"

I lean in and speak quietly to her. "Look, I don't know what you're getting at here, but you're playing a very dangerous game."

She stares me directly in the eyes.

"Don't worry, Alex, it's no game. Your secrets are safe. Unlike all of you, I don't have any interest in putting innocent people in danger. Although it appears you at least had a change of heart, didn't you?"

I lean back, and she mirrors me again. Then it hits me.

"Are you the one spreading the rumor about a big story regarding Frank Douglas?"

"No. But if *I* put it all together, it wouldn't take much for someone else to do so," she says. "I mean, I'm very new to this. Think about what a seasoned investigative journalist would be capable of finding out."

I swear under my breath. “I told Frank that running for office was a bad idea.”

“No kidding. The only reason he got away with keeping his identity a secret all those years was that façade he put on with the billionaire playboy stuff. Any rumors were dismissed as tabloid fodder. But once he entered politics, people started getting interested in *him*. Who is Franklin Douglas III, really? It wasn’t just a fun ‘who’s he dating now?’ scenario anymore.”

I sigh. Again. I seriously need to stop that.

Once more, the server approaches. “Have we decided?”

I’m still a bit sideswiped by everything, but Summer seems unfazed.

“I think I’m going to have the Chicken Fraind, sauce on the side,” she says. “How about you?”

“You know, I’m suddenly not very hungry. How about a small salad with raspberry vinaigrette?” I say as I hand the waiter our menus.

“Fine choices,” the server says. “I’ll get those right in.”

Summer smiles as he walks away. “Well, you certainly don’t eat like Sawyer. I think he ate a burger and fries every chance he got.”

“He’s basically still a kid.” My smile fades as I think about this ‘kid’ spending the rest of his life in a supermax prison. Thanks to me.

Summer’s smile is gone now as well. “That must’ve been difficult, arresting your friend that way.”

“I’m not sure we were ever really friends. More like adopted brothers. Rivals, in many ways.”

"So you're saying it wasn't that hard?" she asks.

I take a big swig of my drink as I mull it over. "It was the hardest thing I've ever done."

She looks at me with... sympathy? Empathy? I'm not sure. But she seems to genuinely care. Then she reaches across the table and holds my hands.

"It's okay. I know it wasn't easy, but you did the right thing."

What's going on here? It's not feeling much like an interview anymore.

"I know we agree that vigilantes are dangerous and need to be stopped," I ask. "But I don't get it. Why are you on such a crusade against them?"

Her expression darkens. "Off the record?" she asks, offering a brief smile. I thought that was supposed to be something the *interviewee* said.

I nod. "Off the record."

She exhales slowly and pulls her hands back. Part of me is actually disappointed when her soft skin no longer touches mine. Okay, more like all of me.

"My brother, he... he was collateral damage during a fight between some *heroes* and villains," she starts. "The criminals probably hadn't even done anything so bad, but some masked crimefighters—including your former friends, Frank and Sawyer—went all-out as if the fate of the world depended on it."

"When you say your brother was 'collateral damage,' you mean he...?"

"Yes. And I've hated anyone in a mask ever since."

Wow. Makes sense. Just like my family being killed by criminals when I was a child led to me spending half my life fighting bad people. I'm not going to open old wounds by asking her the details, but if it was anything like when my parents were gunned down in a hail of bullets during a mob hit, I know how traumatic it is.

She looks at a thin-banded, silver watch on her wrist. "Would you judge me if I ordered a drink?"

"Not at all," I tell her.

"What if I order two?" She laughs.

"If one is for me, I wouldn't object. I'm supposed to be on duty, but as you've so eloquently reminded me, there's not much to do these days. I think I'll text my team and tell them I'm out for the rest of the day."

"I happen to be off today, too," Summer says, standing. "I'll be right back with those drinks."

CHAPTER 6
SAWYER

Nightmares.

The courtroom is closed except for those vital to the case, and my real name will never be mentioned. I'm referred to simply as "Defendant 9242001." Other than that, it's an ordinary trial with a judge, a jury, and the prosecutor—a woman who is clearly looking to make a name for herself and probably wants to become DA someday. She doesn't waste any time painting me as some kind of monster.

"Your honor, members of this esteemed jury," she says. "Our goal here is singular: to ensure no one is above the law. Good, bad, or ugly, those who violate the 'Counter-Vigilante Act' can only be labeled one thing: criminals. Defendant 9242001 has violated laws put into place by not just the United States but the world. He has proven, time and time again, that he does not trust our law enforcement to do their jobs. He has arrogantly decided he knows better."

The jury is comprised of people of all ages, races, and genders. I risk a glance, hoping to find someone who might be swayed, but it's like staring at an ad for hemorrhoid cream. Disgusted looks mingle with nods of approval. Honestly, all that's missing are the pitchforks.

"Who among us hasn't seen the destruction caused just days ago in Queens? City blocks that will take years to repair and millions in taxpayer dollars. All for what? A teenager stole a bike, and Defendant 9242001 thought it would be better to turn one of America's greatest cities into Armageddon than to let the boy go and allow the police to do their work."

It goes on like this for like twenty minutes. She even throws in some things that happened years ago to show that I supposedly never had any regard for public safety or collateral damage. Never mind that I wasn't even Black Harrier back when those things happened because she's out for blood, and I can't fight that without incriminating Frank and Alex. Not that I'd necessarily have a problem with Alex being punished due to his task force arresting me and landing me here in the first place. That would be some karma right there.

My lawyers' opening statement does little to convince anyone, but they try.

It gets a lot harder for me when the prosecution brings out the witnesses.

At first, it's not so bad since it's just a bunch of people who saw me beating up criminals and preventing crimes—nothing horrible in and of itself, but still against the law. Then she moves on to people who witnessed the task force chasing me through the streets of New York. Still not so bad, although some people sustained minor injuries during the chase. Cuts and bruises, stuff like that.

"State your name," she asks as a guy with the worst bowl cut I've ever seen takes the stand.

"Roger Michael Scott."

There's a little laughter, chuckling, and whispers among the jury members. I even hear a quiet "That's what she said."

The judge smacks her gavel. "I will have order."

Everyone clams up, and the attorney leads Mr. Scott through his swear-in.

"Tell us how you know the defendant."

He points to his nose, which is quite crooked. "He did this to me. Five years ago, I was minding my own business. Sure, I was probably pretty suspicious standing around in an alley, but I was just having a cigarette. And last time I checked, that ain't illegal."

Holy crap.

I know this guy. I beat him and a dozen of his buddies up for trying to rob a woman—maybe worse. It was my birthday. That was the year Frank got kidnapped by Chef Maléfique. It literally takes everything in me not to stand up and say what really happened. But instead, I lean over to one of my lawyers and tell her briefly about my experience that night. I can't believe our helmets don't have some kind of dashcam.

"Thank you, Mr. Scott," the attorney says. "That'll be all."

Next comes the law enforcement officers involved in apprehending me, including members of the Counter-Vigilante Taskforce. They were all witnesses who saw my helmet come off when I was fighting them and Justice, so they were able to identify me as the Black Harrier.

Somehow, Alex was off the hook and didn't have to testify. I don't know how he worked that out... maybe he had Eaglestar's help. Or maybe with all of the others testifying, it wasn't necessary, and he made up excuses for not being here. More than likely, he'd have trouble facing me. At the very least, it would be uncomfortable for him.

Next, she brings in the guy whose motorcycle I sto—er, "borrowed" to get away from Alex and his goons. It's only then I realize I never bought him a new bike. I was pretty busy after that and just never got around to it. Yeah, my superpower is being able to copy and remember things I see, but that's not automatic and does take some effort. It's not like a notification system reminding me of things I need to do. Still, I'm disappointed in myself for not making it something more worthy of my attention.

To make matters worse, he describes how he was on his way to a job interview at the time, and I made him late. Then he didn't get the job, and his life went into a downward spiral after that, supposedly leading to him becoming depressed and now on the verge of a divorce. I mean, there was no guarantee that he would have gotten the job even if he had been on time, but I guess I still bear at least partial responsibility.

Then I realize I also never got a new TV set for the old

woman whose apartment I crashed into. They'll probably bring her in next. Based on our previous encounter, she's gonna let me have it. I actually smile at the thought of how feisty she was, swinging a frying pan at me and screaming her head off.

Instead, the prosecutor brings in her star witness for the killing blow. A young woman in a uniform takes the stand and is sworn in by the bailiff.

"Please state your name and occupation," the prosecutor says.

"My name is Amanda Vasquez, and I'm a paramedic with Empire Emergency Services."

"And can you describe your experience on the evening when Black Harrier was chased through the city by the Counter-Vigilante Taskforce?"

"Uh. Yeah. Sure. So, there was this emergency call to an apartment building that Black Harrier had run through and terrorized the tenants in trying to escape the CVT. Some neighbors had checked on an elderly woman after the commotion. They found her on the floor of her apartment and called 9-1-1. When we arrived on the scene, it looked like a tornado had blown through—smashed window, broken TV, and dishes."

"And the woman?"

"She was unresponsive."

I feel my chest clench, and it's hard for me to breathe. When I left her apartment, she was fine. In fact, she had no problem swinging heavy objects at me.

"Was she alive?" the prosecutor asks.

"Yes," the paramedic replies.

I'm able to breathe a little better when I hear that. But my heart is still pounding.

"But," she adds, "she'd suffered a heart attack and was unconscious. We tried to stabilize her, but her vitals weren't good, and we needed to get her to a hospital immediately."

"Were you able to do that?"

"No, ma'am. Traffic was a nightmare. Backed up for blocks in all directions."

"Just normal traffic, or...?"

"Objection!" my lawyer shouts. "Leading the witness!"

"I'll allow it," the judge says. "Please continue, Ms. Vasquez."

"It was worse than normal traffic. Much worse. There were multiple accidents due to the high-speed chase that had occurred."

More fallout that I'm responsible for. I never even thought about it. Maybe Summer was right about vigilantes. About me.

"And who was involved in that high-speed chase?" the prosecutor asked.

"Objection. Hearsay."

"Overruled. The police dashcams have already been entered into evidence," the judge says.

"I'm sorry. Can you repeat the question?" Ms. Vasquez says.

"And who was involved in that high-speed chase?" the prosecutor repeated.

"The Black Harrier."

"And what happened to Mrs. Wilhite?"

Ms. Vasquez swallows hard. "By the time we reached the ER, she had fallen into a coma."

"Do you know how she's doing at this point?" the prosecutor asks.

"Objection," one of my lawyers says. "She's not one of this woman's doctors, your honor. She's not a doctor at all."

"Overruled," the judge says, annoyed now. "I'll allow it. Please answer the question, Ms. Vasquez."

"I was at the hospital yesterday after bringing in another patient, and I checked on her since I knew I would be testifying about it here today."

"And what did you discover?"

"She, uh..." She gets a little choked up. "Her family had decided earlier that day to take her off life support."

"So she was...?"

"She died that afternoon."

When I hear that, I feel like I've left my body. It doesn't seem possible—doesn't seem real. I didn't directly kill her, but... how can I not feel responsible for her death? The prosecutor is right. I am a monster.

I deserve whatever is coming to me.

I wake up in a cold sweat.

My lawyers really did a decent job with counter-questioning, but the writing was on the wall. When the judge read my guilty verdict a short time later, I wasn't surprised. I'd been holding out hope that I'd be sent to a regular, local prison. But no such luck.

It hit me pretty hard.

But not as hard as that guard hit me with his club.

I rub the back of my head and wince. That's gonna leave a lump for sure. I wonder how long I was knocked out. It feels like forever.

I shift my weight but can't find a comfortable position. It's no wonder since I'm chained up in a solitary confinement cell. And since the chains hang from the ceiling, my arms are stretched upward. I can't even lean against a wall, much less lie down.

I feel like this is some kind of inhumane torture that the UN would disapprove of. Can't holding your arms up for this long result in permanent damage? I try not to think about that and focus on my surroundings. There has to be some way to ease the discomfort, at least a little.

However, there's just nothing. Metal walls, metal floor, metal ceiling. And it's freezing in here. The door has a small window at about eye height if standing, but I can't see anyone beyond it. I'm sure there has to be guards outside.

"Hello? Anyone out there?" I call.

Nothing.

"Can I get an aspirin or something? I feel like my head's gonna explode."

The only sound is water dripping from somewhere in the room. There are a few puddles. Does that mean there's a leak? That can't be good. We're thousands of feet underwater. If there's a rupture, I can only imagine that the pressure would eventually build, and the whole side will cave in. Right on me. Then this place will be history.

Maybe that wouldn't be such a bad thing.

You know, when I was sitting on the other side of the ocean, being responsible for locking "bad guys" away in the Trench, I thought it was the best thing ever. Now, inside, I realize no one deserves this. Capital punishment would be kinder than life here.

I listen to the drip-drip-drip, remembering the idea of Chinese water torture. Is that still a politically correct thing to say? I guess? They invented it, I think. Well, regardless, I consider *water torture.* Maybe it's on purpose. Perhaps there's just a garden hose running through the conduits above me, trickling in through an intentionally cut slit in the ceiling.

Either way, it's driving me nuts! Which, I suppose, is the point.

"Hey! Forget the aspirin. Someone, get a plumber in here. I think there's a leak. And that's a lot of water out there."

The door opens, and a couple of guards stomp in—Ernie, thankfully not among them. They're carrying a high-pressure hose. Ah-hah! I was right.

But what happens next makes me wish I wasn't.

"Here's your water," a guard with a handlebar mustache says. He cranks the lever in front, and the blast hits me square in the chest. It's both extraordinarily forceful and cold. Also, it stings like falling in a red ant pile—which I did when I was eight and on vacation in Florida with my mom and one of her boyfriends. Not fun. The ant pile or the vacation.

"Now shut up," the other guard says.

After a heavy breather, I'm able to squeak out my patented snark. "Is that a 'no' on the aspirin, then?"

They carry the hose back out and slam the door shut, but not before the first guard flips me off.

Well, at least I know where the water came from, and it's not outside. So I feel a little better, all things considered. But the cold I'm feeling now makes me think I was lucky just to be freezing earlier.

"Good afternoon," a voice says somewhere in my cell.

I spin frantically, wondering if a third guard entered and I'd missed it, but then I spot a screen inset into the wall beside the door. I hadn't seen it previously since it had been covered by a metal panel that's now slid open into the wall above it.

"You remember me," Crosscircuit says onscreen. I never realized just how punchable his smug face is.

I try to cut through my brain fog to remember everything I know about this guy. Real name, Sean Meyers. Worked for Douglas Industries back when Frank's dad was in charge, which is not a good thing. Big Frankie Jr.—good, ol' grandpa—only *appeared* to be a respectable business leader and philanthropist. He was the head of a criminal empire that controlled most of the underworld in New York and a good deal of it in other places around the country and the world. When Frank found out, he had a... well, *problem* would be an understatement, I guess. Once he realized his dad's criminal dealings had led to his mother being killed in an assassination attempt on Big Frankie Jr., he decided to make sure the intended target paid the price.

In case you're not picking up what I'm putting down, Frank killed his dad. All of which was revealed to me, along with the fact of Frank being *my* dad, by a crazy supercriminal who was trying to drive Frank insane. Did it work? Not all the way. But... maybe a little?

When Meyers was rejected by the Guild, despite being a world-class genius with unparalleled technological skills, he decided to work for Douglas Industries. Maybe he knew the truth about Big Frankie Jr., maybe not. Either way, he knew he'd have access to more advanced tech and resources there than he could get anywhere else. And he used his smarts to steal materials, divert shipments, hack into classified servers, you name it, to get what he needed to build all manner of robots and drones. By the time Luis Chen—Frank's right-hand man—found out what was going on, it was too late. Crosscircuit had become a full-fledged supervillain.

When Alex was still Red Kite, he and Frank helped the Guild put Crosscircuit in the Trench. But that didn't keep him down. He still managed to stage that huge Mega Mech-Apocalypse in New York and other cities I was talking about. We assumed it was being perpetrated by a copycat since... how could he possibly be doing it from the bottom of the sea? But it turned out that not even being incarcerated in the world's most secure prison could stop him. He had left behind autonomous robots to build more autonomous robots to do his dirty work while he was here in the clink. Spooky, if you ask me.

And I think that brings us up to now.

"What'ya want?" I ask, almost too exhausted to talk. My arms hurt more from being extended and supporting my full body weight than anything the guards did. God, my shoulders ache. Plus, don't forget I'm now soaking wet on top of being a popsicle. I figure the temperature here is probably a toasty forty degrees or so.

"I couldn't give you a proper welcome earlier thanks to the whole 'guards knocking you unconscious' thing. I apologize for allowing that to happen. I didn't realize they were going to be that rough."

"*Allowing* that to happen?" I scoff. "Seriously?"

He smirks, the corner of his thin lips drawing back to create a dimple on his pale cheek. "Oh, I'm very serious. As you doubtfully surmised, I have a great deal of influence here in hell, despite being part of the incarcerated masses."

I readjust myself to try to return blood flow to my hands.

"If you're such a big shot around here, why aren't you gone?"

"Alas, even I can only do so much."

Alas—who says that? Seriously, do these supervillains have a school the Guild doesn't know about? "Hello, evildoers. Today we will be learning the art of pretentious speech."

Crap. Apparently, I've missed a whole part of his monologue. Now I'll never know what he—*shut up and listen, Sawyer.*

"... And escape is currently beyond my capabilities. But not by much. I have a plan, and most of the parts are in place. I was missing but one small piece of the puzzle."

Oh, good. I didn't miss the revelation of his evil plot.

"And that is...?" I ask.

"You."

My heart drops, and my body instantly warms as my heart rate climbs. "Me? Why me? What makes *me* so special?"

"Humility. Fun. That wasn't a trait you learned from your father, now, was it?"

Father? He knows? How does he know?

"Yes, yes. Imagine that. The world's smartest person figured out the world's worst-kept secret. Now, if we can move on? For my plan to succeed, a series of events must be orchestrated with exact timing. And some of them will require actions that need to be duplicated precisely. Others will involve the input of long, complex codes—codes that we may only have a quick glimpse of."

This guy knows more than any of us have ever even considered. "That still doesn't explain why I'm so important."

"Nice try," he says. "But you know *exactly* why. You may have fooled everyone else into thinking you're just a well-trained, hard-working individual. But your parentage is not the only secret I've uncovered. Your special ability—your *superpower*, if you will—this I've known for some time now. I just needed to ensure you ended up here to assist me."

I laugh. "You're trying to convince me my being here was your doing?"

"Please. It only required minor manipulations on my part. A slight nudge, if you will. You don't truly think a fresh beat cop would naturally be handed a position at the head of a national task force against masked crimefighters, do you?"

He got Alex the job? My head is spinning. Does Alex know? Was Alex duplicitous in this whole thing? Working with more supervillains than just Battlegear?

"Now, now. Don't sell yourself short! You got most of the way here all on your own."

Thanks for the reminder. "Okay, so now I'm here. What makes you think I'm gonna help you?"

He smiles fully this time, both sides of his pencil-thin mouth nearly touching his ears. "Other than the fact that I'm your only chance of escape?"

"I don't wanna escape. I belong here. I deserve it after everything I've done."

"Ah, the system got to you already." He shakes his head. "Sad. I thought you had more resolve than that. Well, if the carrot of walking free isn't enough for you, then I suppose it's time to trot out the stick."

"What? You're gonna have Bullshark beat me up again or something?"

Visions of my fight with the big hunk of cartilage flood my brain. I'm not too tough to admit it frightens me a little. I've rarely taken a beating like that in all my years of crime-fighting.

"Hey, I'm not an animal. But I'm not saying

that *won't* happen if you don't fall in line. However, that's not what I was referring to."

A momentary gush of relief fills me inside. "I seriously doubt there's anything you can do to force me to go along with anything."

"Red hair. Tight waist. Full lips. Not an ounce of alcohol in her blood—not anymore."

"What?"

He rolls his head around like he's tired of the games. "Megan Vincent ring a bell?"

My heart leaps into my throat at hearing Mom's name. But I try to play it cool.

"Who?"

"Ah, so it won't matter that I've contracted the Rifleman to blow her pretty little brains all over that Samsung microwave in your kitchen?"

Samsung? Do we have a Samsung microwave? I thought they made TVs. How does this guy know more about my life than I do? And who the hell is the Rifleman?

"You can try to play games all you want, *Sawyer*, but that's not going to change anything. You see, I've already ordered the hit for one week from now. The only thing that will stop it is a code word from me. And I'll only give the word if I'm walking on *terra firma* by next Wednesday."

Now my heart's pounding so hard I feel like it's going to explode.

"You can't." I shake the chains as if somehow they'd magically grown weaker over the span of this conversation.

"I already did. Now, are you going to assist me or not?"

My skin is on fire now. All memories of being cold are gone. I can feel my blood boil in my veins like I could rip these steel chains apart. I clench my jaw, holding back a long string of expletives that aren't gonna help me or my mom. And I can't afford that. Not with her life at stake.

"What's the plan?"

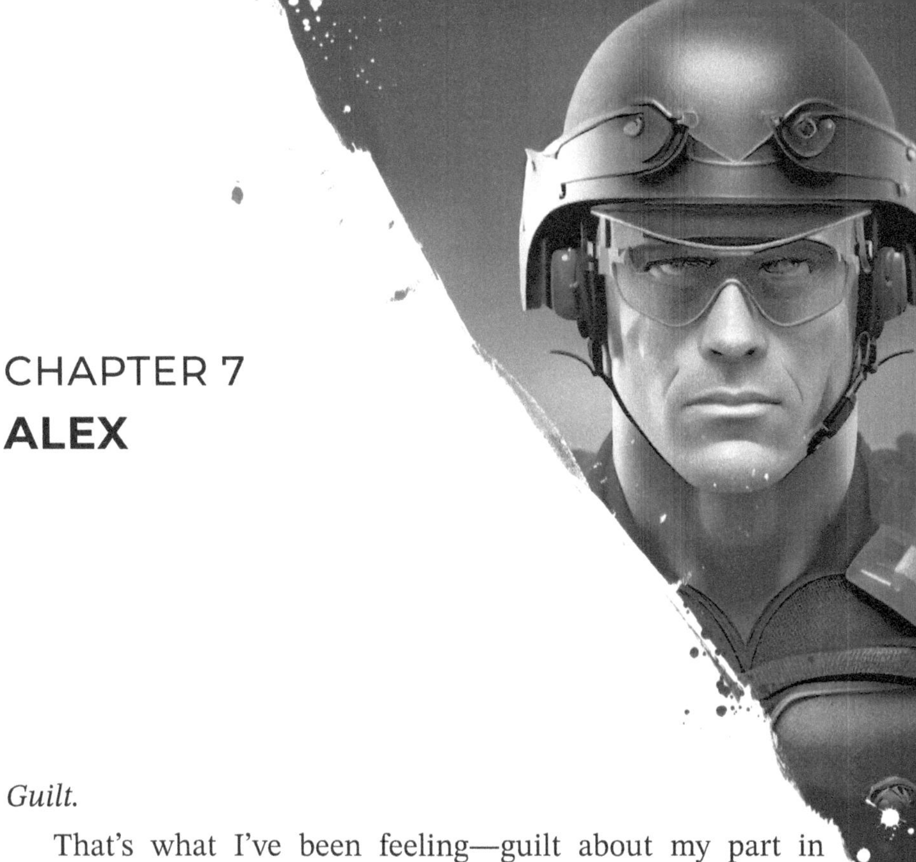

CHAPTER 7
ALEX

Guilt.

That's what I've been feeling—guilt about my part in putting Sawyer in the Trench. And in using his former bully, Logan, to do it. Maybe the worst part is that Logan was formerly a supervillain, running with a gang called the Neon Knights. It's becoming more and more apparent to me that the rules in this little game are made up and dependent upon feelings and interpretation of laws.

It should've been crystal clear the first time I was introduced to Battlegear, *another* supervillain who created the Neon Knights, as my new co-worker. A guy I now know as "Eric" and have on speed dial, in fact, and even hang out with on occasion. How am I supposed to feel like I'm in the right under these circumstances?

And now, to top it off—God help me—I am attracted to

Sawyer's ex-girlfriend, who—unless I'm completely living in a fantasy world—is coming on to me. I'm not one of those guys who thinks every woman is dying to crawl into bed with him —quite the opposite. If anything, I've gone through life being pretty clueless about anyone being attracted to me unless they beat me over the head with it using a baseball bat. With my history of being orphaned, growing up in a home, reaching eighteen without being adopted, and then being rejected by my mentor-slash-father-figure, I haven't exactly developed a lot of self-esteem.

Even cruising around town on Harrier's many overpowered motorcycles, kicking bad guys all over New York, I still never felt like anyone special. And finally becoming Black Harrier and a core member of the Guild after years of dreaming about it turned into a nightmare. I guess when you work with the best, it's hard to feel great about yourself, no matter how good you are.

Bad guys. Somewhere along the line, I'd forgotten that the Guild was trying to do *good.*

I'll have to put a pin in that like I've been doing for the past month or more. Right now, Summer, wearing a stylish leather jacket and black jeans, is sitting across from me, basically doing everything except flashing a neon sign above her head saying, "Alex, I like you." And I don't know what to do about it. I positively know what I *should* do about it. I mean, it's not like figuring out the right thing to do is all that much of a challenge. But *knowing* the right thing to do and *doing* it hasn't always been my strong suit.

For someone—anyone—to be interested in spending time with me is very difficult to ignore, whatever the circumstances. For that person to be one of the most attractive, intelligent, good-humored individuals I've ever met makes it nearly impossible to resist.

It doesn't help that I'm lonely. Desperately lonely. Yeah, I have my task force at the station, and we sometimes go out for a few beers at Reilly's after work. But even my police partner Hank and I haven't exactly been best friends. Plus, he's still out on leave until he recovers from being shot by Justice.

Justice. Wow, I haven't even thought about him recently. I hope he doesn't go after Sawyer in the Trench. That would compound things exponentially. But he's not the only one in there who'll have it out for Sawyer. What was I thinking?

My brain feels like a chihuahua chasing a mouse on speed.

All of this is essentially an explanation—or an excuse, maybe—to deflect responsibility for why I now find myself out on an actual date with Summer Valentine, despite me knowing full well both how really, really wrong it is and how bad it looks. It's not like I'm planning on having a relationship with her or committing to anything serious. We're just two adults with similar interests and backgrounds going out to a nice dinner at a small Italian restaurant off-Broadway and spending some time together. Platonically, of course.

Yeah, you've got a lot in common with her, Garner. Keep telling yourself that.

S.O.L.

After dinner, we find ourselves walking around Heather

Garden—one of New York's most romantic places. The colorful trees and bushes, along with the smells and the cool night air, have the two of us at ease.

"What was it like?" she asks. "Working with the Black Harrier."

I look up at the stars, trying to find the right way to answer the loaded question. "Exhausting."

She laughs. And it's a cute laugh. One I'd expect to come out of someone with her looks. "You know, it's funny. When Sawyer and I were—"

She stops short.

I look over at her, and she says, "Sorry."

"Sorry? For what? Go on. I'd like to hear it."

She smiles. "Well, when he and I were together, I'd always thought he had some weird curfew or—sometimes—that he couldn't wait to get away from me."

"Sawyer might be dumb sometimes, but no one would be *that* stupid."

She laughs again. I like being the one to elicit that sound.

"Every night around 9:30, he'd have some lame excuse why he had to leave wherever we were. Him doing what he did explains so much."

I nod. I have to admit to liking the fact that they apparently didn't spend too many nights together. "That was one of the hardest parts. Lying to everyone all the time."

She doesn't say anything, but I can tell she's thinking deeply about something.

"I can imagine it feels like a betrayal," I say after a few minutes. "Like, why couldn't he trust you enough to let you in?"

"That's exactly how it felt. I keep playing it all over again in my mind. Wondering if things could've been different if I'd known."

"Would you have stayed with him?"

After a long pause, "I don't know. Probably?" Another long pause. "Probably not."

"That, right there, is why we... he—everyone who was ever a masked crimefighter—kept it so close to their chests. You never know how someone is going to respond. At best, they accept it at face value. But even then, now you know they are going to worry every day, every night, that something bad might happen."

"And at worst?"

I chuckle. "At worst, they go sell the information to the highest bidder. Or they slip up and mention it in public. *Or* they hate you and want nothing to do with you."

"Right," she says, nodding. I'm unsure if it's just agreement or if she's acknowledging that she falls into that last category.

"Sawyer cared about you," I say. "And I understand why."

"Detective Garner, are you trying to flatter me?"

"Well, I don't just go around buying dinner for beautiful women every day."

"Oh, I'm beautiful, am I?" she asks playfully.

"Let's just say I've never seen an old hag delivering the news on New York television."

That laugh again. "You're not too bad yourself, *Detective*."

Her eyes flash that neon sign again. I might be dense regarding these things, but I'm not clueless.

What are you doing, Alex? What happened to two friends having dinner together with no other agendas?

Before I can answer my self-imposed question, I feel her hand gripping mine. I don't try to fight it. Her fingers interlace mine, her thumb moving back and forth in a soft caress. We walk like that for what feels like the entire night until we end up back to my bike.

"Let's go dancing," she says.

"Dancing?" I laugh awkwardly. "I'm not much into dancing."

"Oh, come on. I know this great new spot. It'll be fun."

I try to make excuses, but she has a way of being quite convincing when she wants to be.

It's just dancing. A little dancing never hurt anyone.

Eventually, I give in, and we're cruising through Midtown. Somehow, she gets us right in, no questions asked. I suppose I'm not the only one who's a little starstruck by her.

Turns out, she also likes to drink, which is something Sawyer couldn't do. And every time she orders a drink for herself, she orders one of my favorites—Captain Morgan and Coke—for me. I lose track of how many I put down throughout the night. And just like my willingness to work with supervillains when it's convenient, it's not lost on me how judgmental I've been about Frank's drinking when I don't seem to be any better about it myself.

I guess I learned from the best.

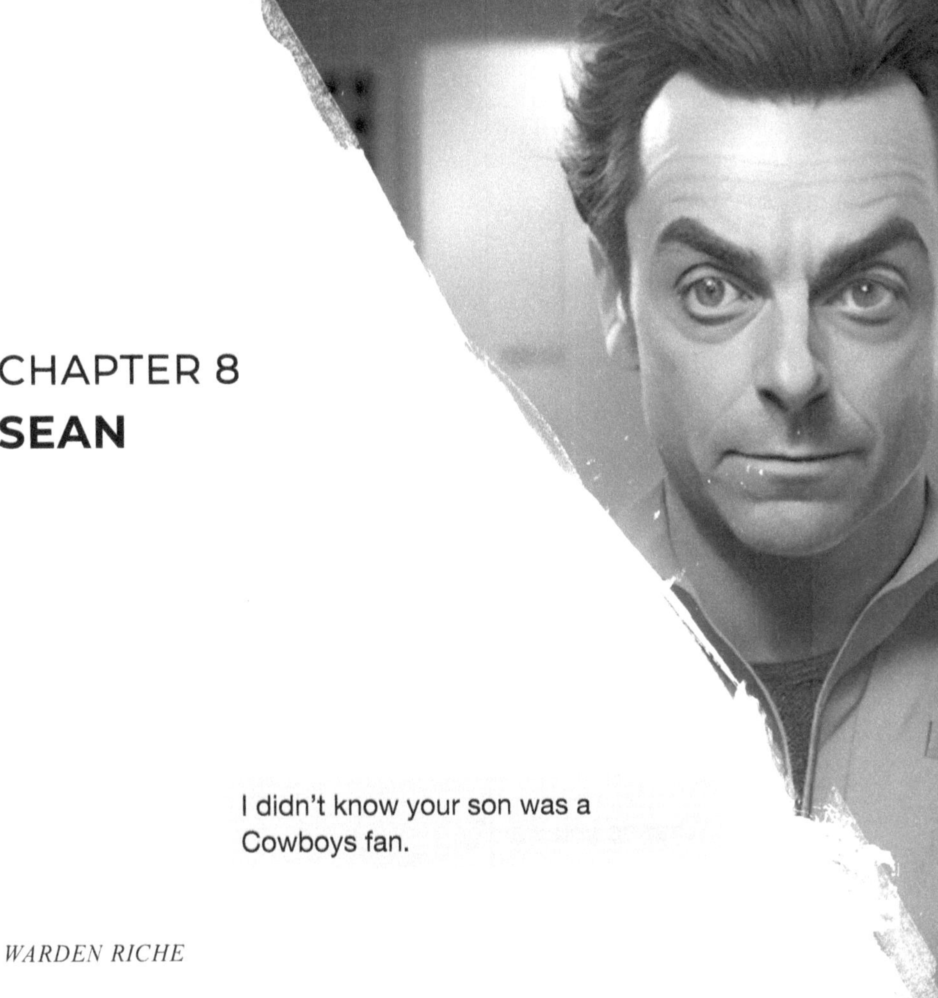

CHAPTER 8
SEAN

I didn't know your son was a Cowboys fan.

WARDEN RICHE

What?

He wore an Emmitt Smith jersey to school today. Old school. I like it.

WARDEN RICHE

You stay away from my son...

Now, Warden. You and I both know I am at the bottom of the ocean.

WARDEN RICHE

I mean it, Meyers.

He has swimming practice after school, no?

WARDEN RICHE

. . .

Your wife is really looking fit after today's Orangetheory class.

WARDEN RICHE

What do you want?

Within hours, I have Harrier released from solitary. He needed to learn his lesson, but he's no good to me if he's pained or injured to the point he can't function at full capacity. Because of my unending mercy, I even have him sent to the infirmary. Seems he's one tough cookie. Even after the brutal beating he took from Bullshark, the nurses find only minor bruises and abrasions besides a broken toe. However, his wrists need some attention. The chains in those cells are no joke. I wouldn't be surprised if he contracted tetanus.

I've made quite the name for myself here, if I do say so. Nurse McGillicuddy relies on me to keep her precious daughter in college. The poor girl enjoys the devil's lettuce a bit too much, and her grades reflect it. Nothing a bit of palm greasing or threats can't handle, though.

My persuasions get Harrier the extra help he requires to heal quickly. My kindness does not extend to everyone, I assure you. This could have landed on the opposite end of the spectrum. Had I wanted him in the infirmary for a while, my good nurse would have seen to it.

It's not as if I'm giving everyone orders here in the Trench. I don't want to give the impression that I'm propped up on some throne, barking instructions, or even sitting at the warden's desk—though the place would run far smoother if I were. I simply send messages, texts, emails—what have you—to the right person at the right time with a hint at what could happen—good or bad—if they do or do not perform a necessary task. Most of the time, that's sufficient to ensure things get done.

Other times, sadly, matters must be escalated.

I am not a monster. I do not enjoy threatening or blackmailing people, or hurting people for that matter. No, I'm not malicious. Though some of my former colleagues are, and many are still beholden to me on the outside. However, my life's mission is far too important to worry about individuals when the fate of the entire world is on the line. Like all geniuses, I know my role. I bear the burden of maintaining a laser-like focus and intensity. As mankind's salvation, it is nothing short of essential.

Everyone will thank me once I save the Earth, and it's all over.

Some would liken me to the Christ child. I attain toward no such honor. Though I will say we have much in common. And unlike him, I'll be expecting apologies from all of you. It may not make sense now—I know it probably doesn't to the feeble-minded. But once the aliens arrive and the fight becomes evident, the world will have a front-row seat, and they'll be grateful I did all of this to prepare. The robots, the battles, the injuries—even the deaths—will all be worth it in the end. I promise.

Then, like a father to a child who failed to understand the warnings of a hot stove, I will comfort you. I will be the salve, taking my rightful place as leader of the world. Nations, presidents, kings—none of these will matter once the realization that we are not alone in the universe becomes manifest. It will require one strong man of capable mind. I shall bear that burden as well.

In the meantime, I'll have to accept that nobody believes me and deal with the moniker of "supervillain" and the accusations of being evil. It's okay. I've never been good with people, so it's not like I'm missing out on friendships or enjoying someone else's company.

I accepted my lot in life long ago—the thankless task, fallen to me because of my superior intellect and capacity to get things done. Only one person could have prevented me from living a life so devoid of proper human interaction, and she died when I was still young. My mother, a saintly woman (as I mentioned earlier), didn't deserve what happened to her. Not long after my father disappeared, she was diagnosed with cancer. By then, I had begun accumulating my vast fortune through investments and entrepreneurship, and shares in my holding company had already split multiple times. It seems quite ridiculous, really—owning a company that doesn't even produce anything. It merely buys stock in other companies. Money that grows money as if planting seeds in rich soil. One must simply predict the winners, and for me, that was mere child's play.

I ensured she received the best medical treatment available. But sometimes, "best" isn't enough. Even the wealthiest, most influential people on Earth fall prey to the spread of that horrible disease. No matter which treatments were attempted, my mother's doctors were at a loss. They tried everything from standard chemotherapy and radiation to radical experimental drugs. Nothing worked. Cancer ate at her from within, and she withered away until she was no more.

I would have gladly forfeited my entire fortune if it meant saving her. The same is true today. I've even developed technology to peer into parallel realities and, occasionally, even communicate with alternate versions of myself. Thus far, I've been unable to find one in which she defeated cancer. Nor has there been a universe in which she never contracted it to begin with.

But alas, I turned out fine. Better than fine.

The cafeteria is throbbing with activity. The goons and henches sit to the left while we masterminds partake of our meals on the right. And as always, Deadeye eats his dinner alone, all other prisoners afraid to bother him. Not only does the entire prisoner population steer clear of sitting at his table, but the adjacent tables are also empty. After fetching my tray of gruel, I come to an abrupt halt before him.

Deadeye—whose real name I discovered is Mason Mordare—was the U.S. Government's premier assassin. Former military special ops and given both genetic and cybernetic enhancements, he abandoned that post and decided to work for the highest bidder. His story, like mine, is birthed out of tragedy. Whereas my mother was taken from me at far too young an age, his wife and two of his children were involved in a devastating car accident.

Only his eldest son remained alive and in ICU. When Deadeye's meager savings ran out, he was left with no choice but to seek alternative financial gain. Ultimately, his child has lived many long years in a coma. As I've said, no amount of money can truly defeat the inevitable.

Broken and alone, Mason Mordare considers everything he does vital to his survival and maintains hope that his son might awaken someday. Even the simple act of eating appears important when he does it. You can see the purpose in every movement and feel his sinewy arms coiling like cobras, ready to crush your windpipe or stab you in the eye with an eating utensil.

"Mind if I join you?" I ask.

He ignores me, as expected, and continues shoveling the slop down his gullet. I permit myself to sit across from him, confident that I'm not worth killing until he knows why I'm bothering him.

I leisurely swirl my spork in the gray, viscous meal, watching for any indication that he's paying attention. Apart from his jaw steadily chewing, his face is a statue.

"Have you given any more consideration to my proposition?" I ask.

The only sign he's even heard me is the steady slowing of his jaw. Then, with only his eyes, he looks up—the first acknowledgment of my presence. "Of course I have."

"And...?"

"*And* I told you I'd give you my answer when I'm ready. If I were ready, you would have your answer." He returns to his dinner.

I reach across the table and cross my spork over his as he lifts it to his mouth. "Unfortunately, it's getting down to the wire, and I'll need to make alternative contingencies should you choose not to assist."

He glares at me before placing his spork down. His spine straightens, but he remains stoic and silent.

"Would it help if I answered some questions?" I ask.

"If I had questions, I would have asked."

I smile. "Perhaps you don't know which questions need answers."

He drags a finger across his nose with a sniff, then flicks my spork away and picks up his own.

"Maybe if you knew more about my plan, you would—"

"One more word, and you'll get more than a 'no' out of me."

I join him in silence, retrieving my spork and wiping it on my paper napkin. Then I take a few bites.

I can't help myself. I am running out of time and didn't get to where I am by accepting a non-answer. "I understand that your son is—"

He slams his hand down on the metal table so hard that the entire cafeteria goes quiet. The only sound is a spork—my spork—clattering against the floor. No one picks it up. Nobody moves at all. The entire facility looks at us. Deadeye returns their stares, eyes roaming in all directions, and as he does, they all return quickly to eating. Soon, their own conversations respark, though most speak in hushed tones.

Between my fingers is the handle end of Deadeye's spork, less than a millimeter from piercing my hand. Thankfully, it was a warning, not an attack. As he pulls it back, it scrapes the metal table, sending chills up my spine.

"I'm going to assume you're smart enough that that was the beginning of some bribe, not an attempt to threaten or blackmail me. Either way, I don't care what your plan is. I know how intelligent you are and what you're capable of. As I already explained to you, there are other factors influencing my decision. Once I've made up my mind, you'll be the first to know."

He stands, tray and utensils in hand, but his gaze never leaves me.

"Even think about threatening *or* bribing me again, and

you'll be dead before you know what hit you. That's more than a promise. It's a guaran-damn-tee."

After a long stare proving why he carries the name Deadeye, he calmly walks over to the bin for dirty dishes, where he deposits everything. Without looking back, he exits the cafeteria while everyone watches without trying to be obvious about it.

Most other prisoners glance at me again once the door swings shut.

"Show's over!" I shout, leaning over to grab my spork from the ground. I clean it again and take another small bite. I focus my hearing until I recognize the sounds of those around me returning to their previous states.

My heart pounds in my chest, the blood accumulating around my ears. Just when I feel like I'm the Lord of the World, someone always puts me back in my place, making me realize I still have work to do. And I'll have to play the game until I've gotten everything I need.

But these fools have no idea what I've been able to do on the outside from within. Once they take a gander at my robots, once they know I've saved the world, things will be different. Then, even Deadeye and people like him will bow to me.

Or they'll be dead.

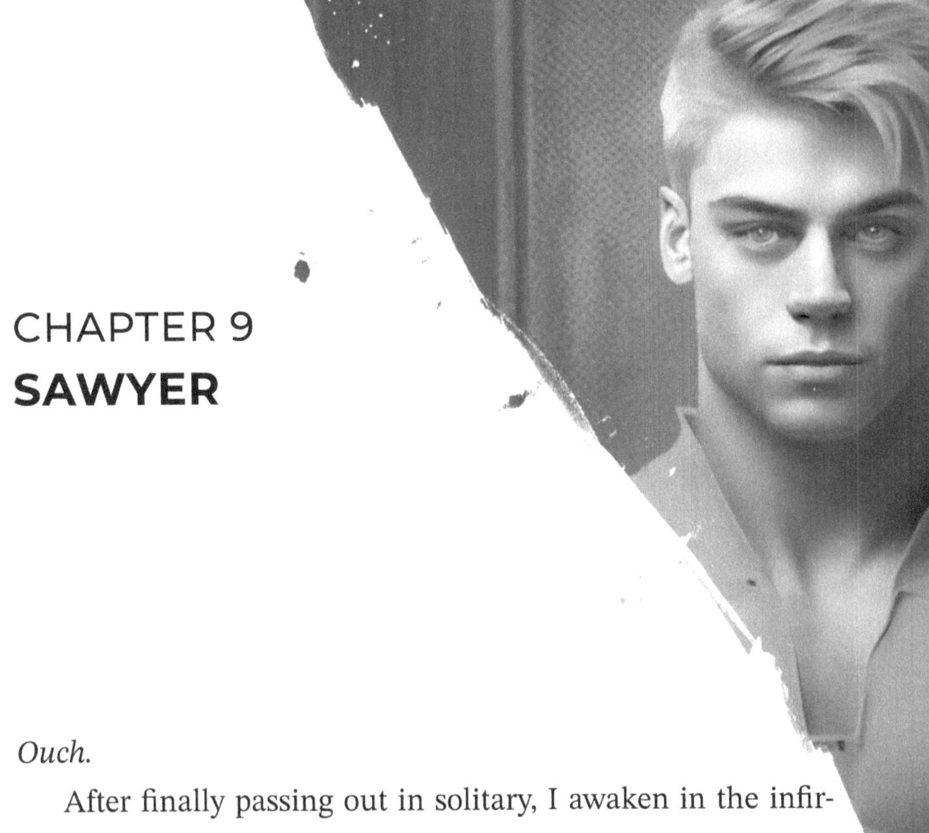

CHAPTER 9
SAWYER

Ouch.

After finally passing out in solitary, I awaken in the infirmary with my wrists, arms, and shoulders feeling like Royal Rampage tried to rip them out of their sockets. Oh, and I think my toe is shattered. And that's with the decent painkillers I see dripping through an IV into my arm. If that's how it feels after just a few hours, I can see why Frank was so traumatized and injured after being held prisoner in a similar way for weeks.

The infirmary isn't much different from a regular hospital. If they'd knocked me out before I left for the Trench and I woke up here, I'd never known I *wasn't* in a standard hospital. Well, until I got a look out of one of the portholes, I guess. That pretty much gives it away.

I try to sit up. Fantastic. I'm strapped down to the bed.

"Hello?" I call out to the empty room.

"Shut the hell up!" someone responds. "I'm trying to sleep."

Guess the room isn't empty.

I hear the door open, and an inmate who apparently works in the infirmary comes over to check on me. His butternut eyes are the same tone as his skin, and there's a kindness there I haven't seen since being here. He's a bit on the heavy side, and gray has snuck into his hair and beard.

"Welcome back to the land of the living," he says with a slight accent—maybe Argentina or Brazil? "I can help you feel better, but I needed to get your permission first."

I've seen a lot of prison movies, and that question carries a weird connotation I'm not sure I'm comfortable with. I mean, to each their own, but like—

"So, do I have your permission?"

"What do you mean?" I ask slowly.

"I have the ability to heal minor injuries if you'd like. But some people prefer not to have me use my powers on them."

I breathe a relieved sigh. Then I realize who this guy must be. "Mender?"

"The one and only. You know of me?" He seems surprised for some reason.

"I know you kept a lot of criminals in business when they should've been down for the count. I didn't know you were in here, though."

"The long arm of the law finally gets us all in the end, don't it?" he says.

An argument burbles to my lips about how I'm not one of

"us," but then my prosecutor's voice echoes in my mind. A single word, over and over again: Criminal.

"Guess so," I agree. "And I assume you know who I am?"

He nods.

"And you still wanna help me?"

"This place has changed me, ese," he says. "I'm not the man I was."

"That's good to hear," I say.

"Well, I'm still sorta doing what I always did, right? Only now, instead of getting rich off it, I do it so I don't have to mop floors or clean toilets."

He chuckles.

I've always hated even the *idea* of this guy. Call me superficial, but now that I'm on the receiving end of his powers, he seems like such a nice dude.

Then it dawns on me what he's actually saying. "You can use your abilities? In here?"

He shows me his wrists. Something similar to the inhibitors I'd worn wrapped them—silver bracers with a green-glowing light. Mine had been red.

"I guess you'd call these 'hibitors.'" He chuckles again. "Lets me heal, but only in this room. Once I step outside, they stop working."

I nod, my brain already spinning, wondering if there's a way I could use them to my advantage—not that my powers are real powers anyway, but who knows?

"And you can heal me?" I ask.

"Broken toe, some minor abrasions. Yeah, no problem at all."

I can't help but think what having him on the Guild's team would've done for us all those years. To return to the Aerie after a fight with La Cucaracha or Abaddon and have Mender waiting there to heal us? That would've been a game-changer.

"Sounds like a good deal to me," I tell him. "Permission granted."

He moves closer.

"Do I have to... do anything?" I ask, feeling a little weird.

He shakes his head, then rests a hand on my foot. A faint glow emanates from it, and warmth spreads across the area. It starts like an electric blanket and then gets hotter. A lot hotter. I wince a little, but a second later, the sharp pain is gone.

"Wow," I whisper.

He smiles.

"You get a lot of 'business' in here?" I ask. If you haven't noticed, I've always been super uncomfortable in this sort of situation, resorting to stupid small talk. Even in Ubers, I'm always the dummy asking, "How long you been doing this?" or "So, is this a full-time thing?"

"Fights happen in the Trench all the time. I mostly heal some bruises and speed up recovery on broken bones and such. But I can't do major stuff like repair organs or bring someone out of a coma."

"Too bad. That would probably come in handy around here."

"Oh, you have no idea," he says like a kid talking about Pokémon or Minecraft or something. "Last year, the Torturess got into a fight with Coldsnap. Without powers, they were pretty well matched. But Coldsnap—she's a killer. Almost took the Torturess's head off with one of the guard's lightning sticks. She was out cold—haha. I didn't even mean to do that —for a month. So how does your toe feel? A little better?"

"Much. Thanks."

"So, I can continue?" he asks.

"Yeah. Go ahead and do your thing."

He closes his eyes and places his hands on my shoulders. The same warmth, the glow, and the pain there and in my wrists starts to dull, then fade. By the time he's done, I'm just a little sore, like I'd spent a hard day in training.

"How's that feel?" he asks.

"Better than extra-strength pain reliever, that's for sure. Thanks, Mender."

That's a sentence I never thought I'd say.

"*No problema*. And call me Jesus." He pronounces it the Spanish way, but it still strikes me as funny.

"No. You're messing with me, right?"

"Nope. Guess mi mama knew what she was doing when she named me, right?" He laughs.

"I guess I'll see you next time I get my ass kicked, Jesus." I purposely pronounce it Gee-zus.

"Hopefully, you won't need me again." He pats me on the arm and walks away.

It's amazing how well "heroes" and "villains" can get

along when they're not out to get one another. I think about Mender and what kind of life he probably had in order to use his gift to help bad people instead of good. He probably grew up in a neighborhood like mine. I wonder how I would've turned out if Frank hadn't come along? Would the gangs have finally gotten to me? Would I have used my abilities to crack safes and steal tech instead of fighting crime?

A lightbulb goes off in the old noggin. I guess I have a pretty good idea of how I would've turned out, assuming I'm right about Justice also being Frank's son. But why did Frank wind up finding me instead of him? I guess I owe my mom's sleazy lawyer ex-boyfriend Derek more than I've ever thought about since he was the one who brought me to Frank's attention.

Somewhere out there is an alternate universe where I became a criminal with my abilities instead of Frank training me to be a hero. And Frank may have even taken me down himself, not knowing who I was. And then I would've ended up... here? Now my brain is hurting more than my toe ever did.

A doctor walks in as Jesus/Mender exits the infirmary. And not some weird supervillain in a costume; she looks like a *bona fide* MD. Her blonde hair is in a bun with two sticks holding it in place. She looks absolutely professional with her studious, black-rimmed glasses, but also—if I can say it—super sexy in a red blouse, white coat, and pencil skirt. And heels. Wow. I don't know what would possess someone to wear high heels in a place like this, but my barely-out-of-teen-years brain won't complain at all.

"He's all good," Jesus tells her.

"Thank you, Mr. Degollado." She clacks over to my bedside and places her hand gently on my arm. "I'm Doctor Taylor. Are you feeling well?"

I nod, my mouth suddenly not working right. What can I say? Attractive women are my weakness. One thing I did *not* inherit from Frank is his rapport with the opposite sex.

She's busy poring over my file on a tablet. Without looking at me, she asks, "Ready to enter peaceably back into gen pop?"

I nod again.

She looks up. "I'm going to need verbal confirmation."

I nod a third time, but she gives me a look over the top of her glasses that makes me realize what she'd just said. I squeak out a "Yes."

"Good. Then up you go."

She pulls the IV out of my arm with less care than I would have liked, then tapes some cotton over the puncture wound.

The doctor points. "Your jumpsuit is over there."

I slowly sit up, and I'm about to crawl out of bed when I realize I'm just wearing a hospital gown.

"Don't be shy," she says. "Nothing I haven't already seen."

I clear my throat and stumble out some incomprehensible response. She doesn't watch me while I get dressed, but she doesn't turn away either, which makes me seriously self-conscious.

Wait... did she mean that as in she saw me naked? Or like, "You've seen one; you've seen them all?"

My back is toward her, but my butt would be flapping in the wind if there was any. Not that it's flabby. I mean, it wouldn't actually be flapping. God, is it hot in here?

Finally in my orange one-piece, I give her a wave that she utterly ignores and exit the same door I'd seen her enter through. I haven't seen this part of the prison yet, and wonder why there isn't a guard to accompany me. However, it's just one long hallway leading to the prison cells with a single locked door that says "Staff Only."

How do I know it's locked? I tried it. I'm curious—what can I say?

As I pass, I hear it open behind me. Turning, I see a middle-aged black man with a receding hairline step into the hall.

"Mr. Vincent," he says with a slow Texas drawl. Sounds like a good old cowboy. "Join me for a moment?"

My blood goes cold at the sound of my name—my real name. No one is supposed to know that in here.

I stare at him before taking a couple of timid steps. "I... uh... yeah. Sure."

"Thank you kindly," he says, stepping aside and waving me in to walk in front of him through the threshold.

Inside is a stark difference from the metal walls, floors, and ceiling I've grown accustomed to in the other parts of the prison. A plush eggshell carpet lines the floor, making me feel like I'm walking on a cloud. Several wooden desks filled the space, each with a man or woman hard at working doing... something: paperwork, computer work. The walls are adorned with artwork. Classy stuff—probably reprints of things painted in the 1500s. I like it.

"Right this way," the man says, gesturing for me to continue toward a door in the back.

I lead the way, which is odd. But he doesn't protest, so I assume I'm heading where he intended. Once at the door, he steps up beside me and opens it. A plaque on the wall reads "Warden Gregory Riche."

I have vivid flashbacks to all those times I'd been sent to the principal's office for something I didn't do. Then I think about the person chiefly responsible for those occasions and realize it's the same person again: Logan Andrews.

"Go ahead; take a seat." Warden Riche motions toward a leather chair that wouldn't have looked out of place in Frank's offices. He then makes his way to a rolling wet bar. "Can I fetch you a drink?"

"I'm not twenty-one yet."

"I won't tell if you don't," he says with a smile. "Besides, you're already in the worst place on Earth. What kind of consequence you worried about?"

Another run in solitary, I think but don't say.

"I... okay. Yeah." I try to think of anything I'd ever heard Frank mention. "Scotch. Neat?"

"Ah, a Scotch man," he says, reaching for a bottle. "I like it. Same here. I think you'll find this to be one of the best you had." He pours two glasses and hands one to me before taking a seat at his desk.

I sniff the diarrhea-colored liquid and try my hardest not to make a disgusted face. People drink this?

"Go on. Give it a sip," he says. Then he watches me—just stares. I have no choice but to do as he asks. Is this what peer pressure is like?

I take a small sip, and my mouth catches fire. This is the best? Yikes.

"Cask-strength," he says. "Nothing like it. No nonsense. Just straight from the barrel to the bottle." He takes a long pull of his, and I wonder how we could possibly be drinking the same thing.

"Yeah," I say, my cracking voice barely slipping past the burn in my throat. "It's great. Thank you."

"I'm Warden Riche. You can call me Greg."

I nod, expecting him to continue. Does he want me to actually do it? Like... now? Since he still hasn't talked, I figure he must. "Thanks, Greg."

Oddly, that gets him going again.

"And you're Sawyer William Vincent. The Black Harrier. I—"

"I'm sorry, but... you're not supposed to know that."

Riche smiles. "There ain't a soul behind these walls I'm not exhaustively familiar with. It's my job to know things I ain't supposed to know." He must sense me growing uncomfortable. "Now, don't worry. I'm not gonna out you or put anyone in undue danger. Truly, I want you to know I'm on your side."

"My side?" I ask.

He takes a sip of the Scotch before placing the glass on his desk with a clink. "Absolutely. I've been a big fan since the start. I realize that wasn't you, but still, that uniform you wore demands respect. It's an awful thing they done to you, and I aim to correct it."

"You do?"

"Why so skeptical?" he asks. "We're on the same team, ain't we? Out there in that yard—that's your doing. All them criminals, locked away, allowing the world to be safe for another day... Without you, I wouldn't have this job. So, that said: Thank you."

Huh. I hardly know what to say. "You're... welcome?"

"Here's the thing." He sighs long and hard. "I can't show favorites 'round here. So, if we meet in the halls, you're just another scumbag. In fact, I may even have to be harder on you than the rest, just for show. But just know..." He pounds his fist against his chest three times. "In here, you're my hero."

I'm so caught off guard and confused by all of this I don't respond. What is happening?

"As you know, there are a lot of bad people in here. Very bad. Over the years, many have tried to escape." He leans forward in his chair. "Believe me when I say there *is* no escape."

I'd begun to settle, but with those words, anxiety creeps

back in. Does he know about Crosscircuit's plan and, furthermore, my involvement in it? Or is he on a fishing expedition?

"I just wanna make sure you don't get wrapped up in the wrong crowd," he continues. "Things change, you know? Times change. Who would've thought a year ago one of the Guild's founding members would be locked in the Trench? Even if you're not Frank...."

Ho-lee... he knows about Frank, too?

As if he read my mind, he nods. "Yes, I know all about the history of the Raptors family. I consider Frank a dear friend, and I hope he succeeds in his endeavors for mayorship. Should he do so, this whole thing—you in here, the task force..." He spits that word like he'd swallowed cat piss. "It'll all be a thing of the past. A bad moment in time."

A bad moment in time. Yeah, I'd say.

"So what am I getting at here?" he says. "I'm sure you wanna know."

He pauses again as if waiting for me.

"Yeah."

"You keep your head down. Choose your *friends* wisely. Consider where you been and what you done. If you wouldn't associate with them on the outside, don't let the inside change who *you* are inside. Make sense?"

I nod slowly, thinking about how buddy-buddy I was with Mender.

"Good. I'm gonna try to get this all figured out, Sawyer. Don't you worry your little head. In no time, you'll be back in

New York with your ma. And who knows, maybe Summer will even forgive you."

Out of nowhere, a bit of anger washes over me. "What is this? Are these some kind of veiled threats or something?"

He sits back in his chair. "Threats? Golly. No! I'm sorry if it felt that way. I just want you to know you've got a true friend here. You ever need to talk, don't hesitate to reach out to me."

I eye him with a big side of suspicion. Despite his words, I can't help but draw a correlation between Crosscircuit's mention of my mother and his. The problem is, I don't have much choice here, and this guy runs the show despite whatever Crosscircuit might think.

"And how do I do that?" I ask.

"As I said, I know everything that goes on in here. Everything. For example, say someone was planning some elaborate escape, and you caught wind of it. Well, as a *friend*, I'd want you to tell me about it. Do what you've always done: help stop the bad guys from getting free and hurting more people. Understand?"

My mouth feels like I swallowed a ball of yarn. I smack my lips together, but there's absolutely no saliva. I take a sip of the whiskey and immediately regret it.

I nod. "Yeah. I understand. But that still doesn't tell me how I reach out to you."

"Just tell one of my guards," he explains. "I'll hear of it sooner or later. Now, why don't you finish up that drink and get on out there? Keep your nose clean and ears open, and this place will be far better off for it."

I stare down at my drink. Finish it? I hardly wanted to start it. But he's watching like a mom on Christmas day, unable to contain her joy at her little baby experiencing the joy of her gift.

I figure the best idea is to just down it in one gulp. Taste it once instead of a bunch. I toss it back, and bam! I'm hit with the most intense feeling of warmth. Seconds later, my head starts to spin.

"That a boy," he says, rising. "Now, let's get you back to things. Glad to see you're feeling better after that tuss-up with Bullshark."

I try to rise, but sway a bit. He grabs me by the arm, escorts me to the door, through the offices, and deposits me back in the hallway where he'd found me. Now a couple of armed guards are there to usher me through double doors at the end of the corridor and down another long hallway with no doors or windows.

"So, where are we headed, guys?" Am I slurring?

Silence.

They're dressed like black Stormtroopers. Like, black armor, not like Finn or whatever. Shiny armor that honestly looks way weaker than my graphene, but since I don't have my armor, it's good enough. It's hard to tell whether they're just following the rules, if they're not answering because they don't like me, or if someone has ordered them to ignore me. Heck, maybe they can't even hear me through those helmets.

Not that it makes much difference.

We walk, and I'm grateful for them holding onto me. I've never been drunk before. I'm not really sure I am, but I'm definitely buzzed or something. Before I know it, my mouth is moving again.

"Did you catch the big game last night? Not me. I was passed out while chained up, soaking wet in a dingy metal room." They don't even glance at me. "Actually, now that I think about it, I have no idea what time it is. Morning? Afternoon? Hard to tell in here, you know?"

One of them finally responds, spitting a mouthful of sunflower seeds onto the ground before us. "You wanna end up back in the infirmary before you even get down to the yard?"

Okay. So we're going to the yard. "That would be a *no*."

"Then shut the hell up."

I take his advice until we arrive at another large set of double doors with the word "yard" printed on a sign above. The seed-eating guard punches a code—265917—into the keypad inside that compartment. I retain that number because, well, I can't help it. Apparently, those inhibitors can't be bothered with a "power" as weak as mine.

Instead of walking me in, the other guard shoves me through the doorway.

"Hey, you treat all the ladies like this?" I ask as the doors slide shut behind me. Man, no respect for banter around here.

I turn around to yet another set of doors. When they slide open, I'm surprised by how large the area inside is. In an ordinary prison, the yard would be an outdoor area where prisoners can get some fresh air, exercise, lift weights, or play basketball. Obviously, that's not the case with the Trench being miles below the ocean. Prisoners of all shapes and sizes still do those things, but the "outdoor" part is nowhere near a good description. There's some astroturf resembling grass, but most of it's covered in spongy flooring like on modern playgrounds.

No slamming heads happening here—which I don't understand. These are the worst of the worst of the worst down here. If one happened to kill another, who would be upset?

Looks like we're on the facility's top floor with a large dome overhead, lit up from the outside with wide-view spotlights in an attempt to approximate the daytime sky. But the effect is not a good imitation at all. It's scary when you look up and see the darkness of the water and the occasional undersea creature swimming by. But I guess there's not much they can do, nor are they probably worried about the mental health of a bunch of degenerates. I pretend it's a cloudy day and keep my eyes down. Not to mention, in my currently inebriated state, the bright light hurts like hell when I look into it.

All I can say is it's a good thing my claustrophobia went away once I got out of that tiny cell in the sub on the way down. I don't know what I'd do if it continued to happen even out here.

I stagger around a little and finally decide my best course

of action is to stay close to the wall. As I stumble through the crowd of yardbirds, all I get is a few looks from some of the meanest of the bunch. Most of the others pay me zero attention. Honestly, it's almost insulting. I can count at least a dozen criminals who I personally had a hand in sending here, and they all know who I am by now. It's just weird.

Scanning for Crosscircuit, I notice quite a few more familiar faces. Bullshark is at the weight bench—as you might expect—lifting an incredible amount with no effort at all. I don't know his Power Rating, but if he's that strong with the inhibitors, it's gotta be really high. Royal Rampage sits in a corner on a high ledge overlooking the area, glaring down at Bullshark. That looks like a fight just waiting to happen.

I also notice Justice across the way, looking like he's talking trash to some other prisoners who don't seem interested in giving him the time of day. Without his costume, he's not much to look at: kind of stringy and covered in tattoos. His bright orange hair hangs limply to one side, and I'm sure these guys aren't taking him the least bit seriously. I'll have to keep my eye on him to make sure he doesn't get himself killed. If I don't get myself killed first, that is. Redhead or not, I'm not ready to accept one hundred percent that he's my brother—or half-brother—but it sure sounds like he's Frank's son. If that's true, I'll have to decide when and how to let Frank know.

Do I get phone calls in here? Do phones even work? That feeling of claustrophobia begins gnawing at me. What if I never get out? What if this is my home forever?

Breathe, Sawyer. Breathe.

I feel someone staring me down. You ever get that sensation? Like, you just know someone is watching you even though you don't see them? I turn to confirm my theory, and there he is, but it takes me a minute to figure out who it is without a costume. The man is seated on the bleachers, a ratty paperback in hand, glaring up over the pages at me.

I've never seen him without his helmet, but it has to be Deadeye, from what I can surmise based on his stature and body language. It turns out I can remember that kind of stuff, too, though I've never really thought much about it.

Stand in awe of the superhero who can recognize people he's only seen with their faces covered. Almost seems like a joke of a power. Hey, but it's one that still works in here despite the inhibitors. I'll take that as a mark in the "win" column.

I spot Crosscircuit holding court across the yard. Fury starts bubbling up in me after his threats against Mom if I don't cooperate. I do deep breathing exercises as I approach him, which makes me more than a bit dizzy from the alcohol. But still, anything I can do to make sure I don't try to kill him. I'm not sure if I believe him, but that's a chance that I can't take. Most people spending their lives in a place like this are unhinged. You don't start a career as a supervillain if all your marbles are polished and in the bag.

I can't help but wonder how much the warden actually knows. Cop-types are good at bluffing, letting people think they know more than they really do. He was probably hoping I'd slip up and offer information. Problem is, even if he *was* threatening me, out of these two, it would be Crosscircuit who would be most likely to go after my family and friends.

But am I seriously ready to switch teams just hours after arriving here? Maybe? I could be here forever. If so, what good is it to be besties with a warden who made it clear he wouldn't treat me any differently from the other inmates?

For now, I have to play nice with both parties. The last thing I need is to do anything to slow down the process. I've gotta compartmentalize things in my brain and keep my anger toward Crosscircuit in check until I know the plan. After that, I can decide whether to put my eggs into his basket. Once the escape is over and my mom is safe, *then* I can kick his ass all over the place.

When I get near, he motions to the dozen or so convicts standing around him in a semicircle, and they all scatter. I'm not sure if that's supposed to make me feel special or if it's a standard way for him to do business.

I recognize a couple: Yonder, a dude who can teleport as far as he can see, and Rally, a lady who used to dress sort of like a NASCAR driver. Her superpower is she can drive really well. Sees things differently and can plan several moves ahead. Handled a lot of bank robbery getaways until she got caught by Omar the Defenestrator.

Crosscircuit smiles his creepy smile at me, but I don't return it. I'm not gonna hurt him—yet—but I don't have to be nice. Maybe there's a way the warden can stop his plan to kill Mom if I let him know. If that's the case, this guy is toast.

"Okay, I'm here," I mutter. My mouth feels numb.

Crosscircuit claps. "Smart decision."

"Yeah. Okay. Well, I realize you didn't wanna talk while someone could be listening, but we're alone. Give me the details so I can start working on things."

I wondered if we were truly alone. Was the warden listening in even now?

"Hold your horses, cowboy," Crosscircuit says. I get the impression he learned to interact with people from watching TV and movies. He just doesn't talk like an average guy.

"The sooner we start, the better. How the hell do you expect to get out of here?"

"Have you no nuance, young Sawyer? You can't cook the dough until it's been properly kneaded."

I want to tell him I was gonna knead *him*, but I hold my tongue.

"First thing's first," he says. "I understand we haven't always been on the same side of the law. However, I believe we've always both had the world's best interests at heart."

It's like a replay of the warden's speech. "You have a funny way of showing it."

"Pish." He waves a hand dismissively. "Sometimes, horrible things must be done for the greater good. How many soldiers have been sent to die in order to defeat evil or even to merely protect American interests?"

I shake my head. "Sounds like you should run for president."

"Funny you say that. It has crossed my mind."

"You're insane," I tell him.

He tilts his head and tsks his tongue. "Maybe you're not the man for this job."

I take another deep breath before continuing. "I don't even know what the job is."

"Well, it's simple. I'm going to open up an inter-dimensional portal that leads from the Trench to Schenectady. We're going to step through, and *voila,* we're out of here."

"Wait, seriously?"

He rolls his eyes. "No, of course not, you idiot. This plan is very complex and has a lot of moving cogs. I will explain it in stages as we go and give each person only the details required for them to accomplish their part. I don't need anyone forgetting anything or trying to help where they aren't needed. They'll only get in the way and slow things down or, worse, bring things to a grinding halt."

"As you said yourself, I don't forget things, so you don't need to worry about that part with me."

"Yes, well, out of everyone on my crew, you're the one I trust the *least*, being a big hero and all. So, the less you know at any point, the better. If you ever decide to take a chance and turn on me, I need you as clueless as I can keep you."

Is that a hint that he knows about my conversation with Warden Riche? Or is he trying to gauge my reactions to figure it out?

I look around, wondering where all the guards are.

"Don't worry," he says. "The guards are in my pocket, just like everyone else. They have mothers, too, you know."

My fists ball unintentionally; it takes everything in me not to strike. The simple act makes me teeter to one side, and I have to shift my weight to catch myself from falling. "Whatever."

"Are you drunk?" he asks, sniffing me. He smirks. "I applaud you! Most people can't get alcohol in here without me. I might have to keep my eye on you."

"Just tell me the first thing I need to do."

"Each guard has his—or her—own access code. They use them to open doors and gates and check out medicines or foods. All kinds of things. I need you to start watching them closely and memorizing their codes."

"265917," I say.

"Excuse me?"

"265917. That's the guard's code."

He narrows his eyes. "Which guard?"

"Uhh." Crap. I don't know which guard. They all look the same in that armor. "Uh. He likes sunflower seeds."

"This is why you little chicks need a mother hen," he says. "Now—"

"Why can't you just ask one of them for it?" I ask. "If they're in your pocket."

"Nuance, little bird. Nuance. Sneaking Killbaka a pack of cigarettes is one thing. Planning a prison break is something else entirely. If a guard were found to do something that blatant, they would not only be fired but probably end up here as a prisoner with the rest of us. Leverage can only get one so far."

I sigh. "Fine. But wouldn't I only need to memorize one, so we can use it for all the doors we need to pass through?"

"I hope you're not planning on questioning everything I tell you, or this could end up taking far longer than it should. And you know what that means."

He makes a *tik tok* sound as his finger goes back and forth.

"I just—"

"Nah-uh! Shhh. Listen," he barks. "Just to give you some confidence in my ability to execute this plan, I'll explain this part to you. Not every guard can open every door or gate. Only the ones in the sections they're assigned to. It's part of the security protocols for this distinct contingency."

I guess that makes sense. This can't be the first attempted escape, after all.

"But what ab—"

He holds up his hand. "Uh-uh-uh. What did I say? That's not part of your job, so don't worry about it. Don't even think about it."

I clench my jaw shut. "Got it. Go on..."

"And secondly, if we use the code of a guard who isn't currently on shift or is known by the system to be in another section of the facility, it will set off all manner of alarms."

"Okay-okay, I get it."

"Fantastic. Is there anything else I can help you with to set your mind at ease?"

"Actually, I—"

"I wasn't serious. Get over near the guards and start snooping. We need to get on this immediately."

"Now?"

"What part of *immediately* was unclear?" he asks, shooing me away like a bug. I turn to walk away when he adds, "Oh, I almost forgot. I have something for you that should be of great assistance."

I turn back to him. "What is it?"

Crosscircuit's smile really is pretty creepy.

I hope it's something good.

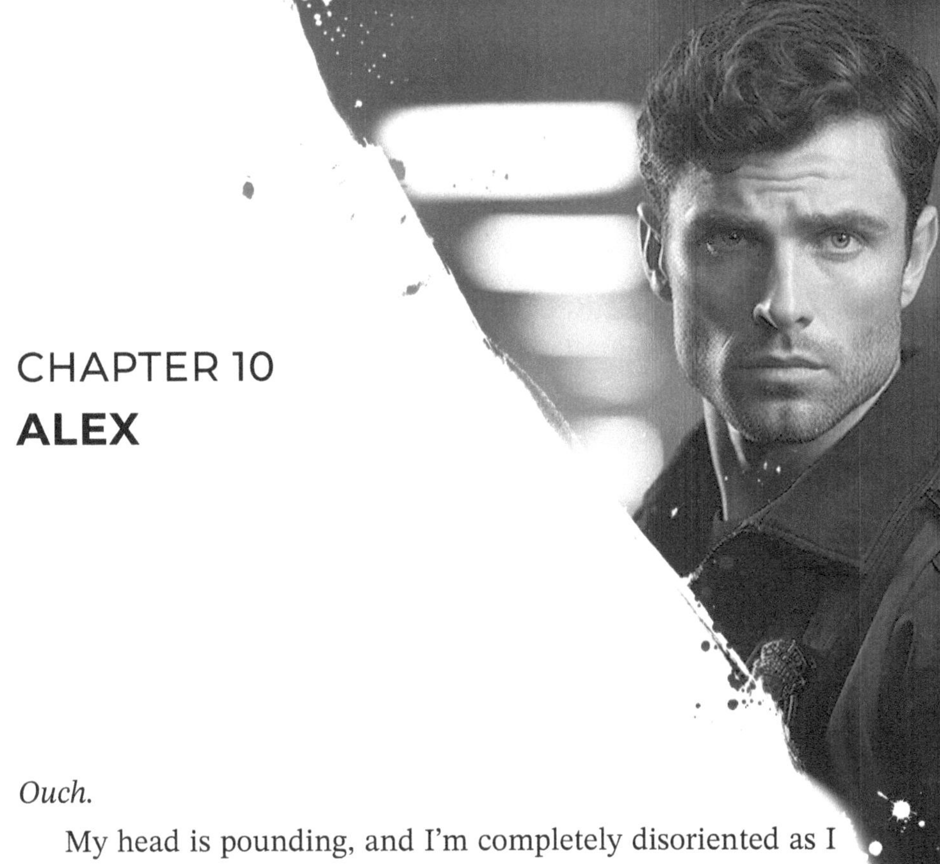

CHAPTER 10
ALEX

Ouch.

My head is pounding, and I'm completely disoriented as I try to open my eyes in the blinding light of morning. Everything feels off as things begin to come into focus. The silhouette of my bedroom TV is in the wrong place. Hell, my door is in the wrong place. On top of that, my mouth feels like it's full of cotton, and I'm one bad odor away from losing everything in my stomach. What the hell did I do last night? Who was I—

Oh, no. No, no, no, no, no, no, no.

I roll over in an unfamiliar bed in an unfamiliar bedroom. Lying next to me, still sound asleep, is Summer Valentine. A completely naked Summer Valentine. A completely naked Sawyer's Summer Valentine. And—I peek under the covers, YEP—I'm not wearing any clothes, either.

This can't be happening. I would never do this to Sawyer. Would I?

Oh, who am I kidding? I *did* do this to Sawyer. What—I'd arrest him and have him put away for life in an inescapable hellhole of a prison, but I wouldn't sleep with his ex? I need to reevaluate my life. What kind of person have I become?

I have to get out of here without waking her up. This is too much to deal with and *way* too awkward to handle with a pounding head. Even thinking about my queasy stomach makes me gag. How much did I drink last night?

What's the best way to do this? As I roll over, my body starting to hang over the edge, I feel like I'm in some stupid situation comedy. Rolling begins to pull the blanket with me, so I transition to a sort of wormlike scoot, but the bed shakes with each movement. I stop and take a deep breath before continuing more slowly. The mattress springs make weird popping noises. *Why does it sound so loud?* Summer stirs and drapes her arm around me.

I lay there, still as a... very still thing. I don't know. I can't think of anything that's still right now. My mind is reeling.

When I'm confident she's soundly back to sleep, I lift her arm in steady increments, stopping each time she stirs. Finally, after what feels like an eternity of halts and starts, I manage to dislodge myself from the bed without waking her. Then, she inhales, and I freeze like I am midway through breaking and entering when a spotlight hits me. To my relief, she rolls over and starts snoring away. I want to say that it made me less attracted to her, but unfortunately, I find it kind of endearing.

Dammit! What the hell is wrong with you? Get it together, Garner.

I need to face up to the fact that I screwed up. Bad. Now I have to fix this. But not, like, right this second. When I'm feeling better and thinking straight.

I creep into the bathroom. It looks like a Sephora bomb went off. There's makeup, toiletries, and other beauty products taking up every millimeter of counter space. After closing the door, I relieve my full bladder and splash my face with water.

Ugh. My breath smells like a tiny, alcoholic rodent gave up on life in my tonsils. Managing to find some mouthwash—I hope it's mouthwash—among the sea of bottles and containers, I swish it around in my mouth. I wonder if she has an extra toothbrush.

Time to put my detective skills to their best use.

I scour the medicine cabinet, then the drawers under the sink. I should probably ask before rifling through her stuff, but I really need to get out of here before she wakes up. In the bottom drawer, I find a couple of toothbrushes still in the package. I'm just going to assume she bought extras while they were on sale and not that she entertains so many guys she needs a stash. Not that there's anything wrong with that, of course. She's a fully grown adult woman. Okay, now I'm feeling jealous at the thought of fictitious swarms of men. I need to get out of my own head. My aching, throbbing head.

Toothbrushes. One is red and black. Maybe it was for Sawyer. It certainly makes me think of Red Kite. But she didn't know he was Kite then. Or Raptor. Or did he buy it himself to leave it here?

Blue and white it is, then.

I peel the cardboard painfully slow in hopes of not disturbing sleeping beauty. Sparing a second to lean in and peer through to the bed, I check on her. Back turned. Fast asleep. Phew.

My next search entails locating the toothpaste. More digging. More guilt. How could anyone possibly need all these bottles and containers and… what the hell is that? Must be some feminine hygiene thing. Nothing I've ever bought, that's for sure.

Amy didn't go overboard on the products and was a little —okay, a lot—more organized with her stuff.

I've never been with anyone like Summer before. Not that I'm *with* her. I'm not with her. I *was* with her last night. But not like with-with. Man, I'm panicking now.

The only tube of toothpaste is gone—squeezed to the point of looking like a steamroller flattened it. Who has extra toothbrushes but no toothpaste? Usually, the final bit lasts longer than the whole tube itself, but not this time. After going through more trouble than I would cooking a gourmet meal, I finally get a tiny dab of paste onto the bristles. I brush and then wonder what I should do with the toothbrush. Take it with me? That's just weird. But I can't leave it here, or she might think it's one of hers and use it. Or notice I used a toothbrush without asking, for that matter.

This is ridiculous. I wrap it up in some toilet paper, and

along with the packaging, I shove it into the bottom of the small, overflowing trash can in the corner.

Nice, Garner. You're a real professional sneak there.

Why am I feeling more and more like a criminal? I'm an invited guest. This is perfectly fine. I can pay her back for the toothbrush if I have to. How much could it be? A dollar ninety-nine?

The muffled sound of my ringtone goes off. Crap! Where's my comm device? It's going to wake Summer. I rush back into the bedroom as quietly as I can—but of course, my shoulder hits her dresser. I suck in through my teeth and rub at the spot while I frantically search for my pants. It doesn't help that neatness is *not* one of Summer's endearing traits. I can only assume she wasn't expecting me—or anyone—to come home with her last night because she didn't take the time to tidy things up.

That's actually pretty reassuring. Maybe she doesn't have guys over all the time. Yeah. That's what I should be focused on.

Clothes are splayed about the room, draped over every surface, and piled on the floor. Following my ringtone, I finally locate my pants and yank my phone out of the pocket. Then I hit the answer button as I exit the bedroom and close the door behind me as silently as possible.

"Hello?" I whisper.

"Yo, Alex. Why you whispering?" It's Battlegear. I mean, Eric. Of course it is. Who else would call at the worst possible time?

"I'm just... not somewhere I can talk loud. What's up?"

"Did I wake you up, bro? I'm sorry." The apology rings true. This guy is desperate for me to like him.

"No, it's fine. I was already awake."

I get self-conscious when I realize I'm still completely naked and standing in the middle of her loft. Especially since she has floor-to-ceiling windows and it's surrounded by other tall buildings, so any number of neighbors can probably see me right now. I grab a throw pillow off her sofa and press it against me to cover up a bit.

Great, now I'm going to have to get this thing dry-cleaned for her.

Eric can tell I'm lying. "Wait. You're with someone. Dang, you dog. Oh, man, now I feel terrible."

"Forget it, Eric. Just tell me why you're calling," I say, trying to keep the frustration out of my voice.

"I know it's your day off, but we finally have a situation. The others tried texting you, but you weren't answering—wink, wink. You devil. I told them I'd try to call while they headed out to the scene."

I look at my phone and see I have seventeen missed texts from my team members.

"Great. We go weeks without having to do anything, and then the one time I—"

"So, who is it? Someone I know?" he asks. "Is she hot?"

"Eric, it's none of your business," I tell him. "What scene? What's the scene?"

"Oops, sorry. Is it a dude, then? Because, if so, I'm totally fine with—"

"Just tell me where I need to go." Nope. No hiding my frustration that time.

"Geez, dude, you don't have to be rude about it. It's on Madison Avenue, right near Douglas Tower. I'm sure you can't miss it."

"Douglas Tower?" I ask. I hope it's not Frank. Please don't be Frank.

"That's what they said on the call. Why?"

"Nothing. Thanks. And sorry about the... attitude. I'm a little hungover." It's weird enough to have a conversation with a former supervillain without apologizing to the guy for a minor slight.

"Understood. Been there many times."

"Be there as soon as I can."

"All right, later, bruh—"

I hang up and tiptoe back into the bedroom, then the bathroom. I know I have to go, but there's no way I can show up looking and smelling like a dive bar. I turn on the shower and step in. I need to hurry, but the steaming hot water feels so good on my face that I close my eyes and stand there, letting it hit me.

Suddenly, the shower door opens and scares the crap out of me. Summer stands there, wearing nothing but a smile.

"Hey, you," she says.

"Oh, sorry. I tried not to wake you, but work called and—"

She puts a finger over my mouth and steps in.

This situation isn't going to be resolved anytime soon, is it?

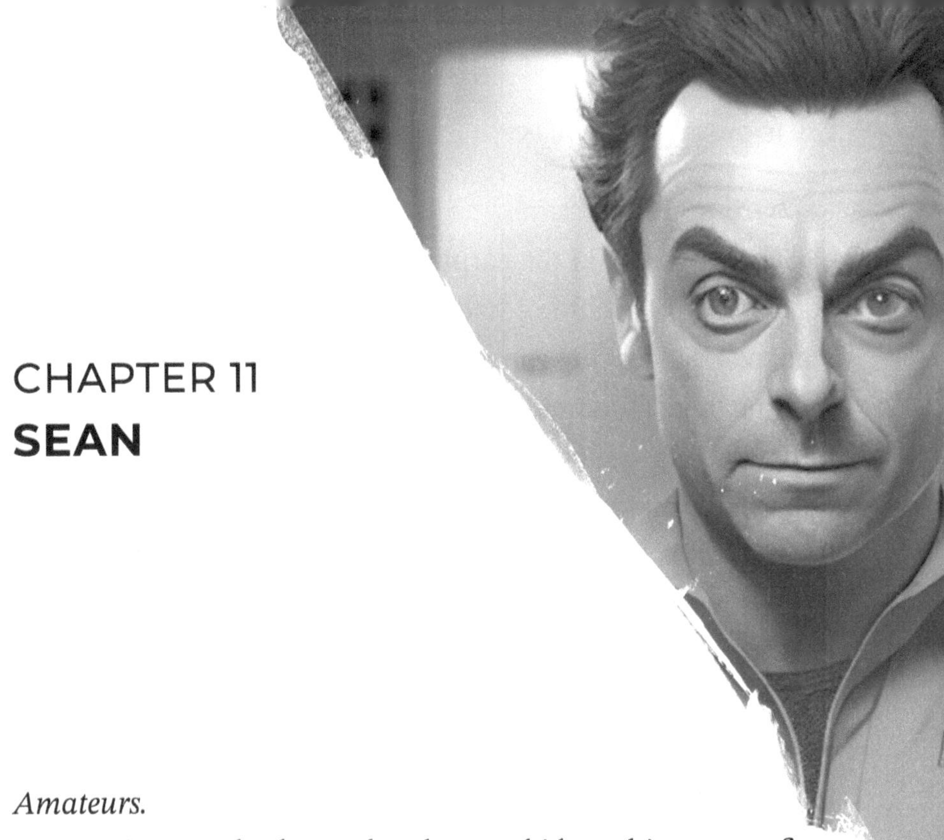

CHAPTER 11
SEAN

Amateurs.

Harrier stands there, drunk as a kid on his twenty-first birthday. I have no idea where he got the booze since I didn't provide it, but it proves he's more resourceful than I gave him credit for. Resourceful and stupid.

I hand him the little gift I created for him using spare parts and black-market materials I've acquired here in the Trench. Since Harrier's fundamentally powerless and used to utilizing technological crutches, I've provided him with a little "side-kick" of his own. It'll be quite useful.

He grabs the small, red and black ball drone, which powers up upon his touch.

It's barely the size of a golf ball and will fit snugly in his jumpsuit pocket. "All you'll need to do is ensure it's not found when being searched. I can think of at least one orifice in which it'll nicely cram."

"Gross," Harrier says.

Then I pass him the earpiece. It's a work of art, especially considering what little I had to work with here. I cannibalize whatever gadgets my connections gain me access to. It's taken months, and I'll admit, there were times when I wasn't sure he'd wind up getting caught. However, as soon as I heard Eaglestar was cracking down on masked crimefighting, I figured it was only a matter of time.

The whole Raptor family is nothing if not defiant and arrogant.

"What's this?" he asks.

"It's for you to use during the escape since I know you rely heavily on your equipment to be effective. A mini-drone to assist you in scanning the area and fighting."

"Who am I gonna be fighting?" he asks.

"I see what you're doing there—scratching for more information. It's quite all right. I can't blame you. And don't worry. You will not go in completely clueless. You may end up fighting any number of individuals, including guards or fellow prisoners. But optimally, there will be no bloodshed should everything go according to plan."

He examines the drone from all angles. I can tell he's intrigued despite acting annoyed and reluctant.

"How's it work?" he asks.

"Ah, that's the shining glory of it. It's voice-activated. Think of it as a flying Alexa device."

For some reason, he rolls his eyes. I certainly wasn't expecting that.

"Great," he groans. "Just when I thought I was through having those voices in my head all the time...."

Quite the revelation accidentally spilled. "What exactly does that mean?"

"Never mind. I suppose it has a name?"

"Of course it does," I say.

"Of course it does," he repeats with much less enthusiasm.

"Robotic Enhancement Drone for Combat, Intelligence, and Tactical Efficiency," I say with a sprinkling of glee.

"That's gotta be a stupid acron—oh, you *have* to be kidding me."

"Clever, right?"

"Shouldn't that be pronounced 'RED CITE'?" he asks. "Even a little drunk, I know that."

"No, the 'C' is for 'combat,' so it sounds like a 'K'."

"Does it, though?"

"You have to admit, it works."

"Does it, though?" he says again. Despite his protestations, he places the earpiece in his ear, and lets go of the drone, allowing it to lift into the air.

"Fabulous, isn't it?" I ask, desperate to see that twinge of adoration I know is coming.

"I'm not admitting anything at this point," he says. "Tell me more about it."

My face goes red. How dare he... *No, Sean. It's fine. The boy wants more information about your little technological wonder. Give him what he wants.*

"It's full of cameras, microphones, and sensors," I say, keeping all signs of frustration at bay. "It can use the data it collects to create a three-dimensional map of the area. I'm developing some glasses or goggles that will allow you to see what it sees, but I don't have all the components I need to complete them. For now, know that it can warn you about things happening around you and offer advice on how to deal with them."

"Whoa, that looks pretty awesome, bro," someone with whom I'm not acquainted says.

It's a thin man I'd peg for his late twenties. Despite his stature, he's quite sinewy and carries himself as someone who can fight effectively. His various tattoos seem to be without affiliation with any group or gang I've heard of. I remember a third prisoner being brought down with Harrier and that gorilla, but I hadn't been interested enough to bother finding out who it was.

Now, my interest is piqued. A man who recognizes greatness when he sees it.

Sawyer turns and gives the man an odd look. I can tell they know one another, but if my instincts serve me, not well. There's also something else there. Something I'm not quite sure about, but Harrier's demeanor toward our newcomer is a strange combination of reluctance and... something else. Pity, perhaps? It's quite odd.

"Oh, hey, Justice," Harrier says, his voice still slurred. Though I am impressed at how quickly he's gone from lush to lucid.

"Justice?" I say without attempting to hide my bemusement. The man looks embarrassed. "Certainly, a name like that wasn't available for someone new to the game, which, at your age, you must have been."

"I was just trying it out until I came up with something better," he says. "And then I ended up in here."

"Might I suggest a thesaurus?" I ask.

"What's that? Some kind of dinosaur or something? I don't think that name fits, to be honest."

I can't help but laugh. If it was an attempt at humor, it was pretty witty. Unfortunately, it's obvious he's entirely serious. And clueless.

Harrier shakes his head. Additional pity for the man. What *is* the story there? They can't be friends, can they? Hero and criminal? Not likely.

"How you holding up?" Harrier asks this "Justice" person. "I guess if you haven't been killed so far, then it must be going well."

I continue to study this Johnny-come-lately for more clues as to his identity. Justice could be a name for virtually any type of crimefighter. In fact, it may be the most generic name for one I've ever heard.

"It's not for lack of trying," Justice admits. "I've been trying to egg these guys on, but for some reason, none of them will take the bait."

"They've been instructed not to cause any problems until I'm ready," I tell him. It's time for him to understand who occupies the throne around here.

"*Instructed*?" Justice laughs. "What do they care? It's not like anyone's getting out of here."

"Oh, they'll listen," I say, offering a smile of my own. "To *me*. Everyone in here does."

Justice takes a few steps, coming within my personal bubble. It appears he was not lying about his intent to stir up trouble. "And what makes you so special?"

"Have you heard the name Crosscircuit?" I ask him, pronouncing it with a dramatic flair.

"Nope," Justice says. "Doesn't ring a bell. That name's dumber than Justice. Should I have?"

Harrier looks the other way, apparently embarrassed for him.

My lips draw a straight line, but I let the comment go. "I'll tell you what: Look me up when you get a chance to log some time on a prison library computer. Then let me know what you discover."

"What am I supposed to do—write a book report or something? I didn't do that crap while I was in school, and I sure as hell ain't gonna do it in here."

"Then perhaps you can just ask your friend here about me," I say.

He looks toward Harrier. "Well?"

"I'll tell you about him later. I really want a chance to test this thing out."

"You'll tell him now!" I snap. I will not have two newbies outwardly challenging my authority.

Harrier glares at me.

"Fine." He nods and begins. "Our new friend Crosscircuit is a bit of an egomaniac. He thinks that because he's barely better than Battlegear with tech, he should be praised as a mastermind. He's constantly reminding everyone that he's in charge, which means he isn't confident he is. Oh, and he probably has a really small pe—"

"That's enough!" I shout, unable to contain my rage. It's unlike me to be so easily coaxed into this state. He's lucky I'm aware of his state of intoxication, or I'd have him killed on the spot, escape be damned. I clear my throat. "Go. Play with your new toy. See what it's capable of. Then, remember who made it."

As soon as I say those last words, he smirks—that little bastard.

"Yeah, I'll try to find the time," Harrier says.

"It's already been arranged," I tell him. "It's imperative for you to practice with the device. It will also help test the limits of the inhibitor devices. This will be the perfect opportunity."

"Oh, right," he says as if remembering something. "You should get some of those wristbands they use in the infirmary."

"Wristbands?" This is the first I've heard about any wristbands.

"Oh, you don't know?"

Again with the condescension. I should have left him in solitary.

"Of course I know about them," I lie. "But please, tell me what you have in mind?"

"They apparently negate the inhibitors."

"Yes. Yes. I see where you're going. You see, a good leader listens to his underlings. You never know who might have a stroke of temporary genius. Even a blind squirrel finds a nut on occasion."

"I think I found a nut, all right. So you'll get some?"

I sneer at him. "I'll take it under advisement."

"Wait," Harrier says, his drunk mind finally catching up. "What's been arranged?"

"Oh, you'll see soon enough. And don't worry. He won't do any permanent damage because he knows we need you to get out of here." Although, after the barrage of insults, I'm certainly inclined to let it go further than I originally anticipated.

"He? He who?"

I smile at him.

"He *who*?" he repeats.

As Harrier is pattering, Bullshark lowers his weights and stalks over to us. Harrier almost doesn't notice in his drunken state, but the drone gives him a warning—just as it was designed to do—and he ducks just as Bullshark takes a swing at his head.

"Yer gonna pay for gettin' me in trouble, Tweety," Bullshark says.

He too had been sent to solitary. Thanks to a little push in the right direction by yours truly, he just now got out.

"C'mon, I just got out of the infirmary. Really?"

"Welcome to the Trench, Harrier," I say.

CHAPTER 12
SAWYER

Nope.

Crosscircuit can claim he's making sure Bullshark isn't gonna hurt me too badly because of the escape, but I don't trust him one bit. That monster is enraged, and I don't see how he can possibly be thinking straight enough to kick my butt without killing me. From what I know about him, showing restraint isn't exactly his thing.

"Danger at your 4 o'clock," says a voice in my ear.

It helps that the drone warns me when he approaches and feeds me all kinds of information that might help me defeat him. But... and it's a big *but*. Unfortunately, the voice in my ear belongs to Crosscircuit. I never thought I'd prefer Amber or Tiffany, my former helmet hoes. What? They aren't real people.

Also unfortunate for me, I have to do the actual fighting

part myself. While drunk, even. He couldn't have outfitted this thing with missiles or something?

I get the warning from the drone just in time to duck and roll away from Bullshark's first attack. Won't kill me? Bull crap! He's using his weight bar like a golf club.

I jump to my feet and back up as quickly as possible. But then he comes at me like an actual bull.

"A leftward dodge at a negative twenty-seven-degree angle will spare you damage akin to being struck by a bullet at 56% velocity."

None of that data sounds promising, let me tell you.

Luckily, I'm already in movement during that whole speech since by the time it's over, so is the attack. Makes sense since its creator rambles on and on and loves the sound of his voice.

Then Justice gets between us, jumping a few feet in front of me, but Bullshark mows him down like a fullback rolling over a punter while heading for the end zone.

For someone who doesn't care about sports, I'd consider that a pretty decent analogy.

"I got this, man," I said. Much as I appreciate the assist, I don't have time to worry about Justice at the moment. I can't help him if I'm dead, and we don't exactly have a working relationship to begin with.

Oh, great. He's down and not moving.

Another warning from the drone gives me a head start. I leap at the last second and plant my palms on Bullshark's head to vault over him. It isn't as easy as it was in the cafeteria since I don't have the luxury of being tabletop-height. From the ground, it's a challenge. He's gotta be a least a foot and a half taller than me, but the fact that he's hunched in an attempt to tear my throat out with his teeth is a boon in my favor. Yep. I heard it, too—thankful he's trying to murder me. Amazing the things that seem normal after doing this job as long as I have.

I manage to get past him and even give his head a shove on the way. This sends him slamming even harder into the bulkhead than he would've without my help. The sound when his skull rams metal reminds me of a slab of meat hitting the grill at my old job at Big Frankie Jr.'s. But way louder, of course.

And much more satisfying.

He turns back to me, all—I dunno—two hundred of his pointy, stabby teeth showing.

"I'm done playin' games, punk," he growls, wiping blood off his face with his forearm. I don't know precisely how much shark DNA is still in him, but I would imagine that tasting blood—even his own—is not a good thing for me.

"Just one more? Jenga, anyone?" I quip.

"Funny guy." He grinds his teeth, then rushes forward again.

How exactly is this supposed to go without me ending up dead eventually? The guards don't seem interested in stepping in this time and, instead, watch from the outskirts of the yard. Crosscircuit's doing, I'm sure.

"Are they taking bets?" I yell.

"I can hear in all directions for several hundred feet," the drone says. "It appears Officer Ubong has placed a $20 bet in your favor."

"That's encouraging," I say.

"The odds are thirty-to-one."

"That's less encouraging." As I say it, the drone gives me another warning.

"Multiple attackers approaching from your five, six, and eight o'clocks."

Looks like Bullshark's buddies are closing in to give him a hand again. Shooting a look over at Crosscircuit, I see that he's leaning against the wall, arms crossed, a bemused smile on his face. No help there. I'm starting to regret the cracks I made a few minutes ago. Especially the one about his, well, you know.

Justice is on the ground, unconscious. At least, I hope he's just unconscious.

Somehow, the drone must sense the question—or at least realize where I'm looking.

"The inmate called Justice is breathing."

That's a relief. It's not like we're friends or anything, but we might be related. And he is in that condition because of me. Sort of. He's certainly brave, but that wasn't the most brilliant move. And I'm sure Crosscircuit gave Bullshark no instructions about not hurting him too severely like he claims he had for me. I can't believe he took that hit for me. I barely know the guy.

"Closest target is almost within striking range," the drone explains.

I've always been able to hold my own against multiple adversaries, but they're usually just ordinary criminals, and I'd be wearing body armor. I don't even know who these guys are or what disciplines they may have.

I guess this is why I'm supposed to test out my little "sidekick."

"Which one is the smallest?" I ask the drone.

"The smallest incoming threat is at approximately seven o'clock in reference to your current position and direction you are facing," it replies.

That's all I need. I turn, almost doing a one-eighty, and run as fast as I can toward the guy. Even at the speed at which we're converging, I still clock a shocked expression on his face, including his mouth opening in surprise.

I execute a jumping snap kick to his face. A couple of teeth fly out as his jaw snaps shut, and his neck jerks back. He goes down immediately, twisting his leg in the process. I actually may have hurt him a little too much, but in my current state, I'm having trouble judging things.

I run a few more yards past him, then turn around so I can assess the situation from the outside.

"I didn't kill that guy, did I? Please tell me I didn't kill him," I say.

"Negative. Chances of survival are 97.8 percent."

"Oh, thank goodness."

"Subject may suffer paralysis as a result of his injuries, however."

"Oh, don't tell me that. What can I—?"

"Hostile individuals incoming," the drone warns me again. Well, that was quick.

Unfortunately, Bullshark is already racing toward me again. His cronies have also managed to stop their forward momentum and turn to face me. Even at my best and with all of my armor and equipment, this would be a difficult predicament, but with what's left of Riche's alcohol still in me, it's even worse.

Why do these tough guys always need so much backup? And how do they get the reputation of being such tough guys if they have to use help all the time?

That gives me a not-so-bright idea.

"Hey, Bullshark—what's the deal with the backup? Can't take me on alone?"

"I could," he says just as he reaches me. He swings and misses. "But you're not worth the extra effort." He swings again. I duck. "It would just take longer to get to the part where I bite your head clean off." I dodge a third time. "Stay still!"

"Oh, sure! What was I thinking?" I quip. Then to the drone, I ask, "Any suggestions?"

"Yes," it says.

"Well?"

"Run."

"Right," I say as I turn and sprint at full speed in the opposite direction. He's fast for his size, but I can easily outrun him. The question is what I'm gonna do once I'm too tired to run anymore. It's not like I can take to the rooftops.

"Warning," the drone says in my ear.

The next thing I know, there's a blur in my peripheral vision, and I'm tripping forward. My training and quick reflexes are enough to prevent me from doing a complete face-plant into the fake grass, but I still go down at a rapid rate and slam hard. After rolling a couple of times, I see the guy who tripped me, looking down and laughing. He's a speedster criminal called Rush, who's nowhere near the league of Fastlane or Pace, but he's way faster than an average human like me. I had no chance of outdistancing this guy, no matter how much of a lead I had. And the only way he ran that quickly was if the power dampeners are strained or something.

Once again, I am sure I can credit Crosscircuit for that fun.

Before I can really react, Bullshark's crew is surrounding me, and I'm having a flashback to the cafeteria. The circle of jerks parts to reveal a giant silhouette against the bright light coming down from the top of the dome. Once Bullshark leans in close enough, he blots out most of the light, and all I can see are his beady, black eyes and ginormous teeth. He kicks me in the stomach, and I roll over in a ball.

Bullshark lifts me up by the front of my jumpsuit. He's just showing off and playing with me at this point. He tosses me a few yards toward the nearest wall, and I roll again until I'm up against it. I cough and see blood spatter on the wall next to me. That's not good. It's definitely serious. The only question is just *how* serious. Broken ribs for sure. Probably organ damage and internal bleeding also.

Then I puke. Bloody whiskey splashes all over my arms. It burns like hell on the way up.

"I need something," I tell the drone.

When I get no response, I reach up to my ear, but the earpiece is gone. I swear. It must have fallen out when I got hit.

Okay, Crosscircuit, you can stop this anytime now.

Bullshark's shadow covers me, and his minions backing him up make sure I don't get past him again. His hands feel clammy and cold as he picks me up by my neck this time and slams me by my throat. My back pounds into the wall, my feet a meter off the ground. I can't breathe at all, but I'm sure I'll be dead long before I suffocate. As he opens his maw wide, I can only assume he's about to do exactly what he threatened to do.

Then I hear a loud growl from behind Bullshark and some screaming. Bullshark's grip loosens completely, and I slide down into a heap. His whole body lifts off the ground, and I finally realize what's happening. Royal Rampage is holding Bullshark above his head in a move I've seen countless times on wrestling shows. He tosses Bullshark against the wall so hard the metal caves a few inches. The shark man slumps to the turf, bleeding.

Royal Rampage bounds six feet at a time, landing on Bullshark with all of his considerable weight. But he's not done.

Fist after fist rams against Bullshark's neck, chest, and head area. I'll be astonished if he lives through this.

Finally, the guards get involved and rush over, rifles drawn. Probably only because Crosscircuit needs Bullshark for his plan. Several of them hold their weapons on Royal Rampage and shout at him to stand down. Rampage thumps his chest in triumph. Funny enough, none of them have enough balls to shoot or use their lightning sticks.

The guard who'd been cracking jokes at Rampage's expense just a few days ago stands there like a fool. Guess he's not so brave when there're no sedatives involved.

The giant gorilla's rage subsides, and he slowly backs away from the beaten and bloody Bullshark. A couple of medics run out into the yard, Mender among them. They start working on Bullshark.

It might be awhile before he can get to me.

I sit down against the wall nearby, trying to get my breath back and rubbing my neck. Justice is seated across the yard, being tended to by another prison medic. Not far away, Deadeye shakes his head and returns to his book.

And then there's Crosscircuit, striding over like nothing even happened. After looking intently at the wristbands Mender is wearing, he stops just a few feet away and looks down at me, not offering to help.

"Nice job," he says. "Now we lost our muscle."

Without another word, he walks away.

How is this my fault?

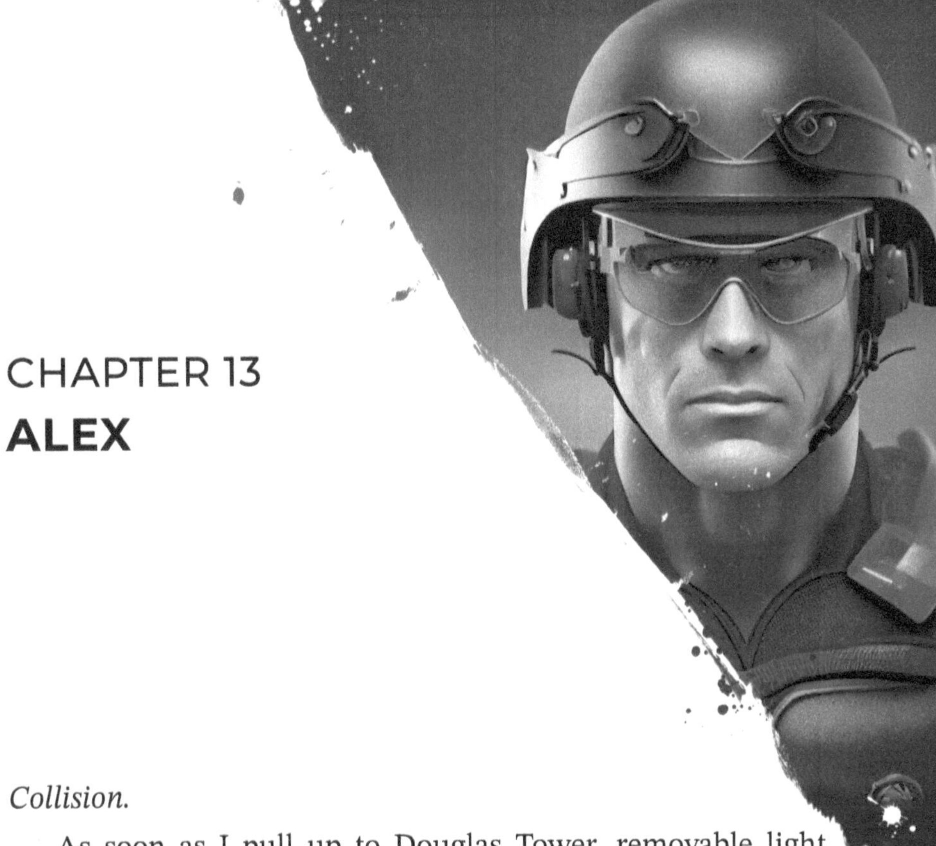

CHAPTER 13
ALEX

Collision.

As soon as I pull up to Douglas Tower, removable light spinning on top of my agency-issued vehicle, something big soars toward my car and smashes through my windshield. I'm not sure what it is since all I see is a hazy shape, and suddenly my airbags go off in my face, but I soon find out.

Blood dripping from my nose, glass shattered all over, Baron Steele climbs out of my back seat. His usually impeccable—and very, very expensive—suit is torn and filthy. Other than his shredded Armani, he doesn't seem the least bit fazed by being propelled through my window at a high rate of acceleration.

"What the hell is happening?" I ask him.

"Bit of a tussle with an old mate of mine turned archnemesis," he says as he sits down next to me in the passenger seat. "Nothin' I can't handle. How are you?"

Small talk? What the hell is wrong with this guy?

"You don't mean Eaglestar, do you?"

"Jonathan and I have had our disagreements, but I wouldn't call him an archnemesis. And, despite my well-formed opinion of him, he's no supervillain."

"Whoever it is, you need to stand down and let us take care of this," I tell him.

"Us?" Baron scoffs, making a show of looking around. Over his shoulder, in the rearview mirror.

"The CVT. And the NYPD, of course."

Baron lets out a barking laugh. "Somehow, I don't think that's goin' to happen, mate."

I felt foolish talking with blood pouring down my face. "It's going to *have* to happen," I said, pushing the deflated airbag fabric away, "since you're breaking the law." I can't believe he's arguing with me. Not only is he a fan of the new laws against vigilantes, but he's also a paid consultant for the CVT.

"Surely you don't expect me to simply stand by and let this tosser use me as a speed bag while you and your mates make a lame attempt at subduing him."

"Actually, I do. We'll get you out of here while we—"

Suddenly my smashed-up car rises into the air, assisted by something—or some*one*.

"Yeah, good luck with that," Baron says as he climbs through the hole where my windshield used to be.

Below on the street, I see a big, rubbery figure wearing bright yellow spandex. Mr. Flexiplex, a former lawyer-turned-

Guild-member-turned-villain who hasn't been heard from in quite a while, seems to be ensuring his return makes a big splash. Stretched-out, noodlelike arms smash my car—with me still in it—*into* Douglas Tower.

Baron Steele leaps off just as the impact shatters about a dozen lower-level windows.

"That's just not right!" the Baron shouts.

"Son of a—"

My vulgarity is cut short as the car rears back like Flexi is going for another bodyslam.

The guy used to be both Baron Steele's attorney and good friend before they had a falling out, and he went rogue. Believe it or not, I *think* it was over a woman. I suppose if wars can be fueled over the love of a woman, then so can super-powered feuds.

"She was mine, Paul! You had no right to take her from me," Flexiplex shouts, confirming my vague memory. His eyes tell the story: something's not right. And, not to make this all about me, but like I really needed a reminder of how pissed off people get when you have an affair with someone they're in a relationship with?

"Bloody hell, you're still on about that, mate?" Baron gripes. "It was last bloody century,' Plex. Give it a sodding rest. And last I checked, you couldn't own another person since the century before that, even on this backwards side of the pond."

I manage to leap through the windshield as Flexiplex smashes the car down onto the sidewalk in an attempt to shut Baron up. It takes every bit of my acrobatics, parkour, and martial arts training to dive-roll on the pavement without being seriously injured.

I didn't get a chance to see it earlier, but the entire city block is demolished from the fight that's been going on for some time now. All while I was busy, uh… showering.

About a block down, Yamo ushers about two dozen civilians to safety. I see no sign of the others.

"Paul, get to safety. We'll take care of this!" I yell, beginning to wonder if we actually can.

"Are you havin' a laugh, Garner?" the Baron responds. "He's tearing up this entire block, and your crew hasn't done jack-all about it yet. What makes you think you can handle this wanker on your own?"

"We'll figure it out. We always do. But you need to stand down, or we'll have to arrest you."

"Christ on a bike. Get your priorities straight. Arrest me? For defending myself and helping you do your job?"

"What do you think the anti-vigilante laws are all about?" I pull my sidearm but don't raise it. It's a foolish move. There's not a bullet I know of on Earth that would affect the Baron.

"Surely not this," Steele says as he tosses a motorcycle at Flexiplex. Plex's hand stretches into the size of a parachute and easily bends backward, then slingshots the bike back at Steele, who dives out of the way. It sails into a giant—and I'm sure *very* costly—LED billboard, smashing it and starting a small fire in the process.

"*Exactly* this, Baron! Look at what's happened to this neighborhood because of this little skirmish."

He scans the street. "Meh, I'm sure Douglas'll pick up the tab. It's practically his front yard, innit?"

"That's not the point!"

The worst part is they don't seem to be able to actually hurt one another. Almost like their powers cancel each other out. This means they're just having a very destructive disagreement that isn't going to end anytime soon.

"Hey,' Plex," the Baron shouts. "I seem to remember you ain't too fond of water." He rips a nearby fire hydrant out of the sidewalk and pulls off the side door of a minivan, then uses the door to deflect the geyser of water toward the Stretch Armstrong monstrosity.

"You've gotta be kidding me!" I yell, thinking about all the wasted water and damage he's just caused to some innocent stranger's vehicle. "How is that helping?"

"It's called a distraction," he replies.

"Last chance, Baron. Stand down!" I point my gun at him as if it means anything.

Steele ignores me and, in one powerful leap, rockets forward into Flexiplex, his meaty fist slamming into the villain's chest. Instead of caving in his rib cage as you'd expect with a normal person, the Baron's fist is wholly absorbed by his target's rubbery body, and he's unable to pull it away.

While Baron tries to extricate himself from Flexiplex's grip, I finally see the rest of my team as they limp over to my position. Every one of them is bruised, battered, and filthy. The twins, who are my weapons guys, look especially rough. Milo has a black eye, and E-Man, a broken nose

"Ya alright?" Yamo asks.

"Me?" I say. "I'm fine. But you guys look like you've been through the wringer."

"The wringer would've been a vacation on a beach in Tahiti compared to this," says Milo.

"Yeah, nothing works on these guys," says E-Man. "Everything we have bounces off the stretchy guy because he's so… stretchy. And Steele's skin makes it impossible to affect him at all."

"Did they attack you?" I ask.

"No," says Yamo. "Not directly, anyway. They've been pretty much ignoring us while they throw cars and stuff and each other. Which, I'll tell you what, is worse 'cause it's so embarrassing."

"Hold on. Where's Logan and Eric?" I ask.

Yamo nods toward the fight, and Logan, who looks like he's in as bad a shape as the rest of the group, if not worse, is running up to the two combatants. He jumps onto Steele's back, but the Baron barely notices. Mr. Flexiplex reaches around with one of his stretchy arms and grabs Logan, pulling him off Baron.

"Stay out of this, interloper!" Plex shouts.

Baron sees Logan dangling next to him and reaches out, presumably to help—I hope that's his intention, anyway. But he doesn't have a chance. Flexiplex tosses Logan aside like a cigarette butt. Logan soars into a nearby wall, hard enough to crumble the cement. He bounces off and lands with no grace at all on the sidewalk. Luckily, he shakes his head in a daze, letting us know he's alive.

"Yamo, can you go check on him, please?" Yamo, who has some medical training, acknowledges my request as she runs over to him. The twins and I have little choice but to continue being spectators in the battle. Yamo said it: this is embarrassing.

A few things run through my mind. One, what would Summer think if she saw me standing here, useless as tits on a bull? And two, in a similar vein, what would Amy think? What have I become? It's a question I feel like I really need answers to.

"Looks like we may finally have a winner," E-Man says, nodding toward the two powerhouses.

Flexiplex's arm looks like a boa constrictor as it wraps around Baron Steele. As Steele tries to break free, it just pulses and stretches, preventing him from being able to pull away. It then wraps around his face, which I assume will prevent Steele from being able to breathe unless he has some additional powers I'm not aware of.

I can only hope 'Plex will let the Baron go once he passes out and won't wait until he's dead before letting up. I guess maybe it depends on how much he was in love with this woman the Baron "stole" from him.

"If anyone has any more ideas, now's the time," I say. "I'm fresh out myself, but we can't just stand here."

A loud sound like a hailstorm fills the air, and Flexiplex is suddenly encased in a block of ice. I turn around, and

Battlegear stands behind me, holding a giant weapon with what appears to be steaming dry ice covering the barrel.

"There," Eric says. "No muss, no fuss. Sorry about the delay, but I had to get down to my warehouse in Queens and dig this thing out of storage."

Flexiplex's arm, the only part of him not in the ice block, goes limp, and Baron finally catches his breath. I decide now's not the time or the place to question why a former supervillain is allowed to have a warehouse full of questionable weapons of mass destruction. Or is it my job to do something about it?

"Is it safe?" I ask.

"What do you mean?" Battlegear says.

"Is he going to be okay after being on ice like that?"

He shrugs. "Who cares?"

I give a look that says I do.

He sighs. "Should be fine. But we *do* need to get his face uncovered in the next minute or so, or he'll suffocate."

"You didn't think you should lead with that?" I say, already in motion.

"Hey, you're the one asking all the questions and taking up so much time."

Eric walks back to the van he'd arrived in and pulls out a small electric saw-looking device. You'd think the van would be as nondescript as possible if that's what he was using while breaking the law, but no. Instead, he has a giant reproduction of Frazetta's "Death Dealer" painted all over the side. I know it's become a thing to say, "shaking my head," but I find myself literally shaking my head.

I stop at Baron Steele's side. "You okay, Paul?"

He slaps my arm away, clearly frustrated and embarrassed.

Behind me, I hear Battlegear's tool cutting away at the ice near Flexiplex's face.

"Be careful," I shout at him. "We don't need a lawsuit because you sliced his nose off or something."

This makes Eric crack up, which probably makes it even more dangerous. I was serious about the lawsuit. Before he got his powers in a freak accident, Flexiplex was one of those accident attorneys with his face plastered all over billboards and bus stop benches.

Baron is halfway down the block before I notice he's up and walking away, trying in vain to brush off his suit.

"Hey, where do you think you're going?" I shout.

"To find another MoonMoney." He points to the coffee shop, which has been nearly leveled. "I still haven't gotten my morning cuppa, and this one is out of commission for a while."

"Oh, no, you don't," I say.

"I thought cuppa was tea?" E-Man asks, having finally caught up to us.

"Yeah," Eric calls down. "Aren't you a coffee guy?"

"Old habit," says Baron. "Besides, it could refer to any hot beverage. Look it up."

"Guys, please, just... shut up," I say, my patience on

thinner ice than Flexiplex. “Baron, you need to come down to the station with us.”

“Ain’t gonna happen, champ.”

I have no idea how we’re supposed to bring in Baron Steele, especially in my team's condition. As much as I dread the idea, I guess it’s time to call in the big gun.

Eaglestar.

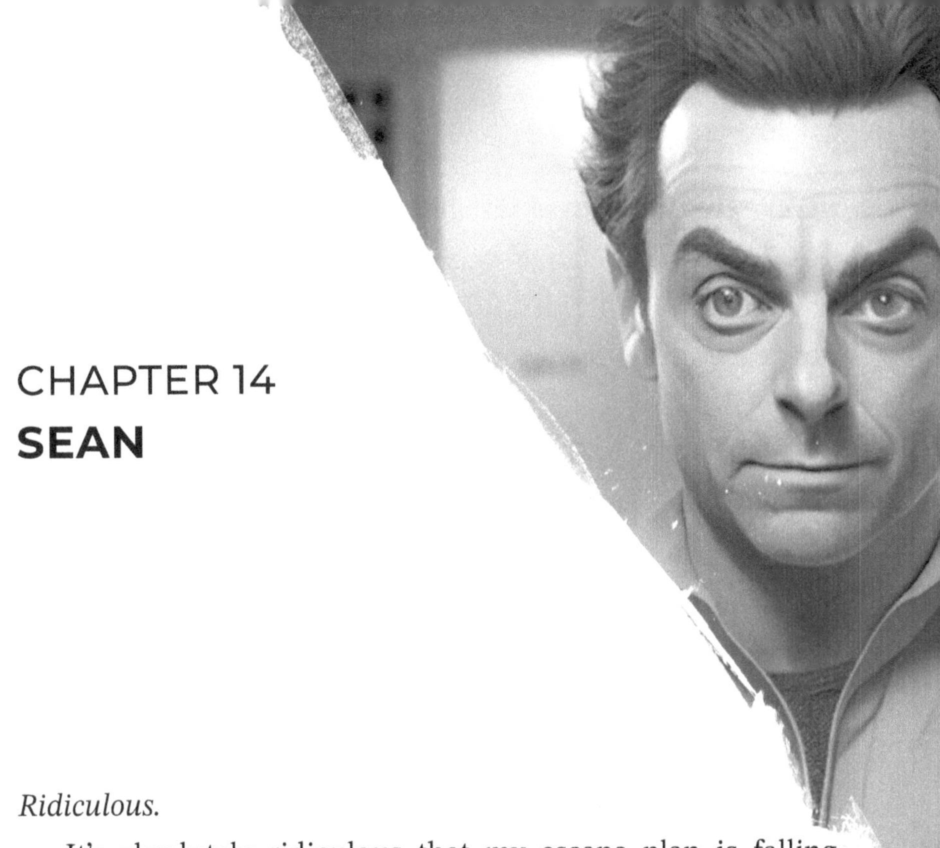

CHAPTER 14
SEAN

Ridiculous.

It's absolutely ridiculous that my escape plan is falling apart after so many months of preparation, especially now that I'm so close to its execution. Bullshark is down for the count, Harrier is seriously injured, and Deadeye appears to be just plain out after seeing what happened to the others. The only person still left for certain in my merry little band of escape artists is Sinsation, who—let's face it—is a few poppers short of a late-night munchie meal. If she's going to be the reliable one in the group, I have a problem on my hands.

I haven't felt this defeated since I snuck out of the house early one morning as a teenager, followed my dad on his delivery route, and then watched him die. Well, I didn't actually see him die, but after trailing him on my bicycle for a couple of hours, I saw him taken by an alien ship, and he never returned. It was just like the man in the immaculate suit. Though my father was strange and unloving, he was normal by all other definitions. My assumption is that he is now deceased, but even if he isn't, I can't imagine he's ever coming back.

I haven't told you that story, have I? I suppose you want to know now. At one point, I believed my father was having an affair, after calculating how long his delivery route should have taken him compared to how long he was gone every day. Not that it mattered to me. I couldn't have cared less and was happy to have him away for as long as possible. In fact, the idea of him abandoning our family was a positive thing in my mind. But it wasn't fair to my mother, and I wanted to assure he wouldn't end up leaving her for some bimbo and breaking her heart.

So I got up early one morning and rode my bike after him. I suppose they don't have milk delivery in most places anymore these days. It was like having Door Dash for milk set up for certain days of the week, only they would leave it in a box on your front step. Seems like a bizarre concept now, to be honest. But just about everyone did it. Some places even delivered hand-churned ice cream.

It turned out he wasn't having an affair. Not that I witnessed, anyway. He was just a languid man. Lazy, if I'm being honest. I could have finished the entire route in half the time if there had been some way to carry all those milk bottles on my bicycle.

But after completing his route, he took a road that led out

of town, and only one place I knew of was located in that direction—a bar where they sold cheap alcohol and played old country music on a jukebox. I started to fall behind once he was no longer making his stops because, as fast as I was on my bike, there was no way I could pedal as quickly as his milk truck could drive. As I alluded, I got to the same point where I had seen that stranger get vaporized by a UFO, and there was dear old dad, stopped on the side of the road.

And *they* were there as well: those same lights in the sky. And when a bright beam shot down, I thought he would undoubtedly be atomized the way the other man had been. But this was some manner of tractor beam.

I watched, helpless, as he was taken up into the sky, flailing around like a lizard maltreated by a small boy. Just before he disappeared into the bowels of the alien ship, he spotted me, and we locked eyes. My final memory of my father was that look of dread and pleading. Then he was gone.

At that point, I knew they were sending me a message. The thing I never understood, and still don't, was why they didn't just take *me*—either time.

As I mentioned before, I wasn't a fan of my father. But I did love my mother more than anything on Earth, and she changed after he disappeared. She had to start working two jobs, and she missed my father—another something I'll never understand. She became depressed. Acted like a different person. And the stress of it all undoubtedly made her illness worsen.

And then, she died.

But enough about my past. Let's talk about my future. My plan has far too many moving parts to be performed by any less than five individuals, including me. And they have to be specific individuals—certain *types* of individuals, I suppose you could say.

I track down Harrier in the sad little room they call the "library" here in the Trench. It's little more than a few sad bookshelves containing a collection of old Tom Clancy novels and self-help books—the latter of which I find endlessly amusing, considering most of us are never going to see the light of day again. We would, therefore, never have the chance to put the advice to any use. To the credit of this hellhole, we *do* have access to reading books digitally. However, even many hardened criminals can't seem to make the adjustment and still prefer printed materials.

The reality is that the library is my command center of sorts. You see, despite their many and varied attempts to keep the computers from functioning as anything but tools to look up information and access ebooks, in my hands, they do whatever I want them to. Not only am I able to access anything I want online, but I can have parts for my robots 3D printed and assembled in automated facilities, log in to banking and investment accounts around the world, and connect with the spyware I created and sent to an employee of Douglas Industries who was looking for a promotion and a raise.

Yes, my friend, it was I who set up the dominoes that are

toppling over and taking down one of the most powerful corporations in the world.

But I digress.

I enter the library to see Harrier reading an old Jack Ryan book, presumably out of sheer boredom.

"Let me save you some time. He takes down the bad guys and saves the world," I tell him.

"I'm fine. How are you?" he says. "Oh, I'm sorry. I thought we were starting our conversation like normal human beings. My mistake."

I ignore the feeble attempt at humor. "We have a problem."

"*You* have a problem," he says. "I have a book."

"You had the chance to be a true hero like your Jack Ryan fellow there. Instead, you—"

"I what? I got my ass handed to me by a freak of nature. And it was *your* fault."

I smile slightly, hoping it will divert his rage so we can converse like gentlemen. "I have seen you hold your own against villains far worse."

"Yeah, with armor and weapons, and not surrounded by more of the world's worst."

"I am disappointed in you," I say. "I believed you to be something special."

"Well, life's full of letdowns," he says. "Just ask your mom."

I bare my teeth at the mention of Glory Meyers. "It's your own mother you should be worried about."

"Yeah, whatever." He goes back to his dime store garbage. Then, he looks up and tosses it aside. "How is it they still let you anywhere near these computers after you used them to control your full-on robot invasion a few years ago?"

I shrug. Sure, I'm still upset that he would blaspheme the most wonderful person who ever graced the Earth, but I regrettably need him. No matter how much it pains me to admit it. "They think they've limited my access. And, truthfully, they have somewhat. Just not enough to matter."

"Okay. Well, good luck doing whatever you're doing." He picks his book up again.

"I knew you'd be fine."

He looks up at me with only his eyes. "Mender can only do so much. What if that brute put me in a coma? What if he killed me?"

I shake my head. "He had his instructions."

"I guess not everyone listens to you like you think they do. Sorry to break it to you, but he wasn't holding back."

"That thought has passed my mind. However, the exercise was still a success."

"A success? Bullshark isn't coming back from that, man. He's done. Caput. And Royal Rampage will be lucky if he ever comes out of solitary."

"Oh, my boy. You still don't understand how this works," I say, grinning. "Royal Rampage is *already* out of solitary."

"What? How?"

"Same way I got you out. Our dear warden has a family. Therefore, he has a weakness which can be exploited."

"You're sick. You know that, right?" he asks.

I shake my head. "No. I am the only one who truly sees what is at stake here. And I am willing to employ whatever tactics it takes. I needed you to test that drone, which seems to work well. And as I guessed, the power inhibitors seem to be strained by several individuals attempting to use their powers at once, which was the other thing I needed proof of. It was a working theory. Rush was only slowed down to half speed."

"I'm glad you benefitted from my pain."

"We *all* benefitted from your pain, you ingrate."

"Ah, we've reached the name-calling portion of the show," he says. "I think we're done here."

"Are you sure? From what I understand, your mother is currently at her spin class on Third Avenue."

Harrier springs to his feet like a jackrabbit and grabs me by the collar.

"Mention my mother, one. More. Time."

I smirk. "I see you understand the gravity of your decision. Go ahead. Pummel me. Kill me for all I care. Without me calling it off, the Rifleman *will* kill her."

"You're lying."

"Is that a wager you're willing to place?" His eyes tell me he believes me, even if he doesn't trust me. He certainly doesn't like me. But that's okay. If the choice were to be made between respect by love and respect by fear, I'd choose fear any day. Fear is a fantastic motivator.

"What do you want?" he asks.

I stare down at my jumpsuit, clenched in his fists. He lets go and backs away.

"I need you to recruit some new members to our team," I say, smoothing out the wrinkles.

"Team? Is that what we're calling it?" he asks.

"Team. Crew. Dance troupe. Call it whatever you'd like. We need a marksman and some muscle, and you happened to have arrived here with both in tow. You appear to have a rapport with Justice and the gorilla, if I'm not mistaken."

"You're not."

"I rarely am."

"Call off the hit on my mother," he demands.

I laugh. "Young Harrier, you are in no position to negotiate. Do as I ask, and your mother will live. Defy me and... well."

His face goes red. Through clenched teeth, he says, "Fine."

"Good, then it's settled. Convince your friends to join our side. It's a win-win, really. We escape. Dear mommy lives to see another day. The entire world is saved."

"You're a delusional son of a bitch."

My jaw tightens as he once again manages to insult my hallowed mother. Before I can express my anger, he asks, "How do you expect me to win them over? After seeing that crap you pulled in the yard—"

"You know them better than I do. I'm sure you'll figure something out."

"And if I don't?" he asks. "What if they say 'no'?"

"That's not going to happen."

"How do you know?"

"Because you can't afford it."

I stand up and try to be as dramatic as possible as I leave, patterned after Deadeye's exit from the cafeteria. I'm sure it's nowhere near as effective, but I'm also sure I get my point across.

CHAPTER 15
ALEX

Sidetracked.

Before I can figure out how I'm going to explain to Eaglestar that his ol' buddy Baron Steele now has to be arrested and that he's probably the only one who can do it, I see Frank standing in front of his building, assessing the damage. There's a giant hole in the side of Douglas Tower, but as far as I know, nobody was hurt because people on the lower floors had long since evacuated during the battle on the street. Thanks to Yamo, who is always thinking about those considerations.

Frank looks even worse than I feel this morning, and I'm sure the wrinkled, unbuttoned dress shirt and slacks he's wearing were what he had on all night—probably after passing out with a bottle of Jack. Or some much fancier, more expensive whisky that someone like me could never afford.

I approach him slowly and cautiously, remembering the

last conversation we had. He takes a sip of what I assume is a Bloody Mary and not just tomato juice, and Frank being Frank, knows I'm there before I even say anything.

"I thought this was what you people were supposed to be trying to prevent," he says without even looking in my direction.

"Uh, yeah. It is. But sometimes, we can only do so much."

"Sort of like when *actual* heroes are in a fight like this?"

"What's that supposed to mean?" I ask.

"Does it truly matter whether you wear a mask or not? I don't think it does. Sometimes when you fight a bad guy, things get destroyed. Sometimes, badge or not, people get hurt."

I try to look him in the eye, but he refuses to reciprocate as he continues to survey the destruction. He points at the MoonMoney. "You know, I own that now? Who's going to pay for that?" Then he stabs a thumb behind him at his destroyed tower. "And that?"

"You've got insurance."

"Fascinating," he says, still unwilling to look at me. "You're willing to pass the buck that easily. So they spend millions, I get premium increases, the entire block has to travel farther for a coffee every morning until it's rebuilt, and that's that, huh?"

"Hey, this was Paul and 'Plexi."

"And you," he says, finally facing me. "You were here. Your team was here. You people did exactly zero to keep this entire street from turning into a Middle Eastern war zone."

"I'm doing the best I can," I say, voice weaker than I wanted.

"Looks like 'the best you can' isn't good enough."

Wow. If there was ever a statement that summed up what I've always believed Frank thought of me, that was it. I don't even know how to respond.

Then I don't need to.

Some guys in suits exit Douglas Tower escorting Luis Chen, Frank's right-hand man. In handcuffs.

Frank notices at the same time I do. He hands me his Bloody Mary. "Make yourself useful."

I take it, caught off guard.

"What's going on here?" he demands of the suits. Frank has a way of asking questions that don't allow someone to not answer, and he's using that particular tone.

I look around frantically, trying to find somewhere to put the damn drink down before I get fired for drinking on the job. From the smell, it's about one-fourth tomato juice and three-fourths vodka.

One of the guys whips out a badge and flashes it at us. "FBI. Mr. Chen is being brought in for questioning."

"If it's just questioning, why is he in cuffs?" Frank asks.

The agents ignore him and start down the stairs.

"I asked you a question," Frank shouts.

I finally toss the drink into a flowerpot and chase after them.

"Do you really think now is the best time for this?" I ask the agents.

"We're not going to stop doing our job just because you let this situation get out of control," one of the agents answers as they shove Chen into the back seat of their black SUV, which I notice for the first time, has US Government plates.

Despite the dire situation, Frank smirks when he hears this. I decide not to respond.

"It's okay, Frank," Chen says. "We'll figure this out."

One agent chuckles.

"I'll get the lawyers down there immediately," Frank says to Chen.

Chen simply nods as he gets comfortable in his seat. Even now, he's calm, cool, and collected. He's always so full of confidence that it borders on egotistical. It's eerie to see him in this position.

Frank wastes no time pulling out his phone and scrolling for numbers. He turns to me. "If you'll excuse me, it looks like I'm going to be a bit busy today." Then he motions to the rubble. "Get this cleaned up."

"Frank..."

He spins on me. "What? What could you possibly think is important right now?"

"Amy," I say, so low it's a whisper.

Frank shoots me a look, and I can tell he knows how to contact her. I'm sure at his prime, I would never have seen him give something away, but it's been quite a while since anyone would describe him as being at the top of his game.

"I'll do my job. You do yours," he says as he turns his back on me.

"Wait." I rush forward and grab his arm as he walks away. "Do you know where she is?"

He pulls away.

"Frank, she deserves to know," I call out.

But he's already talking to one of his attorneys. He tries to enter the building, but uniformed officers block him.

"Can't let anyone in until it's safe," one says.

"I own the damn building," Frank says, pulling the phone away from his ear.

The two officers look at each other, clearly confused about how to handle the situation.

"Frank!" I shout.

He ignores me while the officers continue arguing.

I shake my head and swear.

Somehow, I need to let Amy know her father has been arrested. Somehow, I need to explain to Captain Fernanda how we let this entire street get destroyed. Somehow, I need to defend the existence of my task force.

Not for the first time, I feel like we're in way over our heads. It's one thing to take down a vigilante with a three or four power rating, but when up against a ten like the Baron... what do we even have to offer?

I ponder that question while I walk back to my team.

The twins finish helping a dazed Logan into the back of their vehicle. Yamo is on the phone with someone—I assume Captain Fernanda.

I stop and take one last look at the neighborhood. This

was my street. I practically grew up here. Then I look up to the top floor of Douglas Tower, the Aerie.

I feel a hand on my shoulder. "Let's head back to the station and lick our wounds," Milo says.

"I think I need to swing by my apartment first," I say. I'm covered in shards of glass, dirt, and even some blood. I notice I have little cuts all over me. Nothing serious, but I need to get cleaned up again. "Actually, we've already had a rough morning. Maybe we should all head home and take the rest of the day off. We'll regroup in the morning."

"Don't have to ask me twice," Yamo says. She gives a peace sign as she walks to her car.

Everyone piles into their respective vehicles, but I just stand there looking at mine, which is now a twisted heap of metal.

Then, the last thing in the world I need happens.

Eaglestar slams down on the pavement beside me.

"This didn't go well," he says.

I shake my head. "You don't say?"

"The stretchy one has been detained."

"And the Baron?"

"Letting him off with a warning," Eaglestar says.

"A warning?"

"That's right. Paul has done much to help our cause. We are willing to overlook things this time."

"So that's it, huh? He greases some palms and gets off with a slap on the wrist?"

"You're a cop," Eaglestar says. "Tell me you've never let another cop get away with speeding?"

"That's different," I argue. But is it?

"Is a speeding police officer a danger to his surroundings?" He nods. "We take care of our own. You would do well to remember that."

Without another word, he bursts from the ground with a bang, and I can't even follow his trajectory.

We take care of our own.

I didn't think I could feel any worse for locking Sawyer up. Leave it to Eaglestar to make a crappy day even crappier.

CHAPTER 16
SAWYER

Ugh.

I thought Mender was joking when he was talking about getting out of cleaning toilets, but it turns out that's a job they actually give to the new prisoners. When I was a teenager, I had to clean restrooms at Big Frankie Jr.'s, the fast-food chain Frank owns. I thought that was bad, but that was paradise compared to the bathrooms here in the Trench.

Kind of a weird insight I've gotten as I get older. All the things that seem monumental as a kid begin to come into a clearer perspective as I get older. Yeah, I know, twenty isn't *old* but going to prison has a tendency to speed up the aging process. All the small things like my crush on Amy, my relationship with Neith, and even what I had with Summer—they seem so inconsequential now.

Maybe I'm just overly introspective right now. Can you

blame me? I'm scrubbing dried poo off the back of a communal toilet... in prison... at the bottom of the ocean. A few weeks ago, I was worried about which excuse I'd give Summer for leaving our date early or what I'd tell Mom if she caught me sneaking in at 4 a.m.

The only good thing about my current situation is that I'm in here alone with Justice since he's got KP duty as well. That stands for Kitchen Patrol if you're wondering. And although it's rumored some people make wine in prison toilets, I'd give anything to be cleaning kitchens. Or peeling potatoes. But evidently, it includes cleaning toilets here.

Crosscircuit gave me the task of recruiting a new sniper/gunman for what he colloquially calls "the team." I'm reluctant to ask Justice if he'll replace Deadeye and help with the escape. I know he's probably gonna say yes, but it's extremely dangerous, and I don't wanna do that to someone who could be my brother, even if we've barely just met. Plus, it would suck if Frank lost both of his sons simultaneously. On the other hand, I don't wanna leave him in here to rot, either. Definitely not once Crosscircuit is no longer around ordering prisoners not to make any waves. I don't see him lasting very long at that point, especially if he pisses off any lifers with nothing to lose.

Thanks to Mender doing his thing, Justice looks much better than the last time I saw him. I'm just glad he didn't get seriously injured or killed jumping into Bullshark's path when that monster was coming at me like a freight train.

Neither of us has said a word to each other since getting

here besides the obligatory, "'Sup?" I'm unsure how to engage in a conversation that wouldn't feel forced. But I've gotta start somewhere.

"You ever thought about who your father might be?" I ask him as if *that's* somehow a good way to ease into things.

He stops what he's doing, the scrub-scrub-scrub of his brush quieting. Looking up at me, he says, "Huh? That's a pretty random question."

"You told me you didn't know him," I said. "I guess I've been thinking about what I went through myself, and I was wondering if you felt the same way."

"I... uh." He starts cleaning again. "Sure. Well, yeah, of course I think about it. I don't think a day goes by when the question doesn't at least cross my mind once or twice. Who wouldn't?"

"Yeah. Right? That's how I was, too."

"I take it you eventually found out who yours was?" he asks. And I wonder if that's jealousy in his tone.

"Oh. Yeah. I did."

He gives the toilet a flush before getting back to scrubbing. "And did it feel as good as you thought it would to finally know?"

I think this whole thing might backfire. How do I answer this? I didn't exactly find out under the most ideal of circumstances. He must sense my hesitance.

"We don't have to talk about it," he says. "You just brought it up, so I figured..."

"No. It's fine," I say, flushing my own toilet and moving on to the next in line. "Just trying to think about a good way to respond. Honestly? Not like I thought it would."

"He some kind of deadbeat loser who knocked your mom up at a club or something?" he asks, laughing.

Funny, he's not that far off except for the deadbeat part. My parents met at a club owned by Frank's family; from what I understand, I was conceived in the bathroom. Not Frank's—or my mom's—best moment, for sure.

"Something like that," I agree. "But he's a good guy."

"I don't expect to ever find out who mine is. If he's gone, he's gone for a reason. This long without trying to meet me, he's either dead or doesn't care. Either way, I can't imagine it going well."

"If someone could tell you who he was, though, would you want them to? No matter what might happen once you found out?"

He stops scrubbing again and stares off into space. "Huh. That's a tough one. But yeah. Knowing one way or the other would be better than wondering the rest of my life."

I guess that's the way I felt. My life since finding out Frank was my father hasn't been ideal, but I know I'm better off than before I knew. I suppose all the money helps, too. Even though that does me no good in here.

"If we get out of here, how about I help you try to find him?"

"Really?" he says, genuinely surprised. "Wow, man. That's killer of you to offer. Yeah, that would be great." A moment passes before he adds. "But I really don't think we're getting out of here."

"Actually..."

There's my open door. I feel like a jerk. What kind of a person uses someone's pain to manipulate them? Then Cross-circuit's voice bounces around in my brain, threatening my mother.

After the few seconds it takes for me to have second thoughts, he pipes in. "Actually what?"

I think about what I'm about to do and the repercussions, including the warden's warnings. What choice do I have? He's right. If we don't do something, we aren't getting out of here —regardless of what Warden Riche thinks. Frank isn't gonna win his mayoral campaign. Not a chance. And when Keyes is reelected, nothing is changing. I'm in here for life.

I keep my voice low in case anyone—including but not limited to the warden—is listening. "I know someone who has a plan. And they need another person. Someone with your... talents."

A look of someone who's been betrayed creeps into his features. "Oh. So that whole thing about helping me find my father was just some trick to get me to help?"

He's not as dumb as he looks. *Play this next hand carefully, Sawyer.*

I shake my head emphatically. "No. No, not at all. I meant it. But you said it: without a miracle, we're not getting out."

He thinks about it. "I'd have helped you either way," he says. "Escape, I mean."

"You would?"

"Of course. Why wouldn't I?"

"You barely know me," I say.

"True. But you're my only friend."

"In here, you mean?"

"No. You're my only friend anywhere," he says.

Oof. I'm getting in deep here, aren't I?

"No one back home?"

He shakes his head, leaning on his toilet brush. "I've spent the last year of my life dedicated to the whole Justice thing. Haven't had much time for friends."

"What about before that?" I ask, wondering why I care so much.

"Not really. You don't know what it's like being so different. Imagine you're better at everything you do because all you need to do is, like, watch a reel about it, and *bam!* You can do it."

I don't have to imagine it.

"When I was a kid, no one would even play sports with me," he continues. "Basketball? No way. I'd watch Jordan or Ewing, and no one could stop me on the court. They got annoyed with me. Probably didn't help that I couldn't help the trash talk. I was young. Didn't realize what was going on. Not exactly. Just thought I was really good. It led to a lot of fights."

"Yeah. That's tough," I said, thinking about my own childhood. I didn't have many friends either. Not until Javier. Then my mind starts drifting to poor Javi. I have no idea what happened to him after I got arrested. I guess I should be grateful that he didn't wind up in prison himself, since he was my "man in the chair," helping me every step of the way.

"And those fights? I never lost. Ever. Almost got thrown in juvie for cracking some kid's skull in high school."

"Watch enough UFC," we both say at the same time.

"Right!" Justice shouts.

My heart practically stops. I hope he doesn't realize I have firsthand experience. Not yet, anyway.

"Anyway," he says, breaking into my thoughts. "What do you need me to do?"

Still a little distracted, I say, "Uh… I'll talk to the guy and let you know when he's ready to meet."

"Yeah. Whatever, bro. Anything's better than this." He holds up the toilet brush.

We return to our duty—pun totally intended—and I continue thinking about Javier. Last I heard, he was questioned about me. He wasn't allowed at the trial. But he didn't try to contact me either. I assume it was because he felt guilty, but I wasn't mad at him.

He was a skittish kid. Always was. I can't imagine what it was like for him, being in a police station, getting drilled about where I was. Like I said, I'm just glad he didn't get sent here too. Well, he wouldn't get sent *here.* He'd go to a regular prison for regular people. But still. At least Alex wasn't a total prick.

My thoughts carry me to Alex. I don't understand what

happened to him. He went from fighting crime and being a badass to chasing me around town like that badge somehow made what he and I did different. But didn't it? He was under authority. More than I was. He knew when to stop, when the risk wasn't worth the payoff.

Me? I crashed through an old lady's apartment, and she's dead now because of me.

Maybe I do deserve to be in here.

Then there's my mom. Was Crosscircuit telling the truth? Was she really at spin class? Her son is in prison, and she's exercising? Guilt berates me. What, she's supposed to stop living because you get your ass locked up? Maybe? A little, at least. Perhaps cry for a few weeks.

Wow. That's selfish. I'm glad she's able to go out and live. I'm sure she's heartbroken. All those years of me covering up to prevent her from finding out what I was doing must've made it all the more difficult when she did find out the truth. What a shock that would've been for her.

Makes me wish Frank hadn't broken up with her.

At the thought of Frank, my father, the first flare of anger rises in me. Why didn't he do more? He's one of the wealthiest, most influential people on the planet, and he couldn't keep his own son out of the Trench? He's the CEO of Douglas Industries. The original Black Harrier, for Pete's sake. A core member of the Guild.

"You okay?" Justice asks.

At the sound of his voice, I open my eyes. I didn't even

know they were shut. There's some moisture on them too, and I'm leaning on the gross toilet. God, I hope those are tears.

I clear my throat, wiping my eyes with the back of my wrist. "Fine. Yeah. I'm fine. Just… just thinking."

CHAPTER 17
ALEX

Bzzzzzzzt.

My comm buzzes, and I see that it's Summer calling. And I was just thinking about her in the shower. *No,* not like that. Get your mind out of the gutter.

"Hello?"

"Hey there!" Her voice is chipper, as always. Makes sense. She's not the one dealing with a mental overload. "I just wanted to see how you were doing. I saw what happened after you left as soon as I turned on my TV."

I guess if you work at a TV station, you probably have it on all the time when you're not out somewhere. Makes sense.

I take a seat on my bed and run a towel over my damp hair after taking my second shower in as many hours. "Yeah, I'm fine, thanks. Despite being in a car as it was thrown around by Mr. Stretchypants."

"Sounds like fun. That's... not his actual name, is it?"

I laugh. "No. It's Flexiplex."

"Wait. Is that supposed to be better?" Now we're both laughing, and a bit of my tension melts away.

"It was like a ride at Coney Island but not at all like a ride at Coney Island. You know?"

"I've lived in the city my whole adult life and never been," Summer says, a hint of sadness in her voice.

"Really? Never?"

"Well, when my brother Jeremy died..."

She trails off. "Hey, forget it," I say. "How about when things settle down here, we go together?"

What are you doing, Garner? That's a bad idea.

"Really? How about we go later today?"

Wow. She's moving fast. I should say no. I definitely need to say no. "You know what? How about we go now? I gave my team the rest of the day off. Not much we can do now that Eaglestar took over."

I try to keep the resentment out of the statement, but it's not easy.

"OMG. Seriously? This is great."

"Oh, wait. What about *your* work?"

"Well, no one reached the scene in time this morning—despite me giving them the heads up—so I'll be following up with an up-close-and-personal interview with the head of the CVT himself."

"Uh... yeah. That sounds... um..."

"I'm kidding, Alex. But I will need some details so I can write something up and pretend I was working. My bosses don't need to know I was riding the Cyclone while collecting the information."

"Oh, is that my new nickname?"

Dude, cool it.

"Wow, Mr. Garner," she says. "I didn't know you had that in you."

A "that's what she said" joke dances on my tongue. I think I'll need to see a therapist when all this is through. I feel like a man of two minds, constantly battling between being playful and flirty and realizing I'm making the biggest mistake of my life.

Instead, I smile. "I don't know. As a law enforcement official, I'm not sure about this whole idea of aiding and abetting someone trying to defraud their employer."

"Yeah? Well, I happen to know someone in law enforcement myself. In fact, I'm sleeping with him. I'm sure he'll be there to bail me out."

"You're... what?"

There's a pause on the other end of the line. "I'm talking about *you*, dummy."

"Oh, yeah! Right." I let out an awkward chuckle. "I knew that."

"Are you sure? Because it sounded like—"

"No, totally. I may have had my brain sloshed around a bit when I was tossed around like Matchbox cars."

She's quiet for a second. "Maybe an amusement park isn't the best idea."

"It's the best idea. I need to relax and let go. Besides, I'm a man of my word."

"Never met one of those," she jokes. "All right, great! It's a date, then."

Ugh. Why'd she have to word it that way? We're just going to have some fun.

"Okay, so… meet me at the subway station?" I say.

"Actually, how would you feel about taking the ferry? It looks like it leaves from Pier 11 on Wall Street."

I try not to think about it too hard. The ferry is a pretty romantic concept, but hopefully, she's not making as much out of it as I am. "Sounds like a plan. Meet in an hour?"

"I'll beat you there," she says.

The ride over on the ferry is definitely a better idea than the subway. The train might be convenient, but it's certainly not the most pleasant way to travel. On the ferry, we're out in the fresh air, a cool breeze blowing, and we get a nice view of everything. It would have been worth it even if we weren't going to the amusement park.

And, yeah, okay, it's sort of romantic. So sue me.

We get to Coney Island, which, fun fact, hasn't been an actual island for over a hundred years. They filled the creek between the island and Brooklyn, which made it a peninsula. It has some of the oldest amusement park rides in the country, which I'm not sure is something to brag about. I mean, I think I'd rather trust my safety to modern technology, wouldn't you?

After looking at the different options for parks, Summer chooses Luna Park, which I'm happy about because it's the newest one. And one of the most popular rides there is the Astro Tower. I'm not afraid of heights—how could I be?—but I've never enjoyed those things where you're strapped in and just in free fall. If I'm in control, I'm fine, but I don't like being part of what feels like a death trap created by a supervillain. And, believe me, I've had my share of death traps created by supervillains.

"Two," I tell the pleasant-looking troll in the ticket booth.

It grunts and passes us two slips of paper after swiping my credit card.

"This place is amazing," Summer says as we enter through the openings below several colorful wheel-type decorations.

Funny, I've never really thought of Luna Park as something I'd describe as amazing. To me, it always felt like a glorified traveling fair. But I guess it's something special to someone who's never been there, and I don't want to steal her thunder.

"I know," I say. "You hungry?"

"Literally always," she says.

"Nathan's Dogs. Only way to go."

"You're the expert."

I lead her past all the rides, watching the wonderment on her face. She even tries to get me to forget food for a minute so we can ride the Brooklyn Barge—a sort of pirate ship pendulum sort of thing.

Once I manage to yank her away from all the lights and sounds, we snag a couple of hot dogs and take a seat along the beach. It's a gorgeous day, pretty perfect for this kind of thing.

"How are you single?" she asks before taking a big bite.

I smirk. "I could ask you the exact same thing."

As soon as the words leave my mouth, I wish I could take them back.

Thankfully, she's gracious enough not to remind me that I threw her old boyfriend in prison for the rest of his life.

"You want another one?" I ask after she finishes her wiener in record time.

She pats her stomach. "I couldn't eat another bite."

I take my last bite as well, wipe my mouth, bundle up all the trash, and toss it in a nearby can.

"Rides now?" she asks like a little kid.

"Rides now," I confirm. "I mean, what better time to be thrown around by heavy machinery than right after wolfing down some junk food, right?"

Now, it's her doing the leading. I assume we'll go back to the main thoroughfare, but instead, she points at the other end of the beach. "That."

As I feared, it's the Tower ride.

"Wouldn't you rather do the Cyclone?" I say.

"What are you, chicken?" she asks, even making the bawking noise.

"Yeah. I'm a police officer who used to be a masked crime-fighter, but I'm afraid of that."

She laughs. "Prove it."

Without another word, I take the lead, and she can barely keep up.

Being a weekday, there's not much of a line. We get strapped in.

"Need to hold my hand?" she asks.

"Need?" I shake my head, then grab her hand. "But I'd like to."

"Man, you are something smooth."

"I try," I say, wishing it were true.

Gears and mechanisms start moving slowly beneath and behind us, and it slowly begins to ascend. We laugh and smile while she points out various things around the park she'd like to ride. Once at the top, I brace myself for a fall that never comes.

"What's going on?" she asks.

I try to look down but can't see past my feet—at least not clearly. There's some commotion below us—three guys dressed in costumes. One points a gun at the attendant, while the other points a finger at me. The third just looks menacing.

I swear.

On the ferry, I spotted a few suspicious-looking guys following us closely. But this is New York. Everyone looks suspicious. Makes my job all the more complex. On the ferry, they weren't wearing costumes, but their general build and shape suggests they're the same people.

At the time, I figured they either thought Summer was hot —which she is, not to mention a TV personality—or they knew I was a cop and wanted some revenge. When we exited the ferry, and they disappeared, I chalked it up to paranoia on my part. Guess my instincts haven't left me entirely.

There's a lot of shouting—some park guests have noticed the weapon. All at once, a small stampede erupts toward the beach.

Something odd occurs to me. Them being dressed as villains. Why? Why would they want to take out the guy in charge of making sure superheroes aren't out on the streets and stopping them? It doesn't make any sense.

While the first keeps the pistol trained on the attendant, the big, menacing guy—one with some kind of shockwave power—grabs hold of the tower's base. The ride tremors. Slightly at first, and then we are rocking back and forth like an earthquake hit.

"We're gonna die!" someone on the ride screams.

His fears are echoed by half a dozen more.

"Everyone quiet!" I shout. "We're not going to die."

"How the hell do you know?" one yells back.

"He's a cop," Summer offers.

"Oh, great. If they don't kill us, *you* probably will."

That barb hurts more than a punch to the gut. I know there are a lot of bad cops out there, but I'm trying to do right by the people of this great city.

I do my best to ignore the comment, and the people start screaming again.

I lean over and glare down at Sir-Shocks-a-Lot.

Are they really going to kill all these people just to get to me? I look over at Summer to make sure she's okay—and she's filming everything on her phone.

"What are you doing?" I ask her.

"Somebody has to do it," she says. "Might as well be me. I'm live-streaming it right now, so everyone knows about it."

"Live-streaming?"

I start to protest when the ride stops rumbling, and chaos ensues below. I immediately recognize a group of newcomers as members of the Resistors. They must've seen some kind of alert—maybe even Summer's broadcast.

That means they'd have to be located nearby in order to get here so fast.

What is wrong with me? These people are here to save us, and all I can think about is that it's giving me some intel on how to capture them later.

A soft roar grows slowly from below, and soon Amy comes into view on her rocket-powered wings. She wastes no time forcing the ride's restraints open and grabbing a couple of kids. She zips the kids to safety beyond the park's fence, then returns for their mom and the cop-hater.

Despite the fact that the shocker guy has stopped his assault on the tower, it's starting to lean.

"I have to do something," I say, trying to figure out what I *can* do. I fight against the harness, but it doesn't budge. I feel utterly helpless. Besides that, I'm worried if I move around too much, my shifting weight could cause the tower to lose its already frail structural integrity, so I resign to keeping as still as possible.

Amy flies back up again, and this time she sees me but doesn't look long enough to give anything away, even though Summer knows it all. Using a device on her wrist, she sends a small explosive at the hinge where the harness meets the seat.

"Everyone, hold on," she says as she snaps it off. Hanging from one side, the harness dangles while she takes Summer and the person on my right, leaving me alone high above Coney Island.

Down on the ground, White Hot and Neith easily take down two of the bad guys, the pointer and the big one, as they try to escape. And neither of them is very gentle with their methods. The craziest part is deep down, that makes me smile. Let those idiot criminals feel some pain for what they did.

I'm the last person on the ride—something I think has to have been on purpose. While Amy soars toward me, the third bad guy with the gun shoots at her. The bullet glances off her arm, but she continues up to me, even with her wound.

"Hang on," says a booming voice behind me. I strain to peer over my shoulder at a now giant-sized Firefly, trying to hold the tower up.

Neith and White Hot both turn and blast the gunman simultaneously. In one second, the guy falls to his knees with a new body piercing—an arrow sticking through his hand. And when he came to the beach today, I don't think he expected a blistering sunburn.

By now, the entire park is aware of the situation, and everyone is panicked, screaming and running in all directions.

"Are you sure about this?" I ask as Amy grabs on to me. "If you have a grappler, I can get down myself."

"I don't use a grappler anymore because—hello?—the whole *flying* thing."

"It'd still be nice to have," I say.

"Speak for yourself, Mr. Not-a-hero-anymore. I don't see you saving anyone."

She tries to lift me but winces and pulls her wounded arm back in a reflexive action.

I've been shot plenty of times. It's no joke. Especially when it tears into a muscle as this round did.

"You're going to have to just grab on while I fly down," she instructs.

I look down at Summer, who's still filming the whole thing from the beach entrance.

"I don't know if that's—" The tower lurches to the side, and I almost fall.

"Just do it!" Amy yells.

In addition to Firefly, BlackFrost is now reinforcing the tower with an ice block. But as strong as Firefly is in his giant form, it's not enough to steady something this big. And BlackFrost's ice can only do so much. The sound of creaking metal and cracking ice tells me I have little choice here. And no time whatsoever.

I grab on to her from the front, and she glides down to the

ground. The boosters on her flight suit strain under our combined weight. She sets me down right next to Summer.

A crack-boom echoes as Firefly's strength gives out, and the tower crushes what's left of the ice scaffolding. As Firefly dives out of the way, the entire ride smashes to the ground in a colossal crash, destroying another ride and some other small structures along with it.

Finally, emergency vehicles pull up.

I turn awkwardly to Amy. “I… um…”

"You're welcome," she says.

"You could have been killed," I say. "If that bullet had been just a few inches over…"

"It wasn't," she snaps as she walks away from me, applying pressure to the wound.

Amy spends a few seconds talking to the rest of the Resistors, and then they take off, leaving the villains tied up for the police. The gunman's skin is already blistering up while a paramedic bandages his hand.

The Resistors are smart enough to move off in multiple directions to throw off anyone trying to follow—namely, me. I'm sure they'll be meeting up somewhere later after they're sure nobody is following them.

Summer gets some final footage of them getting away and the fallen tower. Then we both just kind of stand there quietly. Probably in a little bit of shock.

Finally, she says, "So, kind of an awkward way to run into your ex, huh?"

"Uh, yeah, I guess you could say that." I try a laugh, but it comes across as fake as it really is.

"Especially when you're on a date, right?"

This time she gives a fake laugh.

"Not the best look," I say, shaking my head. "I'm sorry, but I'm going to have to go back to work after all today. Gotta file my report on all this."

"No, I understand. In fact, I'm going to have to do the same thing. I'll probably have to use my cell phone footage for the story since we don't have cameras here."

"Yeah. That makes sense."

I'm pretty sure she senses my trepidation. After all, the Resistors were *right here*, and I just sat there like an idiot. Fernanda is going to chew my ass out. Not to mention my team, who are also taking time off on a work day, thanks to me. This is the second time now that I have let Amy escape.

"Hey, don't worry. I'll make you look like the hero that you are." She kisses me on the lips. "Both for this morning *and* this. I promise."

I really can't ask her not to share the video. It's her job. That would be like me refusing to arrest Sawyer because of who he is to me. And we all know how that went.

"I hate to do this, but I need to deal with the officers who just showed up. Mind waiting for me?"

"Oh, well, I actually have another ride." She grimaces, and I try to figure out what she could be referring to.

Just then, a news copter lands nearby with her channel's

logo emblazoned on the side. She gives me another kiss, this time on the cheek. "I'll call you later, 'kay?"

I nod.

"Sorry!" she shouts back as she runs over to the helicopter.

I watch as she climbs aboard, and it takes off into the sky, heading for the Manhattan skyline.

Must be nice.

I stare at it as it disappears into the horizon and think about the fact that I'm in need of yet *another* shower.

CHAPTER 18
SAWYER

Puppet.

That's what I feel like—Crosscircuit's puppet. I barely even know this guy, and he's got me doing his bidding. It's no wonder he's got the whole prison in his pocket. Part of me wonders how far his influence extends. There're always rumors that powerful men and women run world governments behind the scenes. Is Crosscircuit one of them?

With Justice secured as part of the breakout crew, I have to recruit someone who may not be so easy: Royal Rampage. He may be a gorilla who's intelligent enough to talk and reason, but it's not like he's a genius or anything. He's about as bright as an ordinary nine-year-old. So convincing him to help us and explaining what he needs to do won't be easy. But, to quote Mender, at least I'm not cleaning toilets.

Crosscircuit was right. Rampage is already out of solitary and looking no worse for the wear. I approach him in the yard, where he's off by himself again. Like any ape, he likes to sit up high on ledges and places like that. Right now, he's about ten feet up on a small shelf above one of the locked doors.

"Hey, big guy. Remember me?" I ask cautiously.

He stares at me just as cautiously.

"I used to be called Red Kite. Then I was Black Harrier."

"Red Kite," he says. "Red Kite put me in here."

Crap. "Oh, yeah. I get what you're saying. But no. He was Red Kite *before* I was. He put me in here, too."

The gorilla looks confused. He hops down from his ledge, making the ground shake when he lands. He leans into me, sniffing. "You were small Red Kite. Bigger now."

I nod enthusiastically like I'm talking to that brat my mom used to babysit. "That's right. I was just a kid when we met. About this tall." I smile and hold out my hand to indicate my height when I was that age.

He seems more comfortable now. "Little Kite was my friend."

Breakthrough! "That's right. I was your friend. *Am* your friend. And I wanna thank you for saving my life when Bull-shark tried to kill me."

"Bullshark bad. Bullshark bad, mean person. Me teach him lesson."

Across the yard, I see Rush and Bullshark's other cronies staring us down. I know none of them will try anything with Royal Rampage so close, but when I'm alone…

"That's right," I say, turning back to the gorilla. "He sure is. I need to ask you something, and I don't want you to be afraid to tell me 'no.'"

He nods at me. Looking into his giant, brown eyes, I can see his innocence. It makes me hesitant to do what I'm about to do.

"Would you like to get out of here?" I ask anyway.

Those eyes light up when I say that, and he starts pounding his chest and making that high-pitched noise apes do when they are excited.

"Hey, let's keep it down, okay?" I ask, raising a hand to steady him.

He gets a confused look. "They told me I no leave. Not never."

"Well, you're not *supposed* to leave. But I may be able to get us out if you're willing to help."

"I want help. Me help friend, Little Kite. We leave bad place forever."

"That's right. We leave prison, together. But I have to warn you that your life won't be the same as it was before. You will have to hide, so they don't catch you again and put you back in here."

His face droops, and he looks really sad. "That what they do if find me? Put back here?"

I nod. "Yes. They would arrest you again and bring you back."

"Me here already. So it would be same."

Wow. He's absolutely right. We're in the worst place they can put us, and if we get caught, they can't do anything more to us. Not really. It's not like we'd get the death penalty or something just for escaping—wisdom from the last place I'd expect.

"You know what? You're right. We'd be right back where we started anyway, wouldn't we?"

He nods, and this time, he looks like he's smiling. I guess it's a smile, even though it's kind of scary looking.

"It might be dangerous," I say. "There's a chance we could get hurt. Or even killed."

He looks up, thinking it over for a few seconds.

"Me want leave, even if me might get hurt. Please take me with you." He presses his big furry head into my chest.

How can I say no to that?

Okay. Got the team together. Now, it's time for me to do the final bit of the job Crosscircuit has tasked me with.

The guards have all no doubt seen me talking to Crosscircuit, Justice, and Rampage. They've gotta be a little suspicious, which works in my favor if my plan is to go well.

I find Ernie, the guard who escorted me from the sub, and another officer standing by the yard entrance.

"Back up," he says when I get a little too close. He doesn't raise his rifle but lets me know it's there.

"Relax. I just wanna—"

The butt of his rifle shoots out and into my stomach.

"Don't tell me to relax," he says while the guard with him snickers.

I've taken enough gut punches to recover quickly enough, but still, I play it up for him.

"I just wanna talk to the warden," I say, feigning pain.

"Oh, he wants to talk to the warden," Ernie says. "You hear that, Yancy? He wants to talk to the warden."

"Yeah," Yancy says. "Maybe they could get together for dinner and a movie later."

They both laugh like the idiots they are. Little do they know I was having drinks in his office a couple of days ago.

"Can you just get him a message?" I ask.

"What's the message? I'll make sure to send it snail mail. Postman comes around every day, wouldn't you know? Swims here like a damn dolphin."

More laughing.

"Just tell him I've got some info," I say.

Their faces go serious as a clown who swallowed his rubber nose.

"Info, eh? What kinda info?" Ernie looks suspicious.

"Just something I think he'll wanna know."

"Then tell me, and I'll pass it along to him," Ernie says.

I shake my head. "I can't. Riche's ears only."

Ernie nods slowly. "Yeah. Okay. Why don't you come with me?"

I look from Ernie to Yancy and back again. "Now?"

A violent sneer crosses Ernie's face. "Right now."

He steps up behind me, pressing his rifle barrel to the small of my back, and conducts me through the double doors.

I take notice of his panel code. It's different from the previous guard's. Then he punches in a completely different code at the next door. I memorize that as well.

Crosscircuit was right. They have security protocols upon security protocols here.

He takes me into a hallway I haven't been before. I commit that code to memory. After a few steps, he stops. I begin to turn when he sucker-punches me. I'll be honest: I wasn't expecting it. It's not a soft punch either, and it sends me to the ground.

"What the—"

Yancy interrupts my protest with a swift kick to my face. I glance around, but I can't see a single camera anywhere. That has to be on purpose.

"We don't like snitches," Ernie tells him. "If you're smart, you'll keep your stupid mouth shu—"

I shoulder-rush him, a hard drive from the ground upward, catching him under the ribs and knocking the air out of his lungs.

Yancy shouts something, but I shut him up with a kick to the jaw that sends his head into the bulkhead at whip-speed. Hopefully, it didn't kill him, but he's not moving.

With Yancy out of the way, I kick Ernie's rifle out of reach and mount him like an MMA fighter. I bring my fist back, and horror is evident on his face.

"Don't," he says.

"You're working for him, aren't you?" I ask.

"Everyone works for him," Ernie says, scared to the point of soiling his pants. "He knows stuff. He's a monster."

I bring my fist down and grab him by the collar. Leaning in close, I say, "So am I."

I make believe I'm gonna knock him out, then stand up instead. His eyes are clenched shut, but when he notices he's still conscious, he squints.

"Now," I say, brushing myself off. "Tell the warden I need to speak with him."

"Yeah. All right. You got it."

"Good," I say, stepping over him and exiting the way we came, using Ernie's code. Then I point to Yancy. "And tell him he tripped and fell."

A short time later, I'm "enjoying" my first shower here in the Trench. I say that sarcastically, but I really needed one, and it's actually not nearly as bad as I imagined it, given the way everything else has been since I got here. I'd been avoiding it, thinking I'd be standing out in the open with a bunch of other prisoners, letting it all hang out, and being terrified of dropping the soap. Because, y'know, that's what everyone tells you when you're young to scare you into not committing crimes and going to jail, right? And maybe because it's a little true? I really don't know. This is my first time in the slammer.

And I hated taking showers in school. I would go to my

next class after PE all sweaty and smelly to avoid them, which I'm sure my teachers and fellow students appreciated. Then, when I was forced to be on the wrestling team, I did everything I could to be Mr. Slowpoke and not get in until everyone else was getting out. I'm sure they all thought it was because I was afraid of Logan, but the truth is, I just didn't like the idea of showering in front of other people, no matter who they were.

So I guess the whole thing followed me into adulthood. I never had to go to a gym because we had all the training equipment we needed at the Aerie. Now, I'm spending what could be the rest of my life in a place where I'll have to shower publicly, and I'm not loving the idea.

But, as I said, it could be a lot worse. They have dividers between the shower nozzles, so we get a little bit of privacy. And they even give us a towel—as thin and threadbare as it may be—and our own bar of soap. So I walk past everyone, all the way down to the stall at the end, and turn on the water, which is reasonably warm. Makes sense they'd wanna make sure we're able to stay clean since there's no outside and we rely on recycled air. It feels great to be able to stand here by myself and just chill for a few minutes without worrying about an insane shark man trying to bite my head off or a megalomaniac threatening me and my family if I don't do everything he orders me to.

A bit of red trickles down, tinting the water pink. Ernie's blood must've got on me somehow. Gross. But I'm no stranger to the stuff.

We're all set and ready for action. I finally have a chance to take a few deep breaths and come as close to relaxing as I'll probably ever get while in this nightmare factory.

The plan's set, and the team is recruited. I've got three different guards' codes, and since this isn't a huge facility, I'm hoping that'll be enough. I'll keep my eye open for a few more, though.

As I'm showering, I notice the talking and humming dying down, and then I don't even hear any other showers running. It's completely silent except for a few dripping shower heads. And I know immediately something is wrong. I sure could use my mini-drone right now. Of course I don't have it when I could use it most.

I reach for my towel, but it's not there. Did it fall? Nope, not on the floor, either. Peeking out, I see that the room is entirely empty. I don't know what that means, but I know it can't be good. Is this just some prank? Or hazing? Am I gonna have to go all the way back to my cell naked?

I walk toward the exit on high alert, checking each stall as I pass to ensure I'm not ambushed. But I am anyway. A fist clocks me in the side of my head. My first thought was Ernie came back for revenge. But when I don't see my attacker, all the pieces fit together.

Rush.

He was watching me out in the yard, waiting until I was alone.

I stagger a bit but don't go down. In combination with Ernie's lucky shot, I'm not too manly to admit, my face hurts.

"Okay, Rush," I say. "I know it's you. Why don't we deal with this like me—"

Another punch sends me reeling backward. Then another. I put my fists up, but it's no use. The hits keep coming. I won't survive long under these conditions. What I don't understand is how he's doing it. He steps out into the open as the world spins in front of me.

I notice the same cuffs Mender was wearing strapped around his wrists.

"Heard you talking about these," he says. "Thanks for the tip."

I wipe blood off my lip. "They're only supposed to work in the infirmary."

"Crosscircuit's not the only one who knows tech around here," Rush says.

I've spent enough time with Pace—one of my old partners in the original Resistors—to know when a speedster is about to make a move. It's a sort of a tell. Their body rapidly vibrates for just a split second before they spring into action.

When I see Rush shudder, I drop to my knees. The impact when his knees hit me, going fast enough to become a blur, makes my vision go white. But the sound he makes when he trips over me and slides across the wet floor makes all my pain worth it.

When I'm able, I stand and dart over to him. He's not knocked out, but he's moving slowly—which means normal speed for the rest of us. Quickly, I uncuff the bracers.

"You little—"

"What's going on here?" a voice asks from the shower entryway.

Warden Riche stands there, arms crossed and looking put out.

I quickly hide the cuffs behind a divider when he looks over at Rush.

"Just a little accident," I say. "Rush didn't obey the 'Do Not Run' sign. Can't all be model inmates."

The warden eyes Rush. The speedster gets to his feet, nodding. "I'll have to be more careful."

He gives me a look that could melt stone as he smashes into my shoulder and makes his way from the showers.

Riche uses a key to open a locker by the entrance and pulls out a towel. A toothpick bobs in his mouth—which seems like an exceptionally bad idea in a prison. I mean, what if someone grabbed you and got a hold of it? They could treat your eyeball like an olive in a martini. What's this guy thinking?

Or maybe that's the point. He has so much control here that he doesn't have to worry about things like that—like a psyops move. I stare at him right in the eyes. What do I see there? Intelligence? No. Malevolence. Smarts? No. Smartass, maybe.

Nah. This guy isn't that bright. He's just too stupid to realize what a dumb idea a sharp object in a supermax prison is. I'm convinced of that now.

"I thought you and I had us an understanding," he says.

"Did we?"

"We absolutely did. And then you go and get into another fight. *And now another.* In your brief time with us, you've caused a bigger uproar than I've seen in half a decade. And my guess is you had something to do with Ernie and Yancy's current condition."

"Are those the guys from Sesame Street?"

He ignores my comment. "Not to mention hanging out with that ne'er-do-well, Crosscircuit."

"Wow. *Ne'er-do-well.* That's a word you don't hear much nowadays."

His fake smile turns to a sneer, causing the toothpick to stand almost straight up from his lower lip.

"My belief after our last conversation was that you were gonna keep your nose clean in here, and I was therefore gonna be able to leave you be."

"Did I miss my nose? Let me just jump back in there and make sure to wash it really well."

He looks down and shakes his head in obvious disappointment.

"Let me tell you something, son. Lots of tough guys come in here, thinking they're gonna be some kind of comedian. Some even think it's gonna help them stay safe for some strange reason. But that idea tends to go away real quick once they learn that nobody likes or wants a funny guy. We don't need no Johnny Seinfelds up in here."

Not only does he get Seinfeld's first name wrong, but he also pronounces the last name "Seen-FIELD." How clueless is this guy?

"Jerry," I say.

"What?"

"Never mind. Not important."

"Just what is your problem, kid?" He puts his hand on his chest. "You've got the warden on your side. You're supposed to be one of the good guys."

"I *am* one of the good guys," I argue. "But that doesn't seem to matter anymore. Not out there, and sure as hell not in here."

"Why would you say that?" he asks.

"You realize your guards are on the take? Or are you too blind to see it?"

"On the take..." Genuine confusion passes his features. "What's that supposed to mean?"

"I told your little friend Ernie I needed to talk to you. Just like you said. Instead, he tried to kill me. Sometimes, it doesn't matter who you are or what you do. Sometimes, the circumstances force you to make a choice."

"I don't care what you *think* the circumstances are in here. You need to stay outta trouble and report to me. If you know what's good for you. Otherwise, things could get real bad for you. And maybe for the people you love on the outside if you're not careful."

There he was with more threats. This time, I'm hearing him loud and clear.

"You know, warden, you claim to be one of the good guys. But so far, you don't sound any better than the bad guys I've talked to in here."

"That right?"

"Yeah. That's right. It doesn't seem to make much difference *who* I talk to. They all want something from me, and they're all willing to threaten me and my family to get it."

He steps forward, chest puffed out like Royal Rampage. "Nobody else matters in here except me. In here, I am boss. I am God. You'd do well to remember that. You even *think* about crossing me, and you're gonna be paying for it a long, long time. Is that understood?"

"Do you even wanna know what information I wanted to share?" I ask.

He stares at me. "Don't think I'd believe it anyway. You're a disgrace to the Guild."

I can't bring myself to respond, so I just give him a slight nod. He tosses me my towel and turns to walk out.

"Now get yourself dried off and dressed, and go be a model prisoner."

CHAPTER 19
ALEX

Déjà vu.

Back at the station, I stop and grab some coffee in my new office. That's right. I got a brand-new office. No longer am I Harry Potter, thrown into a cupboard or janitor's closet. I even have a window. Although my view is a brick wall right across the alley.

I throw a pod in the machine and wipe out the mug I used yesterday. It's not worth a trip down to the break room to use the sink. As I pull some Hazelnut creamer from my mini-fridge, I automatically think about Amy again. I'd never tried it before she and I got together, but that was all she ever had, and I have to have creamer in my coffee. Now I can't drink anything else.

What would Amy say about Summer and me? It's probably better if I don't think about it too much. It's not like it affects anything. That relationship has not only sailed but sank to the bottom of the ocean.

Aaaand now I'm thinking about Sawyer at the bottom of the ocean. Man, I don't know how I will ever get through all of this.

I look at my comm as it buzzes with a new text. It's from Summer, which makes me feel guilty about thinking about Amy. But I also feel guilty about Summer because of Sawyer. Geez, if I ever go back to being a masked crimefighter, I'll have to call myself Emo-Boy or something.

SUMMER

Everything okay?

Fine. Just got to the office.

SUMMER

Took that long?

Had to stop to take another shower.

SUMMER

Mmmmm. I'll try not to think too long about that. K. See you tonite?

Eric enters without knocking and plops down in one of the extra chairs I now have. As if that's not annoying enough, he props his feet up on my desk, knocking over a cup of pens.

I snap forward and try to catch them before they spill all over the floor. He doesn't move a muscle.

Sorry. Something just came up at work. I have to go.

SUMMER

Okies. Talk to you soon. Bye.

Then a little heart emoji pops up. I try to decide if I'm supposed to send her one back, then decide it's not worth the brain power trying to figure out the right one.

I put my comm away and stare at Eric. "Well, come on in and make yourself comfortable."

I'm not sure whether he misses the sarcasm or willfully ignores it, but either way, it doesn't seem to bother him in the least.

"Was that your new *girrrrllfriend*?"

"None of your business. Let's stick to work stuff. What'cha got?"

Looking slightly discouraged, he says, "Yeah, all right, man. Cool. No need to get testy. Check this out: I think we should go talk to Chen."

"Why's that?" I ask.

"Because I'm pretty sure he knows where the Resistors are, and we're out of leads. After they took off from Coney Island, they disappeared again. We couldn't even follow them with our satellites."

Talking to Chen actually makes some sense.

"Much as I'd like to finally get the Resistors, I'm not sure interrogating Luis Chen is the best way to go about it." I'm also not wild about the idea of going in there with Eric, especially since Chen knows he was Battlegear.

"Why not? We could do the old 'good cop-bad cop' routine."

"You mean 'good cop-former supervillain'?"

I meant it as a joke, but his expression tells me he doesn't take it well. "Low blow, dude." He lowers his feet and starts to stand.

"Hey, there is something I'd like you to do," I say.

He stops and sits back down. "Okay?"

"Can you contact Eaglestar and try to convince him we need to..." I pause a bit too dramatically, "... arrest Baron Steele?"

"Seriously?"

"Yeah." I sigh. "He let the guy off with a warning after utterly destroying a whole city block. Not sure why Saw—" Wow. That was close. "Not sure why Harrier gets arrested and the Baron gets off scot-free."

"Damn, man. That's a big ask. Why me?"

"Oddly enough, you two seem to have a much better rapport than he and I do."

A big smile crosses Eric's face. "Yeah, years of being someone's archnemesis will do that."

He's so matter-of-fact about it, as if everyone has their own arch-enemy they deal with on a regular basis. That's definitely a strange dynamic they have going on. Almost creepy, the more I think about it.

"Honestly, if it weren't for him, I probably never would have gotten into the game."

"It's not a game, Eric."

"Sorry. Yeah. Poor choice of words. But you know what I'm saying. Things could've been much different without him."

I nod. "Probably much for the better."

Eric looks around, worried. "Shhh. Watch what you say, bruh. That dude has hearing like no one else."

At this point, getting fired over something like that would almost be a relief. "Just do it, okay? Use your special relationship to persuade him that fair is fair."

"Sure thing, I'm on it." He seems to be in a better mood when he exits my office since he has something important to do, and I'm the one who asked him to do it, which is a big thing for him for some reason. But now that he's busy doing that, I think I *will* go talk to Luis Chen... on my own.

Driving to the FBI office where they're holding him, the news on my car radio is talking about the fight between Steele and Flexiplex that we failed to prevent. The news people aren't pulling any punches, and the witnesses they're interviewing make it sound like they survived the Apocalypse itself. I mean, yeah, it was a mess, but nobody was really hurt. At least, I hope nobody was hurt. I guess I better find out for sure.

Then they get into the Coney Island debacle and emphasize the fact that the CVT didn't even show up other than me, who was basically a helpless hostage needing to be saved by the people I was supposed to arrest. Great. This is all going to do wonders for our sagging poll numbers, I'm sure.

My comm buzzes, and I'm ready to pick it up, thinking it's probably Summer. Luckily, I look first and see that it's Captain Fernanda. This time, I'm going to ignore her call and deal with the consequences later, for the same reason that I didn't stop by her office at the station like I was supposed to. If she finds out that I'm going to talk to Luis Chen, she's probably going to shut it down. And I'd much rather do it and ask for forgiveness later than go against her after she knows about it.

Typically, checking in at the FBI building would be a huge hassle, but technically, I work for another federal law enforcement agency, so I can show my badge and gain quick clearance. Once I find out where Chen is being held, I'm guided back by an armed guard.

It's one of the few positive aspects of having Eaglestar as a boss. They don't even take my gun because I'm so official.

Chen sits in the interrogation room, which in this case, is just an office with a conference table. He doesn't look surprised to see me when I walk in and sit down, so I have to assume they told him I was here.

"Should I have my attorneys present?" he asks.

"Only if you want them to know your daughter is a wanted masked vigilante."

"I see," he says.

"I'm sure you know why I'm here, Luis."

"To rub in the fact that I've been arrested, perhaps?"

"You think I'm that petty?" I don't know why I'm surprised, given our history.

"There's not a thing I would put past the man responsible for Sawyer's arrest," Chen says.

I nod slowly. "I deserved that."

"You sure as hell did. What were you thinking, Alex?"

Well, those tables turned quickly.

I clear my throat. "Look, Luis, I'm not the one in cuffs."

He shows me his hands, which aren't bound.

"Figuratively speaking. Besides, I had no idea you were being arrested."

"Would you have tried to stop it either way?" he asks. I sense he's just messing with me. Trying to throw me off. Get in my head.

"You're a smart guy, Luis. What exactly do you think I could've done to stop the FBI?" I put particular emphasis on the letters, making sure he realizes how far above my pay grade all of this is.

"Perhaps *you* should tell *me*."

Now I know he's messing with me. It's what he does.

"Let's dispense with the BS. You and I both know Amy would be safer if she were in custody. The longer she's a fugitive from the law, the more dangerous her situation becomes."

"I suppose you think Sawyer is better off in the Trench?"

Right for the gut.

"Look, Chen. I watched her get shot at Coney Island. And it's not like she can go to the hospital. I swear to you, my primary concern is for her safety. I'm hoping I can talk her into cooperating and helping us track down the rest of the Resistors in exchange for a more lenient sentence than what Sawyer got."

"I… appreciate your *concern.* But you couldn't help Sawyer get a more lenient sentence. What confidence do you think that instills?"

It's challenging to keep the anger out of my tone. "An old woman *died* while Sawyer was trying to escape. My partner was *shot* trying to bring him in. And Sawyer appeared to be working with the one who shot him—a known killer. Amy never did anything like that."

"But she could." It was a leading question.

"Yes. She could. Which is why I want to bring her in before she goes too far. Help me help her."

"I'm sorry, Detective Garner. I think you know Amy would never even consider betraying her teammates that way." Then, after a beat, "She's not you."

I chuckle. "I love it. A lecture on ethics from a guy caught selling spyware to authoritarian governments worldwide to help them suppress their people. Talk about betrayal."

He puts up a finger. "Allegedly."

"Ah, yes. The magic A-word," I say. "Because we all know Douglas Industries is squeaky clean. No secrets there."

"I thought we were talking about Amy?" Chen says.

"You're right. We were. And what do you think she would do to save her father?"

He stares daggers at me. Now I'm getting somewhere.

My comm rings, interrupting my mojo. I pull it out, see that it's Yamo, and put it in silent mode as I lay it face down on the table.

"I certainly hope that wasn't a slick way to begin recording this conversation?" Chen says. "I did not consent to be recorded, so nothing I say will hold up in court."

"No recording going on. Just you and me."

"Good. Perhaps some water?" he says.

"This isn't a hotel," I tell him. "Now listen, I may not have had any influence on whether or not you were arrested, Luis, but they'll certainly be coming to me for advice, seeing how I've known you for so many years."

"Your point?"

"My point is I may have information about things in your past that might lead to... additional charges."

His usual frown somehow turns even... frownier. "You wouldn't."

"Try me." It's an effort not to smirk. Not that I want to be a jerk or anything, but I can't help myself. You know how some people just rub you the wrong way no matter what? Yeah.

"You know, I never did like you very much—"

"Yeah, for a guy who keeps a lot of secrets, you sucked at keeping that one. And, by the way, the feeling is mutual."

He sighs. "You didn't let me finish. I was about to say that

I never liked you much, but I did think you were good for Amy when you were together. She seemed happy, and I believed you had her best interests at heart. There aren't too many others who would have understood the life she chose to live."

"Nice try. I know what you're doing, and it's not going to work. I've known you too long to fall for your manipulation tactics."

"Think what you will about me, Alexander. Much of it is probably true. But I believe that deep down, you would never do anything to hurt Amy. And I'm counting on that."

"Of course I wouldn't hurt her. That doesn't mean I won't try to save her from continuing to make bad decisions."

"Save her from herself, you mean?" he asks. "You think you know what's best for others?"

"Maybe not always. But in this case, I believe I do."

"And what about Frank? Will you sit by and watch them arrest him? Take his company away?"

I lean forward. "Frank has been digging his own grave for a long time now."

Chen looks up at the camera in the corner of the room, near the ceiling, as if he's about to say something he's not sure anyone else should hear. I told him we weren't being recorded, but I know him. He only trusts himself. When he speaks, his voice is so low I can barely hear it, even sitting across from him.

"You know something, Alex... there's more to all of this than you realize."

"What the hell's that supposed to mean?"

"You're right that I've kept many secrets, and I've kept them well. When Frank became the head of Douglas Industries and confided in me his plans, they encompassed a great deal. Among them was looking into his father's and grandfather's lives as well as their business dealings, which I obviously already knew something about."

"I know all about their dealings," I say, sure I'm wrong.

"What you do not know about is that there are branches on his family tree that even he was unaware of."

"Yeah. Like Sawyer. And probably other illegitimate kids."

"Yes, like Sawyer," Chen confirms. "And others. But he was not the only Franklin Douglas who had offspring from illicit liaisons with various women."

"Okay, so his dad slept around, too. So what? Typical rich guys, if you ask me. And Frankie Jr. was a piece of crap to begin with."

"Perhaps. But I discovered early on that Franklin Douglas the First—the original—had a daughter whom he took care of financially but never acknowledged publicly or even told his family about. She, in turn, married and had children of her own."

My comm buzzes on the table. He looks down at it.

"Is this going somewhere?" I ask. "I've got things to do, and I feel like you're getting off on quite the tangent here."

"You'll want to hear this," he says. "Trust me." His eyes narrow in a way that somehow assures me he's telling the truth.

I silence the vibration, nodding for him to continue.

"After Franklin died, Frankie Jr. found out about this half-sister of his. He was afraid his rivals might find out about these secret family members and use them against him somehow."

"Okay. And?" I'm getting impatient and can't see how this could possibly be relevant.

"And he was correct. They did find out and decided to send him a message by killing them very publicly in a hail of bullets." He pauses for effect. "While they were eating in an Italian restaurant. With their children."

As he says this, something clicks in my mind. Memories play in my head from my childhood. Of my parents being riddled by gunfire while my baby brother screamed in his highchair in a restaurant. Of me hiding under the table, terrified, as my mother's chair fell over. Of her collapsing to the floor. Of her lifeless eyes staring straight at me. A puddle of blood forming underneath her and running toward me...

I shake my head as my body goes numb. "No."

"You see, Alex, Frank didn't find you and take you on as a partner by accident any more than he did Sawyer. You should understand as well as anyone that everything he does is calculated."

"You can't be—"

My comm starts buzzing again.

"What is it?" I answer with more annoyance than Yamo deserves.

"Alex, we have a problem," she says. "A super-sized one."

I don't respond.

"Alex, we need you *now*."

"Okay. Fine. I'm on my way," I say, hanging up. "I have to go."

I rise, barely able to keep from falling over.

"There's one more thing, Alex. Your brother. I've found him."

I stop in my tracks. I know why he's doing this. He's going to use this information as leverage, so I don't help the FBI. So I don't go after Amy.

As much as I want to find out more, I have to do my job. Plus, he could be lying to save himself. "We're not done here. Not by a long shot."

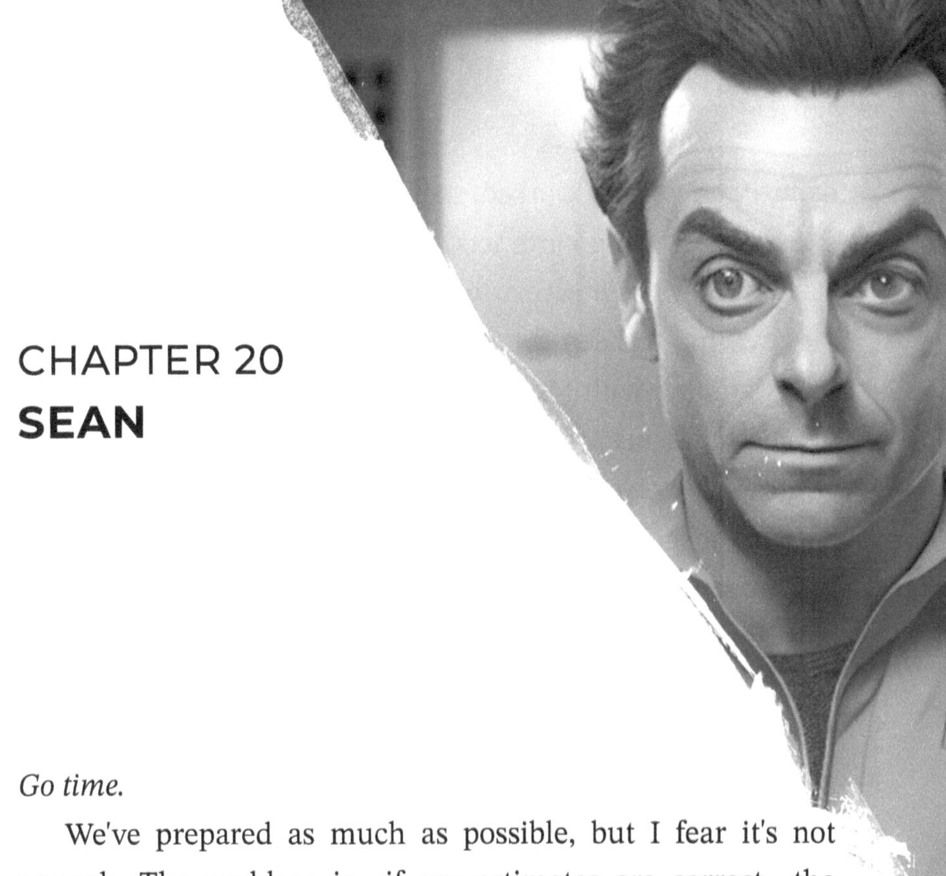

CHAPTER 20
SEAN

Go time.

We've prepared as much as possible, but I fear it's not enough. The problem is—if my estimates are correct—the alien presence will arrive at Earth with no time to spare. As safe as I might be from their terror here at the bottom of the ocean, it would do me no good to be one of the last remaining inhabitants of a planet shared by supervillains.

It's time. It has to be, and I'm smart enough to know it will never be perfect. I must trust these people I've assembled—including the new replacements—will somehow rise to the occasion and pull this off.

Harrier did fine work and quickly, arranging meetings with Justice and the baboon. Yes, I know a gorilla is not a baboon. I'm not that foolish. However, it seems a fitting slur.

The child Black Harrier even went above and beyond, scoring a pair of those cuffs he'd mentioned. It was easy to deduce how they worked. Replicating them was a simple enough task using parts scoured from an out-of-use air recycler I'd been given access to by Officer Ubong. That man will do anything to keep the warden from finding out about his little dalliance with Mrs. Riche.

Justice seems a fine marksman, even if he couldn't hold a torch to Deadeye. And where Royal Rampage wouldn't have been my first choice due to his adolescent thought processes, he has proven his strength rivals and exceeds that of my original tank, Bullshark. That poor bastard is still recovering. So many of his most grievous injuries were entirely out of Mender's league.

Also, I tend to be so good at everything that I can usually make up for the deficiencies of others. But such facts are probably already apparent to you now that you've gotten to know me a bit. I'm confident everything will come along swimmingly.

My team members meet in the library at the appointed time, during the one hour prisoners are allowed to spend to themselves before lights out. While most inmates have returned to their cells, I arranged for storytime.

When I enter the dimly lit room, a couple of stragglers remain, poring over their drivel. The first looks up and sees me, slaps his comrade on the arm, and together, they scurry away. It helps that the second one went by the name of the Sultan before landing here, and I know the location of his every hidden family member in Saudi Arabia.

A short while later, the others join me. Harrier enters first, scanning the empty space. Royal Rampage is hot on his heels like a puppy dog. I fear he's got too big a heart for the task at hand. I'm willing to be wrong; I just rarely am.

"Is fashionably early a thing?" he asks, to which I remain stoic.

I've learned my lesson with the kid. If you allow him an inch, he takes a mile. Acknowledge one quip, and suddenly, he's Andrew Dice Clay.

Next comes Sinsation, hips swaying, and hair bouncing like she just stepped off the set of a photoshoot instead of having spent many years of her life here.

She stares at Harrier from across the room. "Remember me?" she sneers.

"Sin," I interject. "Let us allow bygones to be bygones for the sake of this mission, shall we?"

She looks at me as if I'd suggested we eat dirt. Finally, she says, "Fine. For now."

"For now," I agree. "Now, if you would, please extract yourself from the group as we discussed."

She makes her way to the far corner of the room as if she'd been put in timeout.

Justice enters as this happens, and he can't keep his eyes off her. That is precisely the reason I suggested she stay apart from the crowd. With what I have planned, it will be vital she does not affect those around her negatively.

Justice carries himself like a man twice his age, but it's obvious it's an act.

As soon as he opens his mouth, his immaturity shows. "Who's the hottie?"

"I will murder you faster than your father left you," Sin says.

"How did you kno—"

"Lucky guess," she says, winking.

"Now, now," I say. "Let's all get along."

Justice blows a raspberry noise and stalks to the other side of the room.

If he had half my drive, half my desire for greatness, he could be someone of true talent. But instead, he is content with mediocrity. A shame, really.

Immediately there's tension. None of them truly trust me, and that's okay. I've learned to deal with suspicion and doubt. Once we are free of this metal box, they will understand that I was the man responsible for their freedom. The one thing I did not disclose to any of them was the threat that awaits us when we reach dry soil. Each assumes they'll be on the run, in hiding, but the truth is far graver. We will all be in a fight for our lives, for the very survival of the human race.

"Thank you for your time," I begin. "I know it is precious, and there are many things you could be doing instead."

"We're in a prison, dude," Justice says.

"Your first lesson will be in understanding dark humor," I retort. "Each of you will wear one of these."

I provide them each an earpiece that will allow us to communicate with one another, except for Harrier, who will use the one I gave him for his mini-drone.

"And these..." I hold up one of my bracers. "Empowerment bracers."

Harrier laughs.

"Something funny?" I ask, more than a little annoyed that I gave him the satisfaction.

"Empowerment bracers sounds like something a hipster would wear while eating vegan muffins and protesting animal cruelty."

Justice joins in on the laughter.

"Have you a better term for them?" I demand.

"I was calling them 'hibitors.'"

"That's not even a word," I say.

"I like that," Justice says at the same time.

"Me like too," Royal Rampage agrees.

"They are called empowerment bracers!" I shout far too loudly.

"Shhhh. We're in a library," Harrier says to another round of chortles.

Children surround me as my best hope of escaping this damnable prison, and they can't begin to fathom what's at stake.

Then I hand out the wristbands that negate the power inhibitors, and things start to go haywire.

I had purposely kept Sinsation from the rest because, as a general rule, the less she interacts with anyone, the better. Against my wishes and her better judgment, she walks around as we all stand in a circle and looks each one of us in the eye, which in itself is quite unnerving. I wonder if perhaps those pheromones of hers have been building up while she's been in the Trench and hasn't been able to release them due to the inhibitors. One of their effects is to increase the testosterone levels of those around her, which will be beneficial as long as we don't end up at each other's throats.

When she gets to Royal Rampage, she stops and affects a wide smile. "*You*, I like. Monkeys make everything more fun. Is your name 'Bonkers' or something? Please tell me your name is 'Bonkers.'"

Royal Rampage turns his head to look at Harrier, confused. Harrier gives him a reassuring look in return.

"No," the big ape says.

"Not much of a talker, I see," she says. "But, then again, I suppose anything you say is more than any other ape can." She lets out a giggle that should be annoying, but instead, I find it titillating due to those damn pheromones.

As she walks past Justice, she just shrugs. "Meh. Whatever. You seem like a typical dime-a-dozen shooter guy. Guns aren't my thing. Though Deadeye and I once had a fling, and that man really knows how to hit a target if you catch my meaning."

"It's not the size of the rifle as much as how you pull the trigger," Justice says. "Luckily for you, my rifle is perf—"

"That'll be enough of that," I bark. "Sin, if you'll please."

"I'm not through yet."

But when she gets to Harrier, there's a problem. Her face twists in suspicion, and she sniffs him. Harrier, to his credit, stands calmly with his arms crossed.

"Something I can do for you?" he asks her.

"You're the wrong bird," she says. "Too short. Too scrawny. Too... young."

"I don't know what you're talking about," he replies.

"You weren't the one responsible, were you?" she asks. "Black Harrier's been around for years. Decades. When did you start fighting criminals, when you were in diapers?"

"How do you know I just don't physically age? Like Eaglestar?"

She holds up a finger and shakes her head. "Uh-uh. I've fought Harrier before. You're not him."

Harrier shakes his head.

"But I *have* fought you, haven't I?"

She looks angry now.

She gets right up in his face. "You're the little red bird who put me here in this cage, aren't you?"

I finally decide to intervene before it gets out of hand. "That's enough. Bygones! We don't have time for this. We're already behind schedule."

"You better watch your back, *Harrier*, if you know what's good for you."

"You can settle this once we're back on dry land," I say, knowing no one will have time for such petty squabbles. "Until then, we work together. *All* of us. Everyone, get to your starting places."

Harrier knows his job and has already memorized the codes I need. I, of course, will execute my parts immediately. Even the crazy lady will do just fine, assuming she doesn't try to kill Harrier along the way. But as I've said, Royal Rampage is even dumber than Bullshark, and this Justice character isn't even a third-rate imitation of Deadeye.

I have to come to grips with the truth. It will be nothing short of a miracle if we can pull this off.

As the others get to their set points in the prison, I use the library computers to shut down specific cameras—well, not shut them down completely since that would be too conspicuous. Instead, I put them on a loop showing empty corridors and closed doors in the places where we need to be. Naturally, I execute my part to perfection.

Things start to fall apart immediately.

"Rampage," I say into my transmitter. "That's not the right spot."

I can see him on my alternate camera feed—the one only I have access to, showing the live stream. He's practically dancing around, looking for his right "spot," as if I meant he was only a few steps off.

"You're supposed to be one corridor over to the east."

I hadn't thought he'd be too stupid to know I can hear him. Though he doesn't talk directly to me, I can hear him muttering "East... east..." and putting both fingers up in an L-shape the way a child is taught to tell his right hand from left.

I shake my head. "Go through the door on your right... yes, that's it. That's your right. And follow the hallway to the end. Good. That's right. Wait! No! Stop!"

Something happens, and he starts slapping at his ear. I watch as the earpiece flies away. He begins stomping on it, smashing it to bits. I have to pull my own away to spare my eardrums from the sound of pounding and squealing.

Ah, yes. Swimmingly, indeed.

With him not where he needs to be to properly take out the guard and allow us to pass into the next section alarm-free, I need to figure out our next steps. Either one of the other team members will need to do the job, or we will have to reassess and designate a new target.

I make the calculations and decide going after the same guard is the better option. But we will need to intercept him before he reaches his fellow patrolmen.

I turn to Sinsation, the only team member still with me, designated to be my protection should anyone become suspicious and suss me out. "You will need to take down that guard in your own unique way."

"On it," she says and exits the library.

On my live feed, I watch her approach the wayward guard. He lifts his lightning stick. "You shouldn't be wandering the halls. It's downtime."

"Oh, but I really wanted to see you," she says.

The guard obviously knows this isn't true, but I can see the pheromones hit him, making him question everything.

She sensually maneuvers her way toward him. "What I'd really like to do is hold that big stick of yours...."

Before he realizes what's happening, she grabs the lightning stick from his hand and zaps him with it, sending him to the ground in convulsions. Once he's lying on his stomach, reeling, she clocks him at the base of the skull, rendering him unconscious.

"No! You were supposed to bring him here first. Now we have to drag him here."

"You told me to take him out," Sin says into her earpiece. "I completed the task."

I groan.

It would be most efficient to have Royal Rampage pick the guard up, but he no longer has his earpiece and is still wandering aimlessly. I swear, if that ape ruins my plans...

"Harrier, I need you to retrieve Rampage from Sector G3 and guide him to G2 so he can help carry the guard here."

"Copy," says Harrier.

Before Harrier can get to Rampage, Officer Ubong turns the corner. "Hey! You! What are you doi—"

His sentence is cut short before he can finish it, the gorilla's huge fist caving in the man's chest. But not before Ubong presses the emergency button on his shoulder.

Alarms blare.

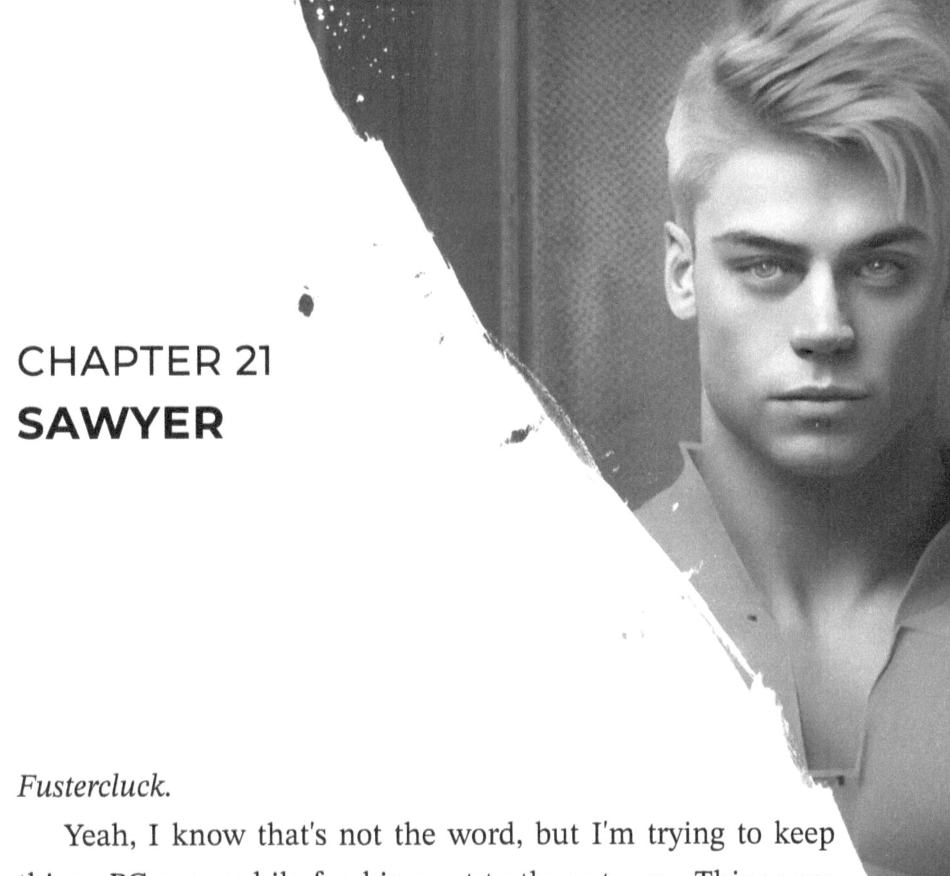

CHAPTER 21
SAWYER

Fustercluck.

Yeah, I know that's not the word, but I'm trying to keep things PG even while freaking out to the extreme. Things are not going well with the escape, and this isn't exactly the kind of situation where you can make a bunch of mistakes. Even a slight deviation from the plan could mean we drown or get crushed under the tremendous water pressure—or both. There's always both, I guess.

In all the years that I've been fighting everyone from school bullies to street punks to supervillains, I've imagined dying in a plethora of violent ways. Becoming a snack for a deep-sea creature after drowning and having air bubbles explode in my brain were not among my fears.

Here I was thinking this was gonna be like an *Ocean's Eleven* movie, and instead, I feel like I'm in a sequel to *Dumb and Dumber.*

How many prisoners does it take to screw up an escape? Just one, but that doesn't prevent the rest from trying.

We're locked in the library. On the screens Crosscircuit has set up to monitor the real camera feeds, we watch guards coming toward us from all directions, many dressed in black, heavy body armor. Luckily, there's only one entrance in and out of the library. I hear an audible groan as Crosscircuit does something to lock the doors electronically, but it's not gonna stop them for long.

I shout at the others, "Get some shelves in front of that door. Quickly!"

They act fast, and Royal Rampage is especially successful at blocking the door with some large bookcases. The guards are already right outside trying to override the digital lock Crosscircuit encoded.

Now we're stuck expecting Crosscircuit to refigure the plan—a plan which I trusted everyone knew, by the way. Several times, he told me everyone knew their part. Everyone understands their roles, and I'm only responsible for mine. Maybe because I'm used to working with professional masked crimefighters like Frank and the Guild, I took him at his word.

My mistake.

An old wrestler used to have a catchphrase: Don't trust anyone. Probably should adopt that in the future. Or maybe I should've trusted the warden instead of some two-bit egomaniacal, lying, thieving, ne'er-do-well. Yeah. That's right. I said it. It's the right word. Riche was right.

I knew my part. Executed the pre-escape plan with perfection.

"We need to just give up," I say. "It's not gonna work. We need to just quit before we all end up in solitary for the rest of our miserable lives."

"We can't. There's too much at stake," Crosscircuit says.

My frustration boils to the surface, and I find myself ranting, despite the possible consequences if Crosscircuit gets angry at me. After everything that's happened since I arrived here, my irritation gets the better of me, and I completely lose it.

"You keep saying that, but what could be that bad?"

"There's no time," Crosscircuit responds.

"Make time."

He sighs. "As we speak, there's a race of ancient aliens inbound for Earth, set to destroy everything and everyone you love."

I freeze. My insides freeze. The stuff inside my insides freezes. But not because of some alien threat. Because... "Are you effing kidding me?"

Crosscircuit shakes his head and goes back to his computer work.

I rush forward and grab him by the shoulder, spinning him around. "You did all this, planned this elaborate prison-break, because of... aliens?"

"That's right," he says. "The greatest threat the world has ever known."

I shake my head. "You've been down here for what—like

twenty years? You can't even see the sky, much less outer space."

The others murmur behind me.

"I have dedicated my life to studying this. I'm absolutely correct. And we are wasting time," he says.

"You've been spouting this since before you got locked up," I say. "I thought you were over it. I can't believe this. And you know what the worst part is? I was desperate enough to buy into it."

"And for that, you will be rewarded with life," Crosscircuit says. "Now, if you'll let me get back to m—"

"Every scientist on the planet says you're wrong," I continue. "The government says you're wrong. The Guild checked it out themselves. *They* say you're wrong."

"What about the Guild satellite station that went dark? Your Arch Angels. When was the last time you heard from them?"

I think about it for a moment, remembering a couple of years ago when a transmission from the Arch Angels—a team of very powerful superheroes stationed on the moon with the ability to visualize space from great distances or something—was cut short. I didn't hear the message myself, but Frank said that Eaglestar said it wasn't much.

Eaglestar flew up there to check on them, but they were gone. Not really anything worrisome since they've been known to wander off now and again. But the mention of them does make me wonder.

"A couple of years ago," I admit.

"And what did they say?" He continues working despite carrying on a detailed conversation. Maybe the guy is off his rocker, but he sure can multitask.

I shake my head. "I don't know."

"That's right. Because their transmission was terminated maliciously. How do you explain that?"

"You don't know that. It could've been a freak accident. A meteor might've struck the towers."

"Do you have evidence of any meteor?" Crosscircuit asks, the words biting.

"That doesn't mean there was evidence of alien involvement."

Crosscircuit looks like he's about to have a stroke because he's so upset, but he keeps clacking away at the keyboard. "You don't know what you're talking about! Nobody knows what they're talking about!"

Royal Rampage whimpers and retreats to the other side of the library. It's sad, like a kid watching his parents fight and being able to do nothing about it.

"Okay, okay. Calm down," Justice says, stepping forward. "Dude looks like a volcano ready to explode."

I know this is gonna sound crazy, but I swear I can see an actual light bulb appear over Crosscircuit's head.

"That's it! Justice, you're a genius. I would kiss you if the thought didn't repulse me so much."

"Me? A genius?" Justice says.

"No, of course not. It's a figure of speech." Crosscircuit switches tabs on his computer and begins a new task.

All this is happening while people pound on the library door, by the way. It's chaotic, but we are all just trying to ignore it for our own sanity.

Scrolling through the results coming up on the monitor, Crosscircuit continues. "I was rehashing the prison's protocols years ago when I first became incarcerated here. I found a contingency for an emergency regarding the eruption of submarine volcanoes."

"What kind of contingency?" I ask.

"The cell doors open, and prisoners are escorted to the escape pods and sent to the surface."

"Submarine volcanoes?" asks Justice.

"Undersea volcanoes, on the ocean floor," Crosscircuit says.

"How many of those can there be?" Sinsation asks.

"Over a million, according to estimates."

"Wow. Too bad there aren't any volcanoes going off down here," Justice says.

"That's the thing." Crosscircuit looks like a man unhinged. "We don't need any volcanoes to *actually* be erupting. We just need the prison's computers to *think* volcanoes are erupting."

Royal Rampage returns to my side, looking oddly like he understands. But then he pipes up. "We make volcano noises, then?"

He starts making a sound like bubbling lava while performing splashing movements with his hands.

I pat him on the arm. "I don't think that's what he means, buddy." I turn back to Crosscircuit. "You think you can do it?"

"I know I can. I'd considered it once before, twenty years ago, but deemed it too dangerous. All those prisoners set free at once: we'd all be just as likely to get killed in crossfire, or heaven forbid, someone do something stupid and flood the place. It would be anarchy. Sheer chaos."

"Just what I want to hear," says Sinsation.

Crosscircuit shakes his head and slams his fist on the table. "It's not a good thing. Some will think the emergency is real. There will be mass hysteria, panic. Others will just want to take advantage of the situation to cause trouble. And it will alert law enforcement on the surface so they can be waiting for us."

"Sounds like our only option other than surrender," I say.

"There's one more problem." Crosscircuit stops working for the first time, just leaning on the desk. "It will also open solitary box 7a."

"What's in solitary box 7a?"

Crosscircuit shakes his head. "It doesn't matter. This is our only chance at this point."

A blast behind me sends us all flying against the far wall. When the rain of gray dust and skittering rubble comes to a stop, a dozen guards stand in the newly blown doorway, guns drawn and trained on us. And more are already coming in behind them.

Sinsation is the first to act, joining in the fray without hesitation. Having fought her before, I know she loves a brawl and is a little on the crazy side. Usually, she lures people into a trap, as she did to me years ago. There were strobe lights and fog machines and all kinds of distractions.

Here, it's just us and a bunch of heavily armed guardsmen.

"Stand down!" one shouts, stabbing the air with the barrel of his rifle.

At first, I think they're gonna fill Sinsation full of bullets, but she stops and blows a kiss.

Immediately, the guard up front lowers his weapon. The others around him become visibly confused, but that's all the opening she needs. Flipping forward, she lands on a guard's shoulders, then claps her hands over his ears, sending him down in pain. Springing off his falling body, she kicks the next guard in the face and grabs his electrified nightstick as he drops it. From there, she's shocking armored and unarmored guards alike, mainly concentrating on the crotch area, which makes me shudder just watching it.

Crosscircuit takes it all in with a giant grin. "I knew she was a good choice. Shall we, gentlemen?"

The rest of us wade into the chaos, shoving, punching, and kicking anyone in our way. Gunfire erupts everywhere. From the corner of my eye, I see Rampage take a round to the shoulder, but that just enrages him.

Crosscircuit—who's never been the physical type—tries to stay in the middle of our group so he doesn't get hit. He seems pretty good at it, probably due to lots of practice. It's also possible that the guards are worried about the consequences of hurting him, even under these muddled circumstances.

Royal Rampage plows through the mob. Bodies fly in all

directions. He could just keep moving, and nobody would be able to stop him. Well, with Bullshark still in the infirmary, I should say.

Crosscircuit gets to a terminal and overrides the security features. "And here... we... go."

He hits one last key, setting off a red alert like on the old *Star Trek* TV show. The lights around the prison even turn red.

"The escape pods are in section B5," Crosscircuit says.

"That's on the other side of the prison," I say.

With the cell doors no doubt already open, we'll have to go through practically every guard and prisoner in the place.

Justice is smart enough to grab all the weapons from the fallen guards. Don't you hate seeing a scene like this in a movie or TV show, and the person or people going through all the enemies doesn't bother to stock up on weapons as they take them down?

Then they inevitably run out of ammunition before they get to where they need to go, and it's *click click click,* and then —you know what I'm gonna say—they throw the gun they're using. As if there's no chance of finding any more ammo with all those armed people around. Plus, I mean, it's a hunk of metal with a grip on it. Swing it around and use it to bludgeon people if you get desperate. Am I right?

Anyway, my point is that we're not so stupid, and Justice loads up on everything he can. He straps them on, shoves them in his waistband, and fills his pockets with ammo.

I concentrate on the nightsticks, picking up two so I have

one for each hand since I'm better at melee than anything else. And, despite everything, I'm still averse to using guns.

"We better get moving," Justice responds, checking the chamber of one of his newly acquired rifles. As we're about to move forward, I grab him by the arm.

"Hey. Let's keep the casualties to a minimum. Most of these guards are just regular guys doing their job."

He pauses, and I can see in his eyes he knows I'm right. He nods. "Copy that."

We tear off from the library, vaulting over a pile of downed guards. Because I'm right behind Royal Rampage when we get through, and the giant gorilla decides to spend some extra time throwing around a couple of guys he doesn't like, I'm the first one to the end of the hallway.

And standing in front of it, blocking my way, is the guy I recognized earlier as Deadeye. He has his arms crossed and, being six-foot-four, he's staring down at me like he's ready for a fight. I'm an excellent hand-to-hand combatant, and I've gotten even better over the years with more practice, but I'm not as good as Deadeye. In fact, now that Frank is older and has so many injuries, he's not even as good.

And I'm not sure Royal Rampage is even gonna be able to be effective against him. He's too quick.

I'm about to swing at him, trying to figure out the best fighting disciplines to counter the moves I've seen him do in the past. But before I can act, he steps out of my way and nods. I stare at him for a few seconds before Rampage grunts behind me.

Cautiously, I step past Deadeye, and he doesn’t interfere.

I guess even though he’s no longer part of the escape, he doesn’t wanna get in the way, either. Shocking, considering what kind of person he is. Or what I assume he is based on past experience. The truth is, I don't know much about him at all. Puts some things into perspective. All this fighting between heroes and villains. Are we all that different?

Yeah. We are.

By now, Justice has caught up, and we take off at a sprint. We reach a door at the end of the corridor, and since it no longer matters which code I use—who cares if anyone is alerted? There's a volcano going off, right?

"Ready, big guy?" I ask Rampage.

He grunts.

"Ready?" I ask Justice.

"Let's do this."

I type in 265917. The first code I memorized. The door slides open, and we all head through.

Then I hear a thud behind me and turn to see a prisoner wielding a makeshift metal club and Justice slumping to the ground, blood gushing from his skull.

"Justice!" I shout.

Before I can kneel and check on him, the attacker comes at me, swinging wildly.

I don't know who it is, but he wasn't sent here for being a good fighter. His first strike comes in at a downward arc. I block it with my forearm—which hurts, but those bones are stronger than most people think. Then, I thrust my lightning stick forward and zap the hell out of him. He drops like a cut electrical wire, flopping around on the ground.

Bending down next to Justice, I swear.

"What the hell happened to him?" Crosscircuit asks as he and Sinsation catch up to us.

I point to the convulsing jumpsuit.

"We'll have to leave him," Crosscircuit says. "He's just going to slow us down."

"No, I can't," I object.

"You can. And you *will*," says Crosscircuit.

"I won't!" I shout back at him.

"Why? How important can he possibly be?" he asks. "He's just another worthless shooter who's too big for his britches, proving to be more trouble than he's w—"

"He's my brother, okay?" I interrupt. "I can't leave him here to die."

Everyone stands silent for a moment, shocked by my revelation. But probably not as shocked as I am that I blurted it out.

"He brother?" Rampage asks.

"Yeah. I can't leave him here."

"We can't all risk being caught just to save him," Sinsation says.

"You can do whatever you want," I tell her. "I'm not abandoning him here. He wouldn't do that to me. I've got an idea. I'll catch up." Then I turn to Royal Rampage. "Please carry him with you, big guy. Please?"

Rampage nods. "I help Kite's brother." He scoops Justice

up, gently putting him over his shoulder. It looks like it takes the same effort I'd exert lifting a sack of flour—and not even a big one.

"Where are you going?" asks Crosscircuit.

"To get help."

"Your funeral," Sinsation says as she starts down the hall.

"You'd better know what you're doing," Crosscircuit warns.

"Go," I say, then head in the opposite direction of the escape pods.

I toss the mini-drone into the air, and it buzzes to life. It doesn't have a very long charge, so I was holding off on using it until we got to the part of the plan where I needed it—which never happened.

"Several lifeforms with increased heart rates approaching from your two o'clock," it says immediately.

Its long warning in Crosscircuit's voice comes just as I'm about to turn, and I roll them over before they even know I'm there. As they fall to the ground, I zap each with a lightning stick to make sure they stay down at least long enough for me to get away. Two inmates. I feel bad about it until I remember *why* they're here. Then I feel like a hypocrite since I'm here too. While running, it's like I have an angel and demon on my shoulders, like in the old cartoons, and one is convincing me that I'm here under false pretenses while the other tells me I deserve it. And to be honest, I'm not sure which I agree with more.

I shake the thoughts free and push on. My only saving grace is the infirmary isn't far. I just have to hope Mender is still in there and not trying to escape or getting beat up somewhere. I pass a bunch more prisoners along the way. Some are content to let me by without conflict. Others I'm able to take down quickly with my shock batons. Except one.

"Hey there, Harrier," Rush says, cracking his knuckles.

"Not now," I say. "Come on. Not now."

"Nice jewelry," he says, pointing to my bracers. "I'll take them back."

He's blocking my only route toward the infirmary, so it seems I have no choice but to lay him out.

"Not so tough without them, huh?" I tease.

"Actually..." He starts vibrating rapidly. "Turns out this system can't handle *all of us*."

There's something like a shockwave that pulses from the walls around us, and Rush explodes at breakneck speed.

My drone gives me so many warnings all at once that I think it might short-circuit. Rush wallops me hard, and I have no doubt half a dozen bones broke or fractured inside me. I can taste blood in my mouth, but I don't have time for injuries. We gotta get out of here, and Justice could die if I don't get to Mender. I roll to my feet, ignoring every stabbing pain. In a crouched position, I scan for him and see him glitching a bit.

"Maybe the system is better than you think," I say as he spasms.

"Nah, you're dead." He darts toward me again, but this time only clips me as I sidestep.

Toward the end of his run, he looks like a lagging video

game. Still for a second, then a quick jump three feet ahead on repeat.

"Wouldn't you rather just escape?" I ask.

"Not unt-ti-til y-y-you're d-dead."

Something's happening inside of him like he's been electrocuted, which gives me a crazy idea. In a hallway made of metal, armed with only a couple of lightning sticks and no other gear, crazy is gonna have to work.

"Fine," I say. "Come get me."

He turns fully toward me, and that fraction of a second before he uses his powers warns me even if the drone can't keep up.

I leap into the air and stab both lightning sticks out to the side. The tips connect simultaneously with the metal bulkheads, and a current of power flows through them and into the walls, making its way into the floor.

I strain to use the pressure from the sticks as they drag slowly downward. My feet dangle just inches from touching back down, and just as I think I can't do it a second longer, I hear a violent scream and see Rush's incapacitated form crumple to the ground, smoking.

Sparks still flying, I use every bit of strength to pull the sticks free. They're stuck like magnets but eventually fall inert.

"Shocking turn of events," I say to Rush's unconscious body as I continue to the infirmary.

As I pass the next clump of guards, they are too busy with other prisoners who have regained control of their powers to do anything about me. It's a fair fight from the looks of it since the inhibitors being overwhelmed means each of the super-powereds only has a fraction of their old abilities.

I almost slip on a puddle of orange slime before realizing it's actually a person. I'm often bummed I didn't get any *actual* powers until I see something like that. Then I'm downright thankful.

I finally make it to the infirmary. Barging through the door, I'm already screaming, "Mender, I need your hel—"

But standing in the doorway holding Mender by the bicep is Warden Riche. "I should have known you'd be part of this. I've had my eyes and ears on you since you got here."

"I don't have time for this, Warden. Justice is dying, and I need Mender to save him."

"I'm sure plenty of guards are injured or dying at the moment too. He's coming with me," he says.

"No. I need him to save Justice. Then he can help the guards."

"That's not gonna happen," he says as three large, armored guards walk up behind me.

Without warning, I leap forward and grab Riche before he or the guards can react. I hold one of the batons against his neck and pull him back. Mender falls free of the warden's grasp, knocking over a table covered in various medicines and tools.

"Move aside," I say to the guards.

As you would suspect, the warden is quick to order the

guards to comply. He's not ready to get hurt for anyone's sake and is suddenly not so worried about any injured guards.

"You're gonna pay for this," he tells me.

"What are you gonna do? Send me to the worst prison in the world?"

I nod for Mender to exit the room, then back away from the guards with the warden still in a chokehold.

"All of you, get inside," I growl.

The guards don't move an inch.

I reposition my lightning stick, more for show than anything else.

"Do it, or his brain gets fried." I don't know if I'd really do that. Killing the warden goes against my code—the only rule I've ever really aimed to follow in life. No killing. Even though Frank killed on more than one occasion, I know he only did it out of necessity or because he'd been tortured to insanity.

Still, killing Riche seems excessively brutal.

But they don't need to know that.

"Last chance," I say.

"Do it," Riche orders his guards, and one by one, they backstep into the infirmary. Then I shove Riche hard into the room, and the door slides shut. I jam one of the lighting sticks into the control panel next to the door and turn on the current, frying the circuits. I have to assume nobody's getting out of there anytime soon.

I tell the drone to locate Crosscircuit and the others.

"Your party is currently heading Southwest in prison section B9," it says.

That's not far from the escape pods, but it's a good run past my old solitary confinement chamber and other potential problems for me.

“Gracias,” Mender says.

"De nada," I respond as I lead the way.

“Hablas español?” he says.

"Uhhh," I say.

"Guess not." He laughs. "What is all this?"

"I'll explain when we get out of here," I tell him.

"Out? Like out-out?"

I nod. "Yeah. We're breaking out, and you're in luck. We're taking you with us."

He stops.

"What are you doing?" I say.

"No one's ever escaped. How? They're not just gonna let us go."

"That's a problem for future me," I say. "Right now, Justice is potentially dying, and I need your help. Can you help? Please?"

"But my powers don't work outside the infirmary."

"They do now," I say. Since I don't need them, I remove my hibitors and give them to him.

"Really?" he takes them and clasps them over his wrists. He shudders like ecstasy itself just entered into the equation. "Wow."

"Come on. We've gotta hurry."

He follows as we pass back through the way I came, climbing over downed guards and prisoners—Rush included.

For a fleeting moment, I hope he's gonna be okay. But whatever. He started it.

I lead Mender around him and wince.

"Are you injured?" he asks.

"There's no time."

"Stop for a second. You could be making it worse."

He's right. I don't know what damage Rush did to me back there, and if I keep pushing, it might not matter if I escape. For all I know, a rib is millimeters away from tearing through my lung.

"Okay. Fine. But let's make it quick."

He looks me over for a minute, then presses his hand against my chest. They glow, and that familiar warmth spreads down my sternum and torso.

"That better?"

I twist my hips. "Much." Then I look him in the eye. "Promise me when we get out of here, you'll use your powers for good."

He nods slowly. "My days of helping villains are over. I promise."

"Good. Let's go. We've got an escape pod to catch."

We find the rest of the team in the cafeteria, where they're fighting both angry guards and berserk prisoners—now with powers! Batteries sold separately.

Royal Rampage lays Justice down on one of the tables in the middle of the chaos, and Mender lays his hands on him. Closing his eyes, his hands glow. Nothing happens.

"He's in bad shape," Mender says. "I don't know if I can—"

"Mender..."

"This is going to take a lot of my power. It will be a while before I recharge."

"Just please save him," I say.

Mender takes a deep breath and gets back to work. After a few seconds, Justice bolts upright.

"Justice, are you okay?" I ask.

"Wow. Yeah." He rolls his neck. Then he lurches forward and reaches for Mender. I turn to follow, watching helplessly as Mender falls over. I barely catch him before he hits the ground.

"Mender..."

"I'm okay," he says. "I'm okay. Just... tired."

"Thank you," I say. "I don't know how I'll ever repay you. Getting you out of here will be a start."

"No," he says, fighting as I try to lift him. "I don't have long left on my sentence, especially with all the help I've given in here. If I escape, I'll be back on the run again. I want to get out the right way and truly help people."

"You're sure?" I ask.

He nods. "If I'm going to keep my promise to you, it needs to be done by the book."

As much as I'd like to have a healer on our side, I can respect the guy's decision.

I nod at him and pat him on the back.

"Stay safe."

CHAPTER 22
ALEX

Panic attack.

I don't get them all the time—only had a couple in my life. But I'm having one now, and I have Yamo's call to thank for that.

As I race in my newly assigned work vehicle to the *second* closest MoonMoney coffee shop to Baron Steele's office, I keep trying to call Eric to find out the details. My heart is racing and feels like it's trying to pound through the windshield. My chest is so tight that I can't catch a breath. My head feels like—well, I'm sure you get the picture.

Luckily, traffic isn't as horrible as I'd been expecting, and for once, most drivers are paying attention to my blinking lights and siren blaring behind them. If I were stuck in bumper-to-bumper on top of everything else, my chest would explode like an alien was hatching out of it.

Eric finally picks up. "Yo, bro."

"Eric, tell me exactly what's going on," I say.

"Well, here's the sitch. I called up Johnny-Boy, and he—"

"Johnny-Boy?" I interrupt.

"Jonathan. Eaglestar?"

"Oh, right. Never heard him called that before. By anyone."

"Yeah, well, don't tell *him* I called him that…"

"The situation, Eric. Please!"

"Oh, yeah. The sitrep. So I contacted him and was like, 'You gotta get Paul, bro,' and he was like, 'I know, right?' and I said, 'How 'bout now?' and he was all, 'Whatever you think is best, bro. Where's he at?' And I said, 'Probably getting some coffee like always,' and he was like, 'Meet me there.' So I hopped in my drone glider—which, dude, you have to try sometime, it's so sweet, like a flying car, but it doesn't actually look like a car, more like something cool out of *Star Wars* or whatever—and got here just after Jonathan did."

He stops talking, and I think we got disconnected until I hear shouting in the background of the call.

"And then?" I push.

"Sorry. Trying to keep up with what's happening. The rest of your—*our* team just showed up."

"Tell them to stand down until I get there," I tell him.

"Will do." I hear him relaying my command to the task force. "Yeah! He's on the phone right now. Yeah. Yeah. Uh-huh. Yeah. Got it."

"Eric, you're killing me. What happened next?"

"So Steele says, 'I had a feeling you might change your

mind, Jonathan' to Eaglestar. And then he throws his arms out like that dude from *Gladiator*. 'So I contacted some friends.' And then, all of a sudden, the Resistors are there, ready to back Steele up. Like, every single one of them. Firefly, Neith, Osprey, White Hot, and BlackFrost. Such a mic-drop moment, you know? Like some serious movie action. And that Neith chick is super-hot in person. I never realized. You think if she doesn't end up going to prison, she might be into me? Anyway, they're all there, lined up like they're best buds with the Baron. Bro, like, what's up with that? I didn't even think he got along with those guys."

"Yeah, well, extreme times can make for strange bedfellows."

"Right. For sure. But he's not, like, sleeping with Neith, right?"

I roll my eyes despite nobody being there to see it. How can this guy be a genius and so stupid at the same time? "That's just a—I'm almost there. Where are you?"

"Oh, there you are!" he shouts. "I can see you. Can you see me?"

I see Eric literally waving at me from up ahead.

"Yes, Eric. I see you. I'll talk to you in a minute." I end the call and jump out of my car.

There's absolutely no way any of that actually happened with Eaglestar. I don't know if all the tech Eric works with finally fried some circuits in his brain or what, but he's delusional at best when it comes to how he perceives their relationship.

However, judging by what I see on the street before me, he did somehow manage to convince Eaglestar to arrest the Baron. And the situation does *not* look good.

Standing in front of MoonMoney with a cup of coffee in his hand is Baron Steele, the members of the Resistors—Mac, Amy, BlackFrost, White Hot, and Neith—flanking him. On the other side of the street, Eaglestar is standing with his arms crossed. Behind him, Eric is still waving at me like an idiot while the rest of my team stands ready to go into action. Luckily, it looks like they have all our big guns with them. I have a feeling we're going to need them and more.

And all I can think about is how much of this neighborhood is sure to be torn up by this fight and how much it will cost to fix it all. On top of that, the chance people will be hurt. Or killed. *Please, don't let anyone get killed...*

A news van pulls up, and a camera crew piles out. Just as I'm about to wave them off, Summer follows behind them, decked out in her best "on-the-scene reporter" outfit. I rush over to her before they can get set up.

"Summer," I say.

"Alex!"

"Hey, listen." I pull her aside. "You can't be here. It's way too dangerous."

"What are you talking about? This is a huge story. I have to cover it!"

"Why? What's so important that you have to put your life on the line?"

"Well, they named me their vigilante coverage correspondent. If I want to keep my job, I have to cover vigilante action. And besides Coney Island, there hasn't been any in weeks, other than the battle I missed while we were… *busy*."

"Vigilante coverage correspondent? Since when?" I ask, a bit of suspicion beginning to burble to the surface.

"A few days ago. Why?"

"You mean right before you approached me at Douglas Tower?"

"I suppose so, yes."

"So, was I just some kind of lead for you?"

"Of course not. I mean, not after that first interview we had at lunch, anyway."

I hear shouting coming from behind me, thankfully deterring my thoughts.

"Hold on. I have to deal with this situation. Please stay out of the way. And don't go trying to interview anyone yet!"

I rush back to the showdown.

"You're coming with me, Paul," Eaglestar bellows across the street, probably not for the first time. Instead of his usual costume, he's wearing the uniform-type business suit with more muted colors. He's never worn a mask, but he's also avoiding an actual costume like he's supposed to.

"I'm not coming with anyone. Especially not a narcissistic, alien-artifact-infused blowhard who thinks he's God's gift to the world. Just trying to enjoy my coffee."

"I've never said that," Eaglestar retorts.

"Oh, but you've thought it,' aven't you? And everyone knows it."

"You're pathetic, Paul."

"And you're an arsehole, Johnny-boy."

At that, I see Eric's face light up. He looks at me with a "see?" expression written all over his face.

Eaglestar's mouth turns to a sneer. "Let's just do this."

"It'll be my pleasure."

The Battle Royale commences. The two strongest people on Earth, going toe-to-toe, fist-to-fist. Unlike his evil doppelgänger, Eaglestar would never use his other powers in a fight like this. Even assuming he didn't have a moral or ethical problem with it—no guarantees, but still—the last thing he needs is more bad press for himself, the Guild, or superheroes in general. And blasting Baron Steele into oblivion with his laser vision wouldn't play well on the evening news.

I just dated myself again, didn't I? Why do I keep doing that? I'm really not that out of touch and old. I promise. Okay, it wouldn't play well on social media. How's that?

A black sports car pulls up. One I recognize all too well. From the driver's seat, Franklin Douglas III steps out, wearing a suit and tie, and looking not at all like the drunk I'd seen the other day.

"Gentlemen," Frank says. "Is this all necessary? You've already destroyed one of my shops today. Must we add another to the list?"

"Stay out of this, Frank," Eaglestar says.

"Yeah. This ain't your fight," Baron Steele adds.

"You see, that's where you're wrong. This is my city. That's my cafe. And I don't like watching it get destroyed."

Frank...

Here I am, about to get involved in what could turn out to be the greatest superhero battle in years, and all I can think about is what Chen told me before I left. If my mom was Franklin Douglas the First's illegitimate daughter, what does that make me? Frank's... cousin? That would certainly explain why he took such an interest in me all those years ago, training me and bringing me on as his partner. But why wouldn't he just explain to me that we were related? That I'm also a—

Ah. Of course. If I'm actually a grandson of the "great" Franklin Douglas, I should probably be sharing that vast fortune, shouldn't I? I can't believe it even took me this long to figure it out. Some detective I am. I guess what I really needed to be was a genealogist. So Frank felt an obligation to look out for me but didn't feel obligated to hand over half of his giant pile of loot.

I better start paying attention here and stop worrying about it for now. This could get messy.

Did I say "could?" It already is.

Eaglestar is a barely detectable blur as he plows into Steele, and the two crash through the MoonMoney. It looks like a wrecking ball has gone through the place after they disappear through the front window. Glass shatters, tables and chairs come flying out and into the street, then Eaglestar flies straight up through the roof of another building a block away, holding the Baron by the back of his expensive suit jacket.

I have to wonder how many businesses or homes were demolished in between. Or, worse, how many people could have been hurt.

Meanwhile, the Resistors form up and take some shots at the Taskforce from behind an ice wall that BlackFrost quickly erects between the two groups. White Hot's blasts are like a flamethrower and cause everyone to scatter and dive out of the way. Neith's arrows seem like they fly faster than humanly possible. How many can she possibly have? Then her tattoos glow, and she teleports from the ground to rooftops and back again. I can barely follow her.

I don't see Mac anymore, which probably means he's shrunken down out of sight. That makes him very dangerous. And Amy—she's headed straight for *me* in her new flying suit.

"Let's go, people!" I shout at my team, finally getting my act in gear.

Yamo and the twins get into safe positions behind some cover with their weapons and equipment, but Logan just runs right into the fray, always eager as a little puppy to see some action. This is someone who's enjoyed beating people up his entire life, and now he gets to do it with superpowers and the full force of the law behind him.

Eric, who apparently has a ray gun for every occasion, blasts the ice barrier with a concussive force that smashes it into a fragmented plume. This is when it finally dawns on me that he's been providing us with all these nonlethal weapons from the beginning. The twins are good at using and fixing them, but I knew they didn't have the know-how to build them from scratch.

The blast sends chunks of ice in all directions. White Hot is hit with one of the large chunks and gets knocked to the ground. BlackFrost—who's not-so-secretly in love with her—freaks out and lets down his guard to kneel and check on her.

Mac appears right in front of Eric out of nowhere, throwing a punch while he grows to full height and then beyond, and the force of the super-punch sends Eric careening back onto his butt. Logan charges at Mac like a defensive lineman sacking a quarterback, and they go down in a flailing ball of limbs. Mac's gotta be twelve feet tall by now, and his head bangs the asphalt hard. I don't think he's dead, but he's at least unconscious, and I'm sure he will have a concussion.

As I'm about to be hit by Amy, Yamo intercepts her with her net gun. Amy falls into a tailspin, whipping around wildly, out of control. And still hits me.

We go down together, Amy on top, then me on top. Bit of a déjà vu, and not in a good way. We shove free of each other.

"Alex, let me out of here," she says. "You owe me."

I watch her struggling for a minute. She's not wrong. But I couldn't be seen freeing a vigilante one of my teammates just took down. Especially not with Summer and her news crew here. The whole world would see it.

"Just let us handle this, okay?" I turn my back to her and run toward the action while she screams some nasty things behind me as she flails in the netting.

Apparently, the irony of destroying a neighborhood to subdue someone because they destroyed a neighborhood earlier is lost on Eaglestar.

What the hell did Eric say to make him change his mind? I was just trying to find an excuse to get rid of him, so I could visit Chen alone. I didn't think he'd succeed.

Eaglestar tosses the Baron a few feet up, then punches him hard as he falls past, like a baseball player self-pitching a ball. Paul turns into a meteor as he plummets into a department store. As you can imagine, anyone sheltering inside comes pouring out, just adding to the danger of the whole event.

Behind them, the Baron wades out of the rubble and doesn't seem the least bit concerned about anyone around him.

"Come down and face me, old man!" he shouts at Eaglestar, who's still hovering in the sky where he punched the Baron.

Slowly, he floats down, lifts a sedan over his head, and slams it down on top of Paul. The metal rends and peels as an unfazed Baron Steele steps through the hole and walks away from it.

"How 'bout we stick to the fisticuffs then?" the Baron asks.

"Fine by me," Eaglestar replies. He winds back like he's going to slap Steele with a haymaker, but the Baron leans in and head-butts before he can swing. I imagine Steele's skull must be one of the hardest parts of his body since Eaglestar appears a little dazed.

The Baron follows it up with a right hook, and Eaglestar

can't react fast enough. Now I know Eaglestar must have had his bell rung because, normally, he can avoid anything he sees coming.

Eaglestar shakes his head, then retaliates with a fist to Baron's face like a piston. Now Steele looks like he's trying to recover.

"Battlegear, full power," Eaglestar shouts.

Eric looks startled. "Full power? But—"

"Now!" Eaglestar yells.

Eric moves a dial on his giant cannon and fires at the same time Eaglestar drives a boot into the Baron's gut. There's a mammoth *crack* as Steele flies backward into a building beside Summer. To my horror, the wall next to her starts to collapse.

As I'm about to rush over, another clang draws my attention. Amy is knocked unconscious when she caroms off the top of a light post while flying in the net and starts to fall. In a split second, I'm forced to make a choice between Amy and Summer, each close enough to save but in opposite directions.

I notice BlackFrost moving toward Summer, so I dive for Amy and catch her before she hits the sidewalk. Since she's unconscious, she doesn't even know how close she came to being lasagna.

Luckily, BlackFrost throws up an ice shield and saves Summer. Large chunks of the building that would've crushed her bounce away harmlessly. The Resistors may operate outside the law, but they're still heroes. Damn fine ones too.

Eaglestar is done messing around. With Steele down for

the count, he goes around at super speed and takes down the remaining Resistors before they can even react. I've seen him move fast before, but it is something I could never get used to. He's a complete blur. They don't stand a chance.

"That's enough!" Frank shouts as he helps Summer to her feet.

Summer sees me holding Amy in my arms. If looks could kill, I'd be murdered several times over. So much for *that* budding relationship. At least I won't have to feel guilty about sleeping with Sawyer's ex anymore.

Eaglestar zips over to Frank, and they glare at each other eye to eye.

"Do you even see what you did here?" Frank asks.

"I stopped a threat."

"You beat up a bunch of old colleagues and destroyed an entire city just weeks after Saw—Black Harrier was arrested for the same damn thing. Are you so self-absorbed you can't even see the double standard?"

"Would you like to join him?" Eaglestar asks.

Frank shakes his head and takes a step away before turning back and punching Eaglestar in the jaw.

Eaglestar doesn't even flinch, while Frank, on the other hand, shakes out his arm and winces.

"Are you through?" Eaglestar asks. "Good. I'll make believe that didn't happen."

"What happened to you?" Frank asks.

"I realized the error of my ways. As should you."

"What are they talking about?" Eric asks, stepping up to me from somewhere beyond.

"I have no idea," I lie.

"All I've realized is that this country needs more than just a new mayor in one city. I won't stop until I am president of this nation, and everyone who thinks like you is stopped."

"We all know you stand no chance at that," Eaglestar says.

"If anyone on Earth knows that Franklin Douglas III gets what Franklin Douglas III wants, it should be you. Don't forget that." Frank doesn't give him a chance to respond as he returns to his car and zooms away. As he passes, he gives me a look, and I realize that was a threat to me as much as anyone.

My team secures the Resistors and puts them in the back of our van. I stand there watching, taking in all the bedlam and destruction. This isn't right. These were two of the greatest heroes the world has ever seen, fighting like hell to kill each other.

An ambulance finally shows up, and the medics tend to Amy. Yamo tries to cuff her to the gurney, but I wave her off.

"You kidding me, Garner?" she says. "After what happened last time we had her in custody?"

"This is different," I say.

She looks skeptical. "You the boss." She rolls her eyes and walks away.

I help load Amy into the back of the ambulance. Once they shut the doors, I notice Summer standing behind me. I tell the EMTs not to leave until I get back, no matter what condition Amy is in, then I turn to face the music.

"Look, Summer, I..."

I can see tears budding, but she does a fine job keeping them dammed up tight. "Don't bother. I saw everything I needed to see."

"No, you don't understand. I like you. A lot. But Amy... she's like family."

"And blood is thicker than water. Yeah, I get it."

"That's not what I mean," I say. "What happened was a visceral reaction to seeing someone I've been close to for years in trouble—trouble that I caused—and I couldn't help myself. I've only known you for a few days, and..." Wrong direction. "Look. I know you don't trust the Resistors, but truth be told, I do. I knew BlackFrost would be there for you, but Amy had only me. I just..."

I trail off, not knowing how to finish my brilliant explanation that's digging me deeper and deeper.

"Is that supposed to make me feel better?"

"What I'm trying to say is that I *want* to get to know you better. I feel like we could have a solid relationship if you're willing to give me another chance."

After a few seconds of silence, she finally responds. "I don't know."

"Summer, I swear, I never intended for you to be here at all. I told you it was dangerous."

She nods. "You did."

"I assure you, there's nothing between Amy and me. Not even a smidgeon. If I had even the slightest doubt BlackFrost would save you, I'd have chosen differently. Please believe me."

Part of me feels like I'm trying to convince myself that's true.

"I need to think about it. My initial feeling is not just to say 'no' but 'hell no'..."

"I like buts..."

She cocks her head at me.

"Not like that," I say. She laughs that amazing laugh.

"We did have fun together."

I nod.

"Besides, I *really* don't want to get back into swiping on those dating apps." She makes a show of doing an exaggerated shudder to drive her point home.

"So... is that a yes?"

"It's a maybe. You're *damn* lucky BlackFrost saved me, Detective Garner. Give me a few days to think about it, and I'll get back to you."

She turns and walks back to the station van and her crewmembers but stops and turns around. "Maybe not all heroes are jerks."

I stand there, stunned and staring, as she saunters toward the van.

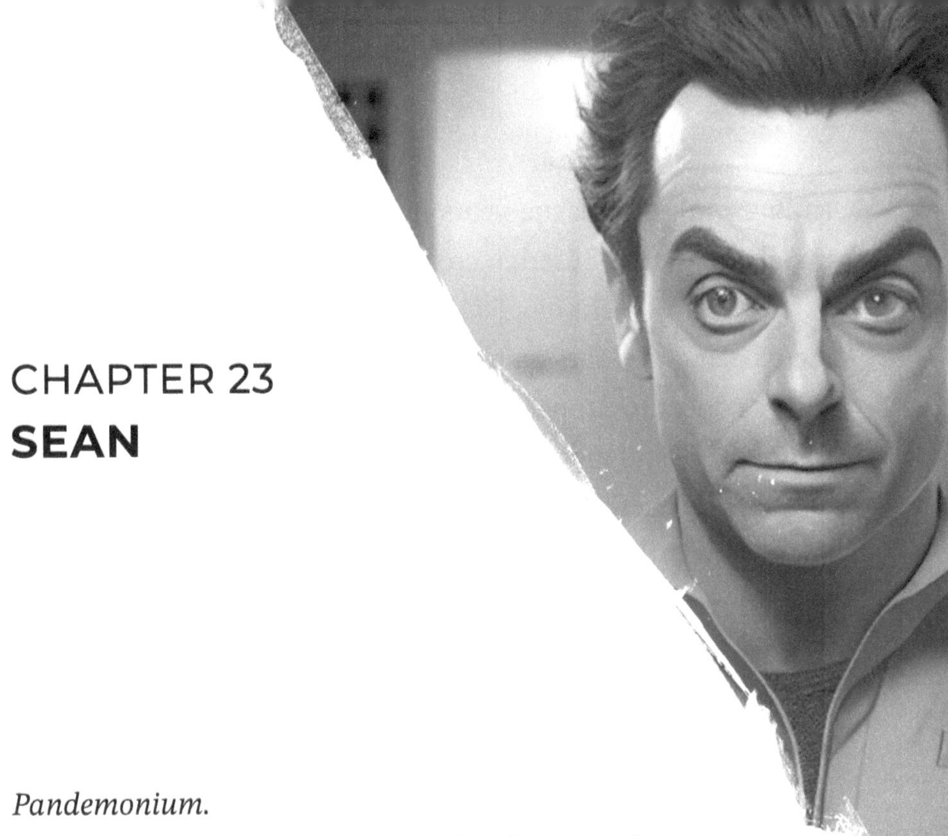

CHAPTER 23
SEAN

Pandemonium.

That's the best word to describe the rest of our escape as we battle through the guards and the other prisoners. When I say "we," I mean the muscle I recruited. I will say I chose wisely. Even Royal Rampage seems the superior choice to Bullshark. He's the closest thing to indestructible I've seen since Paul "The Baron" Steele. Even the bullet he took to the shoulder has not slowed him down.

The escape pods are close. I can taste freedom. I can smell the fresh air. Too bad none of that will matter once the aliens arrive.

This whole ordeal would have been so much easier had I been able to manufacture some robots. But even with my pull and influence here in the Trench, nobody would ever let me near any materials that would allow me to build anything truly useful. It took me years just to collect the few scraps of metal and wiring I used to create Harrier's drone.

Using my technological and mechanical talents, I redirected cameras and guards, as well as opened and closed various doors to funnel them in the right directions. But, even so, there are still many others to deal with.

Harrier uses the codes he memorized by watching the guards over the past few days to open any security doors through which we must pass. That's honestly part of the plan that means very little now that things have gone awry. I was so concerned we'd trigger an alarm by some guard or another being where he shouldn't be. But lo and behold, no one is where they are supposed to be.

Justice—though seemingly worthless at first—uses his excellent marksmanship to take down combatants from across the room, making the far more dangerous and delaying hand-to-hand combat far less than it could've been. Of course, Harrier insists each shot be nonlethal. All the while, Sinsation wields her combination of seduction, acrobatics, and martial arts to get us through the mob of prisoners standing in our way.

Truthfully, I could have used anyone with her fighting abilities since she's mostly powerless without her gear. Still, I've always had a bit of a crush on her, and I have hope once we're out, maybe she'll be open to taking our relationship to the next level. She is a wonder to watch.

Despite primarily despicable people being incarcerated here, most still refuse—or at least hesitate—to hit a woman.

Not necessarily out of any moral or ethical beliefs *per se*, but more because of social norms ingrained in them throughout their lives, from when they first entered the playground in school to the television programs and films they've watched over the years. If they don't want to hit her, she has the full advantage and takes them down without a problem. And if they hesitate, that's all the edge she needs to win.

The prisoners are all incapacitated or drooling over Sinsation. However, the guards are many, and we are few.

"I don't know how there are so many guards," Justice complains.

"Perhaps if we killed some of them, they wouldn't so easily recover," I say, glaring at Harrier.

"No killing," Harrier says.

"Stand down!" one guard shouts. "You're outnumbered."

Justice shuts him up with a slug to the chest.

"I said no killing!" Harrier shouts.

"He'll live!" Justice says. "It wasn't a kill shot."

"Would you two shut up!" I shout.

The sound of a mighty rushing wind passes through the large cargo chamber. Suddenly, everyone is quiet and still.

"Uh oh," I say.

"Uh oh? What's uh oh?" Harrier asks.

When I don't respond, he repeats the question.

"Let me just say I hope none of you ate an apple at lunch," I tell them.

"An apple?" Justice asks. "I had an orange. Is that good? Is an orange good?"

"What on Earth are you all blabbing about?" Sinsation asks as the wind picks up, and behind us, I *feel* a presence, unlike anything one could imagine.

As I turn, the others do too.

From the doorway before us, a creature that could barely be called a man slowly enters. His eyebrows rise like daggers above eyes like emeralds. His ears could be described the same, long and pointed as one would imagine a mythological elf. But an elf, this one is not.

Draped over his wiry shoulders sits a robe made from the softest grass and most brilliant flowers. Its train drags behind him so far I cannot see the end.

The crown atop his head is a part of him as much as my arms and legs belong to me. Woven through skin and bone, a wooden coronet crested with sharp leaves from some long-extinct plant and adorned with berries and cones honors him as the one and only Clover King.

His mouth, pulled back into a permanent snarl, opens, then closes again as if he meant to speak. Instead, he puckers his lips and blows. The gust of wind nearly knocks us off our feet.

"What the hell is that!" Justice shouts.

"Not what... who," I say, barely able to get the words out.

The Clover King is as old as time itself, a force of nature, a druid of old. His power is so great that not even the Trench inhibitors could stymie them. Solitary box 7a acted as a containment field for the ageless, godlike creature. And now, thanks to me, he is free.

And make no doubt about it, he will not recognize what I've done as a kindness to him. Of humanity, he has no regard. No love. No mercy. No care at all.

A guard stands on the opposite end of the room and fires a round that soars right for the Clover King's chest. From somewhere and nowhere, a thick branch shoots out to swat the bullet aside. Then, as we watch in absolute awe, sunflowers burst from within the guard's midsection, blood spurting like tiny fountains from the holes surrounding the stalks. The guard drops unceremoniously to the ground.

"That's 265917!" Harrier says.

"Now is not the time," I say. "We need to get out of here, fast."

All at once, every guard opens fire on the Clover King. Not a word escapes his lips as he accepts the barrage like they're throwing Styrofoam packing peanuts at him.

"This might be our only chance," I say, leading the team toward the opposite end of the room.

Not a single guard takes notice of us as we slip behind shipping crates and through the rear door, leaving the horrific scene that will surely end in countless deaths behind us.

After climbing down a ladder and traversing a long corridor, we reach the hatch leading to section B6, where the escape pods are.

"What the actual hell was that?" Justice asks again.

"That is the world's second biggest threat," I say.

"After the aliens?" Harrier quips, a lilt in his voice.

"We're almost there," I say, ignoring him. "Forward!"

"Uh," Harrier says. "Drone's telling me we got company."

Just then, a fully armored and helmeted guard approaches with the warden himself.

"End of the line, Meyers," Riche says.

"Are you sure you'd like to do this?" I say.

"My family is currently under protection in an undisclosed location. Your reign of terror ends here."

He thinks I don't know that his family has been moved. He's wrong. However, the undisclosed part remains true. Despite my efforts, I haven't yet uncovered their location.

"There's some kind of god lose upstairs," Harrier says. "I really doubt this is worth your time, Warden."

"I told you," Warden Riche growls. "In here, I am the only god."

Justice raises his rifle, and the guard reacts in kind.

"That won't be necessary," I tell him. Then I nod to the guard, expecting him to turn his weapon on the warden if he knows what's good for him.

Instead, he takes his helmet off.

His name is Ernie, and he's been a difficult one for me to manipulate. The man is a workaholic with no friends or family to speak of. He lives a simple, bleak life outside of working here at the Trench, which he seems to enjoy more than is healthy. My only success with him has come in the form of physical harm, and that has become more difficult to hide over the past several months.

"Hold it right there. All of you," Ernie says.

"Ernest, my boy," I say. "We've gotten this far. Surely there must be something I can do for you..."

"You've played your last hand with me, Meyers," he says. "After what that puke stain did to me..." He nods to Harrier. "I'm done acting like you're anything more than some skinny little prick with an ego bigger than a brain."

To that, I take offense. However, there will be a time and place to punish his insolence, and now isn't it.

"Ernie..." I say, a warning in my tone.

"Good job, Ernie," the warden says. "Arrest them."

Ernie turns his weapon on Riche and fires, splattering brains all over the bulkhead.

"What the hell!" Justice shouts.

Ernie's gun is back on us, and this time, directly on Justice.

"Lower your weapon to the ground," he instructs. Justice knows well enough to listen. Truth is, he could pull the trigger faster than Ernie could, but they'd both likely die.

Ernie shifts his weapon to the gorilla. "Tell your pet not to move a muscle."

Harrier motions for Rampage to stand down, and with a huff, he does.

"I've got nothing going for me in life except this job," Ernie explains. "I'm going to be warden someday. Probably a lot faster now that I've stopped this escape from happening, and your guy there killed Riche."

"That's not what happened, and you know it," Harrier says.

"Sure, but the cameras are down. No one here to say otherwise except some prisoners."

"I can take him," Justice says under his breath.

"No," I say too late.

Justice reaches down to pull his pistol, but Ernie shoots first. The bullet grazes Justice's neck but bounces around in the metal, striking the escape pod and causing everyone to duck and cover their heads.

I can tell Ernie is about to gloat when another shot goes off. A small red dot burbles from Ernie's forehead before he falls straight backward.

I look around, not seeing the shooter, only to realize Justice had pulled another pistol with his offhand and fired from the hip.

Perhaps he *is* the crack shot he claims to be.

"Nice shot!" Harrier says.

"You don't mind that I killed him?" Justice asks.

"I guess not everything can be as black and white as Fr— as I want it to be."

Oh, little bird, you're finally stepping out from beneath your father's wings. I have the urge to take a moment to congratulate the young Harrier on his ventures into the real world, but knowing Clover King is on the loose and law enforcement on the surface will already be well aware of the situation, I opt to move toward our salvation.

I examine the damage on the escape pod.

"Is it okay?" Sinsation asks.

"Damage appears fairly superficial, but I can't be sure

without further examination with my instruments—which I don't have—and more time—which we're sorely lacking. We'll have to chance it and hope we make it topside before it springs a leak or, worse, the hull gets crushed."

"Chance it?" Harrier says.

I nod.

"What are our chances?" asks Sinsation.

"Let me put it this way. I don't believe in a deities myself, but if any of you do, you may want to start praying to them."

"Well, the way it looks, we killed the warden and Ernie and hurt a lot of people," Harrier says. "I don't think getting caught is a good thing."

Justice, pulling a bloody hand from his wound, says, "I agree."

I attempt to turn the latch, but it's been damaged by Ernie's stray bullet and won't budge.

"Your turn, big guy," Harrier says to Rampage.

With a grunt of acknowledgment and perhaps a wee bit of excitement, the gorilla grabs hold of the handle. At first, it doesn't seem like it's going to budge, even under Rampage's enormous strength. Then, finally, with a protesting groan, the dial slowly starts to turn.

The others breathe a sigh of relief, but I never doubted it. Well, perhaps a little, but that was why I brought muscle along in the first place, and I always had confidence in my plan. Once Rampage has the hatch open, I enter the pod first, wondering if the others will follow. Sinsation steps in immediately, but then again, she's not entirely sane, so that's not saying much. Royal Rampage is next, seemingly just following Sinsation's lead. But... giant, barely sentient ape. Harrier and Justice both hesitate, apparently unwilling to come along without the other.

"It's now or never, boys. We depart in less than thirty seconds whether you're on board or not." The truth is, it doesn't matter whether they make the trip. Their job is done. I will admit it would be beneficial to have them as backup when we get to land, considering I'm uncertain about what will await us. But it's up to them.

They share a look, and it's at this point that I can see the resemblance. I can't believe I couldn't figure out their fraternal relationship earlier. I should have been able to exploit it before Harrier was forced to reveal it himself. I must be slipping.

Then again, does Justice even know about it? Harrier didn't spill the beans until Justice was unconscious and on the verge of death. Perhaps there is still something there I can work with after all.

The siblings finally step aboard and close the hatch behind them, but Royal Rampage again has to force the door shut. This causes my nerves to catch fire. The structural damage may be worse than I first surmised. Too late now. Once more into the breach.

At the front of the tiny sub is a minimal control board. The escape pod isn't designed to do much more than get people to the surface to be rescued. In fact, it purposely offers very little control other than that because, in a true emergency, most of them would be manned by prisoners. The powers that be certainly don't want them able to float off to Tahiti instead of being recovered by the law upon surfacing.

I disengage the docking clamps and hit the launch button. With force akin to a bullet train leaving the station, the escape pod fires out of the side of the underwater prison and first heads straight out from there. This, too, is by design since, assuming a major emergency would be responsible for their deployment, it would be in the best interest of those aboard to get away as soon as possible. Straight up would be a bad idea. That's the direction things tend to go when they float.

After a few dozen meters of travel away from the Trench, the boosters on the underside of the pod engage, and we begin our upward momentum. That's when something else goes wrong. At first, it's an almost imperceptible amount of water leaking in. But very quickly, it becomes more and more noticeable. I hand Royal Rampage the only flat object I can find—an instructional placard—and instruct him to cover the leak. But I know full well that even his formidable strength won't be enough to prevent water from entering at some point.

Unless I can devise a solution—and fast—the compartment will either flood with water and drown us, or the hatch will completely blow, allowing the water to rush in with so much concussive force that it will instantly kill us. And that's on the positive side of the ledger. If the damage to the sub's structural integrity is too compromised, the immense pressure from outside will simply crush the pod like an aluminum can under an elephant's foot.

Still, it will do no good to panic the others, so I remain calm and mute as I assess the options.

"That doesn't look good," Justice says as he applies a bandage from a first aid kit he found on the superficial wound to his neck.

"Oh, it's perfectly fine. Shouldn't be an issue at all," I lie.

"Shouldn't be?" Sinsation says.

"What does that mean?" Harrier chimes in. "What's the chance we won't make it to the surface?"

"Not as high as you might think."

"We are die?" Royal Rampage says.

"Die? Who said that?" I say, feeling a little hotter than before.

"Stop avoiding the question," Harrier says. "We know what you can do. We want a percentage. You're capable of at least estimating it."

This is where my braggadocio about my intelligence comes back to bite me in the rear. "It's approximately 93% at this point."

Justice lets out a big sigh of relief. "Oh, that's not bad at all."

Sinsation smacks him. "He asked him our chances of *not* making it to the surface, you idiot."

"I know," says Justice.

"That means we only have a seven percent chance of making it," she tells him.

Justice's eyebrows stitch together, then he finally gets it. “Oh, no no no no no no. I'm not dying in here by drowning. That's my biggest fear."

He draws his pistol and points it at my head. "This was your genius idea. Figure it out."

Harrier puts a hand on his arm. "Slow down, there. If he can't figure it out, then there's no use painting the walls because we'll all be dead anyway."

"Yeah, but my last feeling will still be braining this jerk's little egghead before I go, and that will be enough." Justice touches the end of the barrel to my temple.

I pretend to work the controls, so he thinks I'm working on a solution. But I'm not. We can do nothing at this point but believe it somehow holds. All I'm doing is putting on an act, so I don't end up with a bullet in my beautiful brain just before drowning. Or being crushed.

But there is something I need to calculate. If the composition of gases isn't just right in here, we're all going to die of what amounts to a stroke. I find the screen that monitors these things and examine the readings. It is holding despite the leak and the change in pressure. It appears minor enough not to send gas bubbles into our skulls.

At what I surmise to be the halfway point, the water has collected up to our ankles.

"At this rate, if nothing catastrophic happens, we should make it," I say.

"Did you really just jinx us?" Justice says.

"What kind of a feeble mind believes in such ridiculous superstition?" I ask.

"The kind who has a freaking gun to your head, you smug bastard."

"Can we all settle down?" Harrier says. "I remember how long it took to get down here, and based on how things feel, we are going way faster up than we came down. We shouldn't be far."

"He's correct," I say. "I estimate we will reach the surface in fewer than fifteen minutes."

Those next minutes drone on for what feels like days. The water continues to trickle in. The gorilla eventually switches to using his foot to cover the broken seam. Finally, the pod rumbles and shakes, and despite my estimations, we're all knee-deep in seawater. I watch the monitor as we inch upward. Then, we finally break the surface. The hatch blows off as part of the automated process, and a flare rockets into the sky.

"Way to announce our homecoming," Sinsation says.

I sigh. "I had nothing to do with that. Security protocols."

"Well, we sure don't wanna be around when someone comes looking," Harrier says.

It's true, but we also can't just float in the middle of the ocean without a ship or helicopter to take us to shore, or we'll be stranded out here.

Justice finally pulls the gun away from my head once he's sure we've made it, but I don't let him see my breathing relax.

I've come close to death before several times in my life, but

I've never gone for such a long period wondering if it was all over.

"What happens now?" Harrier asks.

I hold up a shaking finger. "First, the four of you need to start bailing water out of here as quickly as possible."

"With what?" Sinsation asks.

"Figure it out," I say. "The original plan was to escape in one of the submarines that travels back and forth to the prison from the surface. It will take me some time to determine how to get out of this predicament. When we set off the false emergency and left in this pod, it sent an alert to the authorities."

"Okay, genius," says Justice. "If we're going to be picked up by the authorities, then doesn't that pretty much mean we just wasted our time busting out?"

"I don't know whom they're going to send to gather us, but there's very little chance they'll be prepared for us, no matter who they happen to be. Or are you done fighting?"

In response, Justice pulls a rifle off his back that he took from one of the guards and chambers a round as if he's some generic action film hero. "Nope."

"Then I suggest you get ready for them in case I can't figure out how to turn off the beacon this pod is surely generating and get us to land."

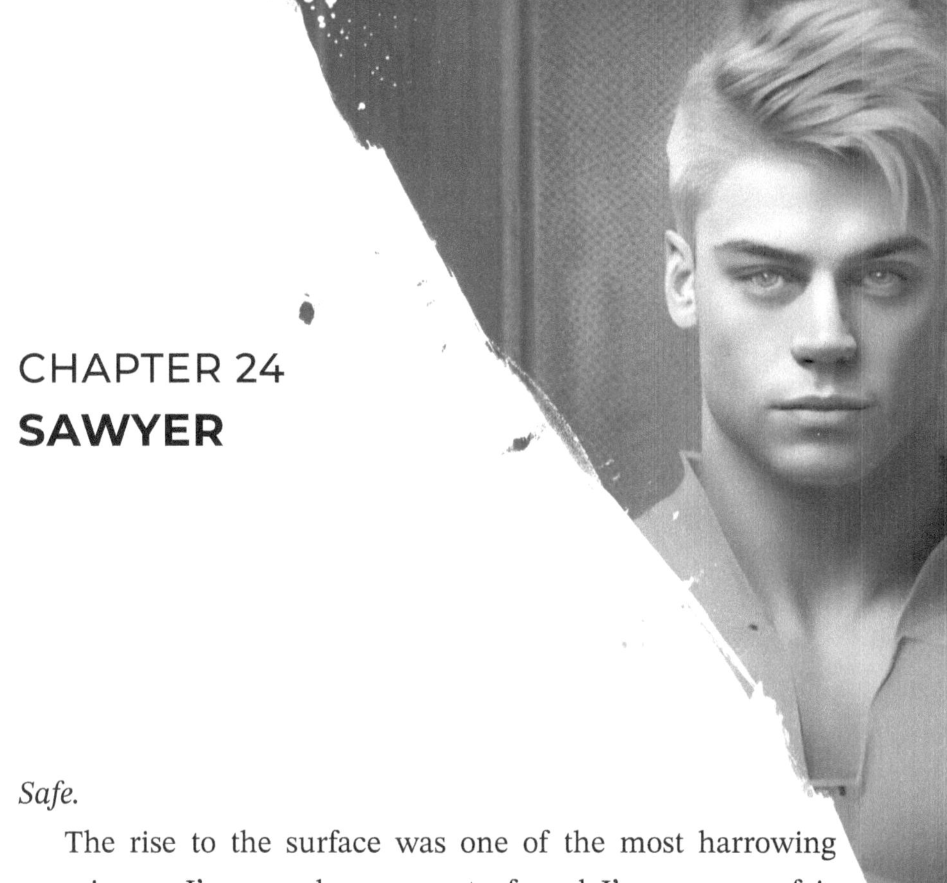

CHAPTER 24
SAWYER

Safe.

The rise to the surface was one of the most harrowing experiences I've ever been a part of, and I've seen my fair share of harrowing experiences. Not only was I worried about us drowning or being crushed on the way up, but if Crosscircuit had died in any way, including being shot in the head by Justice, he wouldn't have been able to call off the hit on my mom.

Despite my burning hatred for the man, he truly is one of the most intelligent people on Earth. Somehow, he managed to take an escape pod designed to simply rise to the surface and escape a place no one has even come close to leaving. I have no idea where we are, but I don't care. It's not the Trench.

Currently, he's at work trying to shut off a homing beacon

we don't even know exists. But I feel like he knows more than he's letting on.

"What's happening, Sean?" I demand.

"Almost safe," he says under his breath. "There!"

"No one can find us?" Justice asks.

"Well, there's still the concern over the flare, but it's long since burned out and..." Crosscircuit makes a show of peering around. "I see no one. Do you?"

"We made it?" Sinsation asks.

Crosscircuit nods. "Congratulations, ladies and gentlemen. You are amongst the first ever to escape the Trench."

"That's good," I say. Now that I know he's completed the task of concealing us from law enforcement or the army or whoever might've been coming for us, I grab Crosscircuit by the front of his shirt. "Make the call, now! Call off the hit!"

"The hit?" Justice asks.

"Our fearless leader here threatened to have my mother killed if I didn't cooperate with this scheme."

"Dude. That's low," Justice says.

"Even for you," Sinsation adds.

Royal Rampage growls low and menacing. His chest puffs up, reminding us just how much of a gorilla he really is deep down.

"Okay, okay, calm down. Relax," Crosscircuit says, trembling beneath my fingertips as he glances around at the entire team who have now turned on him.

"I'm not gonna relax until I know she's safe. Time's almost

up! And if she's not okay, you'll wish Justice shot you in the head."

"It's going to be fine," he assures me. Or tries to assure me. Screw this guy.

Then, part of this whole plan stops making sense. "Wait. You don't have a phone or anything. How are you gonna contact Rifleman?"

"I don't need one."

"How can you be so casual about this?"

I haven't felt this much rage since I was ground-and-pounding Chef Maléfique after he kidnapped Frank and nearly killed him. I feel like I really could murder Crosscircuit right now.

Crosscircuit's face screws up like someone kicked him between the legs. "Look, I... sort of lied about the whole thing."

"*What*?"

"I calculated the best way to obtain your assistance. And I wanted to ensure you cooperated and focused on helping us escape. I don't even think there *is* such a person as Rifleman." He laughs. "That name's almost dumber than Justice."

I grit my teeth, then decide... no, I don't need to hold back on this pile of garbage. I haul off and punch him in the face. Crosscircuit is a lot of things, but he's not a fighter. He falls to the knee-deep water, splashing around even though I didn't even hit him very hard.

"How could you do that to me? To *anyone*?" I growl, wondering if he can even hear me.

The whole thing makes Royal Rampage a bit erratic, jumping and pounding his chest. Water sloshes all over, and the escape pod threatens to tip. Sinsation works to calm the giant beast, but Rampage senses my anger and is more than happy to jump on the hate wagon.

Crosscircuit starts to rise, wiping the blood from his lip with his soaking wet sleeve, but Rampage roars and Sean stays on his knees.

"I really am sorry. But there's too much at stake not to take every measure to ensure I'm ready."

"Yeah, yeah, the *aliens*, right? The big invasion you're gonna save the world from?"

"I know you don't believe me. Nobody ever has. Well, except for that one homeless guy with the tinfoil hat. But everyone is going to now. Because we're out of time."

"What does that mean?"

Just as Crosscircuit says that, a deep rumble begins to rise in the air above. Finally, a massive shadow creeps toward us in the sky.

"Is that the aliens?" Justice asks.

I glare at Crosscircuit. His shoulders slump.

"Unfortunately not," he says.

"Don't move!" comes a voice over the loudspeaker. "You're being taken into custody. Any attempt to save yourself will risk open fire."

"I thought you said we were safe?" Sinsation asks.

"I thought we were."

"Some genius you are, genius," Justice says.

In the darkness, it's difficult to see anything beyond a vague shape. But soon, a portion of a wide metal flying object slides back, and a bright light appears. For a moment, I expect a tractor beam like those old movies from the '50s. From within, a large object descends to drag us upward to a place where we will be poked and probed. Shudder.

Then, a braided metal line descends. When it gets close enough, the whole pod is thrust from the water, clanging hard against it with a reverberating thud.

With a whine, the line ascends, and us along with it. We're jostled back and forth, slamming into the bulkheads and controls. Royal Rampage looks terrified and nearly slaughters Crosscircuit when they bump into each other.

From inside the escape pod, I can see the giant flying ship getting closer, and I spot some alphanumerical writings on the hull. We pass through the opening, and the sound of the door sliding shut below us is deafening.

We're hovering in the air, suspended by the same line that dragged us up here. Finally, the pod is then lowered, and when it connects with the ground, we're hurled around some more.

"What the hell?" Justice asks.

"Was this part of the plan you refused to tell us?" Sinsation asks Crosscircuit.

"Sadly, no."

I slowly stand and climb through the escape pod hatch, which is now above us. We're inside some sort of cargo hold in a military-style VTOL craft. Only thing I know for sure is I've never seen it before.

I begin to climb free when blast doors on the far wall pull back to reveal a man in a suit accompanied by three dozen heavily armed soldiers.

I stare at him for a long while before finally saying, "Mr. Chen?"

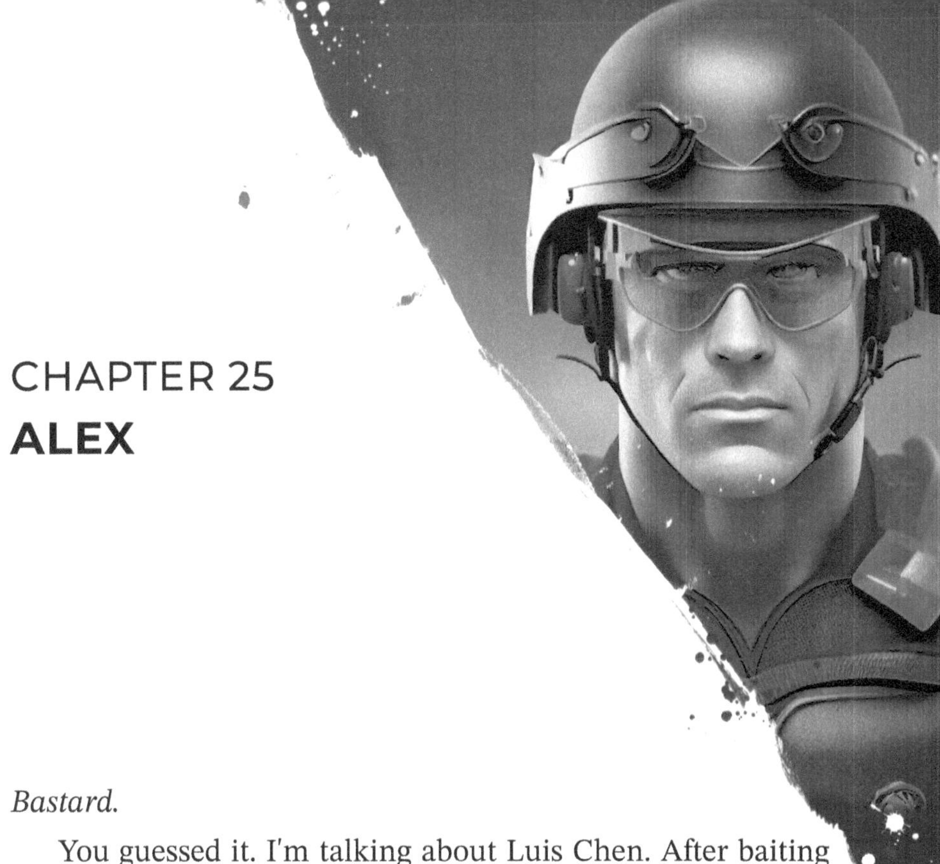

CHAPTER 25
ALEX

Bastard.

You guessed it. I'm talking about Luis Chen. After baiting me with new information about who I am and my relationship to Frank, then slapping me across the face with the fact that he supposedly knows where my brother is, he's disappeared. Some idiot judge let him out on bail because he's a "pillar of the community," and now he's in the wind.

I understand it may not have anything to do with me. He's facing a lot of time in prison, and he's not a young man. But I can't help feeling like at least part of the reason he disappeared is to show me he can—that I should have made a deal with him.

Now, if Amy goes to the Trench, he'll make it look like I set it up out of revenge. All I can say is I'm glad he's been working on the side of the good guys all these years. I'd hate to see what he'd be capable of if he were on the other side.

My phone buzzes, and I see that all-too-familiar Unknown Number. No number on Douglas Industries communicator is Unknown except for one person.

"Yes?" I answer without the tiniest bit of friendliness.

"Alex, it's time to put aside our differences," Frank says.

He's the last person I want to talk to right now, but if he's saying that after our last couple of encounters, it must be important.

"Why's that?" I want to confront him about being his cousin and the fact that he essentially robbed me of my inheritance and the cushy life I could have lived all these years. Not to mention that I need to ask him about Toby, his Red Kite sidekick between me and Sawyer. If I'm related to Frank, and so is Sawyer, does that mean that Toby was as well? His true son, probably? If that's true, then it's no wonder Toby's death at the hands of Chef Maléfique messed him up so badly. In fact, when you think about it, it's pretty amazing he ever recovered.

Or did he?

There's something in Frank's voice. Something I've heard very few times in all the years we've known each other. Panic.

"There's a crisis."

"Isn't there always?" I ask.

"No time for squabbles," Frank says. "Have you looked outside?"

"Huh? What? No."

From my office, I can only see the brick wall across the

street clear upward. Even if the window opened and I could lean out, I'd likely only see a sliver of blue.

"Do it," Frank says.

"Right now?"

"Yes."

I'm moving before Frank even answers. As I push through the bullpen, officers frantically answer phones that seem to be ringing off the hook.

"What's going on?" I ask anyone listening, but no one responds.

After rushing down the stairs, I finally reach the glass doors at the front of the building. Despite being midday, it's so dark it looks like it could be dusk. A storm? Something worse?

Once outside, I see that the darkening afternoon isn't due to clouds.

In the sky above, massive, glowing objects of some unknown material fill the sky—purple and black monstrosities unlike anything I've ever seen.

"Frank, what the hell is that?"

But he doesn't need to respond. I know what they are. Ships. Alien ships. This isn't like the situation I helped stop with the Guild years ago when I was Red Kite. Those were small scouting-type vessels. These are much, much bigger.

"What the hell is going on?"

As if Frank just regained his voice, he says, "I just got off the phone with the president. I know you've been taking all of us masked crimefighters off the streets, but we're going to need everyone we can get."

"Is this...?" I ask, letting the implication of my question linger in the air.

"A full-scale invasion."

EPILOGUE

VRAASSSK

At last.

The stinking ape creatures think they are the apex predator. But their minds are too small—too shallow—to comprehend anything beyond their own little planet. They evolved from the tiny rodents our forefathers snacked upon before the Great Cataclysm that claimed so many of our race. Those of our ancestors who survived took to the stars before a giant meteor struck our home and wiped out most life on the planet. But those tiny warmbloods survived somehow, hiding in hovels in the ground, feasting on insects and grubs, and waiting out the darkness until they became larger, faster, and more intelligent. They grew into tribes, then villages, then towns and cities. They helped return their world to its former glory. Then, they began destroying it once again.

Meanwhile, our people were rescued. Our history cannot

credit our saviors, but they were responsible for shuttling us to our new home on Tuldaria-4. After millions of years evolving at a rate we had never before experienced, we built a civilization the likes of which the galaxy had never seen. We colonized the stars and conquered our neighbors, most of us never giving a second thought to the nearly barren rock we had left behind. But some always believed we should return one day and reclaim our original home—that it had been long enough since the Great Cataclysm for us to return and check on the Hatchworld.

Eventually, we sent scouting ships to see what had become of it. The sun shone once again. The planet had become covered in green and returned to the state it had been in before the space rock had destroyed it all. The ape creatures had recently begun building a civilization of their own, even daring to visit the planet's natural satellite in a primitive spacefaring vessel. Beings had arisen among them possessing special abilities, the most powerful of which was created from our very own artifacts left on the planet, long buried, but uncovered by their scientists and recognized for the powerful weapons they were.

These dynamic beings even managed to fight back against our scouts and hold on to the stolen technology they had found. But this cannot stand. We cannot allow the ape creatures to benefit from our heritage while they continue to scar and disfigure our Hatchworld and pollute it almost to a point beyond repair.

The time has come for us to reclaim our birth home—to

retake our planet and to rid it of the vermin who have produced out of control and overrun her surface. In the name of the Hatchmother, we will come in force. We will defeat the ape creatures.

And we will exterminate them.

THANK YOU FOR READING THE TRENCH

We hope you enjoyed it as much as we enjoyed bringing it to you. We just wanted to take a moment to encourage you to review the book. Follow this link: *The Trench* to be directed to the book's Amazon product page to leave your review.

Every review helps further the author's reach and, ultimately, helps them continue writing fantastic books for us all to enjoy.

Want to discuss our books with other readers and even the authors? Join our Discord server today and be a part of the Aethon community.

Facebook | Instagram | Twitter | Website

You can also join our non-spam mailing list by visiting www.subscribepage.com/AethonReadersGroup and never miss out on future releases. You'll also receive three full books completely Free as our thanks to you.

Other books in series:

NOTE: RAPTORS and HARRIER stand alone with no need to read the other for enjoyment.

Raptors

Sidekick

Superteam

Scions

Baron Steele

Mega-Mech Apocalypse

Harrier

Justice

The Trench

Invasion

Did you love Justice? Get more books by the authors...

2021 *Best Indie Book Award* (BIBA) for Young Adult Fiction. My name is Sawyer William Vincent—I know, it sounds like three first names—but most people know me as the Red Raptor. Well, technically no one knows I'm the Red Raptor, he's just a bit more popular. Wow. Enough about my name. Let me start over. I'm a superhero—the legendary Black Harrier's partner. Not sidekick. I don't care if I'm still in high school. We work together to bring down the city's most dangerous villains. When the Black Harrier gets a mysterious note, then goes missing in New York City, things are pretty much left up to me. But don't worry... I've got this. Piece of cake. If you like Tim Drake as Robin or ever wondered what Peter Parker would be like if he lived in Gotham, Raptors is right up your alley. **From Washington Post Bestseller Jaime Castle and CJ Valin comes a new superhero universe perfect for fans of both DC and Marvel. Actually, it's for fans of anything superhero-related... You're gonna like it. Promise.**

GET SIDEKICK NOW!

In the West, there are worse things to fear than bandits and outlaws. Demons. Monsters. Witches. James Crowley's sacred duty as a Black Badge is to hunt them down and send them packing, banish them from the mortal realm for good. He didn't choose this life. No. He didn't choose life at all. Shot dead in a gunfight many years ago, now he's stuck in purgatory, serving the whims of the White Throne to avoid falling to hell. Not quite undead, though not alive either, the best he can hope for is to work off his penance and fade away. This time, the White Throne has sent him investigate a strange bank robbery in Lonely Hill. An outlaw with the ability to conjure ice has frozen and shattered open the bank vault and is now on a spree, robbing the region for all it's worth. In his quest to track down the ice-wielder and suss out which demon is behind granting a mortal such power, Crowley finds himself face-to-face with hellish beasts, shapeshifters, and, worse ... temptation. But the truth behind the attacks is worse than he ever imagined ... ***The Witcher* meets *The Dresden Files* in this weird Western series by the Audible number-one bestselling duo behind *Dead Acre.***

GET COLD AS HELL NOW AND EXPERIENCE WHAT PUBLISHER'S WEEKLY CALLED PERFECT FOR FANS OF JIM BUTCHER AND MIKE CAREY.

Also available on audio, voiced by Red Dead Redemption 2's Roger Clark (Arthur Morgan)

For all our Aethon Books, visit our website.

ABOUT THE AUTHORS

Follow me on Amazon!

Jaime Castle hails from the great nation of Texas where he lives with his wife and two children. A self-proclaimed comic book nerd and artist, he spends what little free time he can muster with his art tablet.

Jaime is a #1 Audible Bestseller, Audible Originals author (Dead Acre, The Luna Missile Crisis) and co-created and co-authored The Buried Goddess Saga, including the IPPY award-winning Web of Eyes.

All books below are available on eBook, Print, and Audiobook

The Buried Goddess Saga (Epic Fantasy)

Web of Eyes

Winds of War

Will of Fire

Way of Gods

War of Men

Word of Truth

Dragonblood Assassin (Epic Fantasy)

Black Talon

Red Claw

Silver Spines

Golden Flames

Black Badge (Western Fantasy)

Dead Acre

Cold As Hell

Vein Pursuits

Jeff the Game Master (Fantasy LitRPG)

Manufacturing Magic

Manipulating Magic

Mastering Magic

(Science Fiction)

The Luna Missile Crisis

This Long Vigil

Raptors (Superheroes)

Sidekick

Superteam

Scions

Baron Steele

Mega-Mech Apocalypse

Harrier (Superheroes)

Justice

The Trench

Invasion

Find out more at www.jaimecastle.com
https://www.facebook.com/authorjaimecastle

CJ Valin is a writer and artist living in Los Angeles. His award-winning work has included novels, short stories, comic books, screenplays, and non-fiction books and articles. A lifelong science fiction and comic book fan, he created the "Raptorverse" as an homage to his favorite superheroes from childhood.

www.ingramcontent.com/pod-product-compliance
Lightning Source LLC
Chambersburg PA
CBHW020259030826
48979CB00026B/1567/J